UNDER THE KILLING MOON

ROSE BITTERLY

A NOTE FROM THE AUTHOR

Thanks so much for picking up *Under the Killing Moon!* This is a dark horror romance featuring a murderous, morally black MMC. It also deals with themes of child neglect and abuse.

As you might expect, it contains some potentially upsetting material.

Because a certain online bookseller has a history of removing books with comprehensive content warnings, I have opted to put the full, detailed list of content notes on my website, which you can access at rosebitterly.com/content-notes or via the QR code below.

Once you're on the site, just click or tap on the book's title to expand the full list of warnings.

However, there are a few triggers that I did want to list here:

- Graphic depictions of sex and violence
- A subplot that involves the abuse and neglect of a neurodivergent child (there is NO sexual abuse, and the child is part of the HEA)

If you have any questions or would like further clarification, don't hesitate to contact me through the email on my website.

~Rose Bitterly

PROLOGUE

THEO

SIXTY YEARS EARLIER

The first thing I taste is dirt, dark and gritty and metallic. The weight of the earth presses down on me, threatening to crush the air out of my lungs, and the dirt pours into my mouth. But my body reacts as if it knows what to do, and I can feel myself surging upward, clawing desperately through the black loamy soil toward the surface.

I thought I was dead. I remember dying. I remember the hot spark against my temple when I hit the edge of the pier and the sharp, terrible *crack* that I thought was wood and then realized, a second before I sank into the inky darkness of Hanging Lake, was actually my skull.

But I'm not dead, because I erupt out of the ground, sputtering dirt and breathing in the sweet, cedar-scented air of the mountains. I cough and choke, wiping the dirt away from my tongue, and then I slap my hand against my head, feeling for the wound. It's not there.

I cry out, although words don't come. They never have

for me, and it seems whatever happened in the lake hasn't changed that.

So I heave myself up, dirt cascading over my body. I'm wearing the stiff grey suit that Mom said belonged to my father. I don't understand why. I wasn't wearing it when I—

When I died.

I roll sideways until I'm lying on my back, and I blink up at the tangled net of tree branches overhead. They're sparse and spindly, just starting to bloom out. I'm not sure how I can see that, exactly, since it's nighttime. The forest is dark and filled with the usual night sounds—the hooting of owls, the soft hum of crickets. And the moon is full behind the trees, bright enough to cast silvery light over everything.

I take deep breaths, filling my lungs. I'm alive. I'm wearing the suit, the one Mom insists I put on for church services at Christmas and Easter, the only time we go. I can feel my body working beneath my skin: my blood pumping, my lungs filling. It had stopped, though. I remember that. I sank into the lake, and for a moment, I saw my blood ribboning past me, and then there was a terrible flooding feeling in my chest, and then everything stopped.

Because of Kenny Hickman. Everything stopped because of Kenny Hickman.

Rage slams through me, out of nowhere. A hot, violent, all-consuming rage.

He shoved me.

I sit up, moving faster than I expect. My skin is hot and itchy. My fingers clench. The moon bears down overhead.

It wasn't just Kenny Hickman, though. It was all of them. Jack Cooley. Fred Parrish. Maggie Stone.

The rage swells through me again, and this time I jump to my feet, my muscles moving with some grace I've never had before. When I land on the soft, mulchy ground, my chest heaves, and all I can do is remember.

Kenny pushed me, but Maggie was the reason I was there at all. She cornered me while I was at the grocer's, her expression guileless.

Some of us are having a party, Theo. Wanna come?

Her big cheerleader's smile. Her glossy ponytail, curled at the ends. Her big pink bow.

Her loud, braying laughter as I toppled sideways over the pier, as my skull shattered, as the lake swallowed me whole.

I stumble forward and slam my shin against something, a bright burst of pain that, just for a moment, calms the rage. It's a rock, silver in the moonlight.

No. Not a rock. It's too carefully placed, jutting up out of the ground like a tooth.

A tooth among dozens of teeth. I'm in a graveyard.

My rage is swallowed up by something else. Fear. Because somehow I know what I'm going to see on that gravestone as I crouch down, and still it's a shock to find my name emblazoned in the moonlight, carved out in a jagged, unsteady hand:

THEODORE SHORN

And beneath it:

1943 - 1960

For a long time, all I can do is stare at those dates. Then I lift my gaze, blinking at the rest of the graveyard. I know it, I realize. This is the little graveyard near my house, where the graves are marked with stones from the ravine nearby, and where Mom likes to come and pick wildflowers in the spring.

Mom.

I take off in a sprint, tearing into the woods. The air is damp and cool on my skin, and there's not much growth to hold me back. Spring. It's spring now.

Did Mom pick flowers off my grave?

The moon follows me home, a lantern lighting the way.

When I see the familiar, sagging front porch of our old cabin, I feel something like relief. But only for a second.

Because the cabin is dark. Abandoned. There are leaves on the porch, which Mom never allows. She sweeps them off every morning, the *swish swish* always waking me up. The grass in the yard is wild and overgrown. Dead vines crawl along the old sideboards.

I shout for her, but like always, any words lodge in my throat. It's always been easier for me to speak with my hands.

I bolt forward, bound up the porch steps, and slam my shoulder against the door. It's unlocked and swings open easily.

Inside is worse than out. Everything looks like it should —the same yellow couch, the same radio in the corner, the same homemade rug on the rough wooden floors. But it's all covered in a thick layer of dust, and there are leaves on the floor, and a sense that the forest has come inside somehow.

I keen softly, although I know I'm not going to find Mom, not here. I'm not going to be able to tell her I'm okay, that I'm not dead after all. That it was all a mistake. I stumble forward through the living room, heading toward the kitchen. She was always in the kitchen: fixing dinner, washing dishes, sitting at our rickety metal table with her yellow notepad, making her chore list for the day.

And to my horror, she's in the kitchen now.

I stop in the doorway, a terrible emptiness gnawing into my chest. My mother, but it's not my mother. It's a corpse. A skeleton draped in my mother's favorite floral dress, dangling from the light fixture by a rope. The moon shines through the window above the sink, casting her in a soft, hazy light.

The rage comes roaring back, swelling my body with violence. Like my father, even though I never knew him. *Your father has a violent soul*, Mom told me once. *Maybe you'll have it, too. Or maybe you won't.*

I have it. I feel it, that violence, pumping through me like blood.

I stumble forward and wrap my arms around her hips, the bones clacking together inside her skirt. It reminds me that she's not alive, that I can't hoist the pressure of the rope off her throat.

Tears prickle in my vision as I push myself up on the nearby chair. The corpse does nothing, only stares at me with empty eyes and strips of dried-out, leathery skin. *She's been dead a long time*, I think numbly, and I don't know what to do with that information. I don't know what it means that she's dead, and I am not.

I pluck at the rope until it unravels, and then I catch her before she falls. The clacking fills my ears, and I choke back a sob as I carry her into the bedroom. She would hate to be laid out on the kitchen table.

Her room is as neat and tidy as always, although the forest has crept in here, too. Vines push through the window above her bed. Leaves scatter across the patchwork quilt her mother made her long before I was born. I settle her down on top of it and then sweep the leaves away, my body trembling with fury.

It's then that I notice the envelope, propped up on the pillow. My name is written across the front in my mother's perfect, looping handwriting.

My hands shake as I pick it up. The paper feels brittle and warped. Exposed to the elements.

I rip it open, and inside is a letter on her favorite stationery, the one she always used to write thank-you notes after Christmas.

My dearest Theo,

If you are reading this, then it means I was wrong, and I am sorry. But I simply can not live with this grief. Every moment in this house reminds me of you, my sweet boy, and if you did come back to me—you won't be my sweet boy any longer. You'll be like your father, and I don't know if I can live with that pain, either. So I'm sorry to abandon you like this. It is my prayer that you will never wake up and that I will see you in Heaven. But I know there is an equal chance that you are reading this letter, and I owe you an explanation.

The paper trembles in my hand. My stomach flips around. *You'll be like him.* My mother never liked to talk about my father. She said he was dangerous and that he was gone, and that's all I needed to know.

I force myself to keep reading.

Your father's name is Cecil Ashbury. He is a murderer. However, he was very kind to me, and I think he loved me, in his way. He told me, when you were born, the odds were even that you would turn out like him. That you would be a murderer, too. He said he would come back if that was the case and teach you his ways. But if you aren't like him, if you're like me, he didn't want to taint you with his evil.

He said the only way to be sure is for you to die. If you come back, you're like him. If you stay dead, as I will, then you're like me.

My mouth feels dry and sickly. The stationery crumples in my fingers, my mother's words swirling around like the dead leaves on the ground.

My darling, if you're reading this, please seek him out. I believe he is living in Ohio. If you ask enough people about him, he'll come to you. He will not harm you. And please, please, please forgive me. I could not live with the sorrow of your death or of your sins.

With all my love,

Mom

The letter drops out of my hands and floats down the bed. I stare at the corpse that used to be my mother, blood pounding in my ears. My rage spikes, cruel and hot, although it's not rage at Mom. I can feel her grief on the air, like a ghost, and I understand that she did this terrible thing to herself because I died.

Because Kenny and Maggie and all the rest killed me. And when they did, they killed her, too.

My vision tunnels down until all I can see is her corpse, illuminated by a bright shard of moonlight that cuts in through a clean patch on the grimy window. I breathe deep, my body aching with some urge I can't quite identify.

I lift my hand and fold it in the shapes she taught me when I was a little boy, when I didn't learn to speak the way the other children did. "I love you," I say with my fingers, my eyes hot with tears.

Then I wrench away from her, stalking back into the kitchen. The rope is coiled on the floor like a snake, and I kick it with a wordless scream, sending it flying into the ice box. Then I slam open the drawer where Mom kept her knives.

They still look sharp.

I select the cleaver she used whenever she would slaughter a chicken for our holiday meals. I like how it feels in my hand. As a boy, she didn't want me to watch her kill the chickens, and I wonder now if it's because she was worried that I was like my father. But I used to watch anyway, peering through the window. She always thanked them first, right before she swung this cleaver down and separated their little heads from their bodies.

I liked the blood, crimson and glistening in the sunlight like rubies.

I shove the drawer shut and stalk back out to the woods. The moon watches me through the trees with a bright, urging intensity as I pick my way down to our little dock on the lake. Our boat is still there, not that it matters. I would have swum across if I needed to.

The waters of Hanging Lake lap softly against the rocky shore, as quiet and steady as a heartbeat. And on the other side, the lights of Veritas shine in the dark. That's where they live, in Veritas. My murderers. *Her* murderers.

I squeeze the cleaver tightly. I think about the bright, rubied blood of the chickens.

And I wonder if human blood will be just as beautiful.

1

CHLOE

PRESENT DAY

I know I've arrived when I see a big, painted sign on the side of the road, sticking up from a patch of cleared trees. WELCOME TO VERITY HOLLOW! it announces in red, vintage-looking script. LAKESIDE LIVING AT ITS BEST!

Then, in smaller block letters: HOMES STARTING FROM $550K

That number, which, from what I understand, is significantly lower than what my grandparents paid for this house, is unfathomable to me. Equally unfathomable is that I'm about to live in one of those starting-at-$550K homes after spending the first half of my twenties trapped in a tiny, mold-ridden apartment in Boston.

I turn into the subdivision's entrance—a winding, serpentine road covered in dappled light from the surrounding trees, which have somehow been left untouched by the construction. Eventually, the road turns into a residential street, and the houses emerge out of the woods like huge mushrooms.

"Wow," I breathe, peering over my steering wheel. I've never seen the house in person, just photographs, which were impressive enough. But these houses are so much bigger than I was expecting, with their tiered roofs and big picture windows. Half of them aren't fully completed yet; one I pass lacks any siding, and another is just the wood frame with a half-finished roof. But as I reach the end of the block, the street numbers growing smaller and smaller, they become more fully formed. One has a big Range Rover parked in its circular driveway; another has pretty rose-themed landscaping. Between them is 12 Hanging Lake Road, my new home.

My grandparents bought this house five years ago, one of the first in the subdivision. They used it in the summers until my grandfather passed away, and my grandmother decided she'd rather not have to take care of a glittering lakeside mansion. And then she died, too, suddenly and abruptly from a stroke, and I was as stunned as anyone to learn the house had come to me, with no attached mortgage, although I do have to take care of the $1,200 a month in property taxes and house insurance. Still cheaper than my shitty apartment, though.

I pull into the driveway and stare up at the house, sprawling its way through the surrounding trees. My mom used to call it a cottage, which is laughable. This is a mansion, the kind of house designed to host family gatherings—not that my grandparents ever got around to doing anything like that. Five bedrooms, six baths, and a pier that stretches all the way to Hanging Lake.

I step out into the warm, breezy air. I can smell the lake immediately: a soft, steely scent that reminds me a little of rainwater. I can smell the pine, too, and the cinnamon-y scent of sassafras, and a kind of crispness that reminds me I'm up in the mountains and not in the bustle of the city.

A bang echoes through the woods, startling me until voices trail up on the wind. A woman's voice, specifically, stern and chiding. When I glance in her direction, I see the first glimpse of what I assume are the neighbors with the Range Rover, since the woman and two children are currently marching away from the house's porch. One is a teenager, already towering over his petite, blonde mother, his hair turning shaggy for the summer. The other is a little boy, around ten. He's the one who sees me first.

He stops in the middle of the sidewalk and stares at me. I smile and give him a friendly little wave. Good first impressions and all that.

He mimics my movements.

"What are you—" The mother follows the boy's gaze until she lands on me. "Oh!" she cries, correcting herself. "Oh, I didn't realize the Monroes were renting out their property."

I'm not sure she meant for me to hear that, given that the older boy grunts an acknowledgement. Still, I figure I ought to introduce myself. "Hi!" I call out across the gap of our yards. "I'm Chloe. I'm actually moving in."

The woman purses her lips, studying me, eyes sweeping up and down my body, like she's scanning me before deciding what to make of me. I plaster on my nicest smile and cut across the grass toward the family. The woman finally gives me a smile, although it feels fake.

"Blaire Jenkins," she says as I approach, holding out her hand for a limp, awkward handshake. "These are my boys, Owen—" She beams at the teenager, who stares dolefully out at me from under the fringe of his brown hair. "—and Oliver." She nods at the little boy, who blinks up at me with shy, round eyes.

"It's nice to meet you, Oliver," I say to him, and I'm rewarded with a flash of a smile. Then he brushes his palms together and brings his index fingers together like two toy soldiers.

It's the last thing I expect out here, seeing someone speak in ASL. But it's also a bit like seeing an old friend.

"How are you doing today?" I sign back, the movements clumsy. I haven't had many opportunities to practice since I was working as an interpreter, right out of college. The work was too stressful for not enough pay, which I learned quickly enough is pretty much all jobs. At least with the one I have now, I don't really have to talk to anyone.

Still, I've always loved the language, and it feels good to use it again. Especially when the little boy's face lights up in excitement.

"You know sign language," Blaire says, surprise clear in her voice.

Oliver is signing back at me, his hands moving too quickly for me to catch it all. But I get something about the lake, and rowing a boat, and having to do something he doesn't want to.

"Yeah, I studied it in college." I sign the words out as I speak them.

"You don't have to do that," Blaire says sharply. "He hears just fine."

Immediately, I'm struck with a vague sense of unease. Oliver drops his hands to his sides and looks down at the grass.

The older boy, Owen, gives an exasperated sigh. "Can we go? We're gonna be late."

"We're not going to be late." Blaire, however, does give me another fake-looking smile. "Although we should be heading out. It's a bit of a hike into Pinella from here."

Oliver tugs on his mother's sleeve until she looks at him. Then he signs, "Can I stay here? Chloe can watch me."

"No," Blaire says immediately, not bothering to sign the

word. "No, I can't just foist you off on our new neighbor." She gives me another one of those fake smiles. Every single one makes my skin crawl. "I'm sorry about this. Oliver's always trying to get out of his BJJ class. Aren't you, Ollie?"

He doesn't say anything.

"But it's good for him," she continues, pressing her hand down on Oliver's back. "Being around... *other* kids."

The way she stresses *other* gives me that discomfiting feeling again. I shift my weight, already kind of regretting coming over here. I don't like how Blaire talks about Oliver. I don't like the way Owen keeps glaring at me. And I don't really like that this is my first interaction with my new neighbors.

Although it does warm my heart a bit when Oliver signs up to me, "It was nice to meet you. Can I show you my rock collection when I get back?"

"Oliver," Blaire says warningly, but I respond with a quick, "Of course you can." I glance over at Blaire before adding, "If your mother says it's okay."

Oliver beams at me.

"We need to go," Blaire says, corralling Oliver along the sidewalk as Oliver lopes behind them. She bends down to hiss something in Oliver's ear. There's just enough distance between us that I can't make out what she says—

Although not so much that I don't see the way his little shoulders knot up like an old and practiced reflex.

I SPEND the rest of the afternoon unpacking the boxes of essentials I brought with me in my car. The rest of my stuff is scheduled to arrive in a week or two, not that there's a ton of it. My grandma didn't exactly leave the house fully furnished —one of the bedrooms is literally just storage boxes full of holiday decorations, old clothes, ancient paperbacks, and other assorted grandparent-type treasures, and two of the bedrooms are completely empty. But the essentials are all there. A big king-size bed in the master bedroom, a nicely appointed living room and kitchen. There's even a huge roll-top mahogany desk in the smallest of the bedrooms, which, according to family lore, belonged to my great-great-grand-father. It definitely puts my shitty IKEA desk to shame, which is why my IKEA desk is currently in a dumpster back in Boston.

Still, it's vaguely unsettling to be in a sprawling, sun-filled lakeside McMansion instead of a cramped apartment. As I hang my clothes up in the big walk-in closet, the same thought keeps speeding through my head: *This is mine now.* This closet, which is roughly the same size as my old galley kitchen. This bedroom, with its big French doors that open to a Juliet balcony that has a view of Hanging Lake, the water glittering like diamonds in the afternoon sun. The seemingly endless supply of bathrooms. The big living room with its high vaulted ceiling and enormous wall-sized window, which also has a view of the lake. The porch. The dining room. The massive kitchen with its convection oven. The two-car garage.

All of it. *Mine.*

I keep thinking there has to be a catch, although I also pretty much know what it is: I'm in the middle of nowhere. I work remotely, so that's not an issue. But if I want to go anywhere but the lake, I'll have to hop in my beat-up old car and drive. Pinella is twenty-five minutes away, and it didn't have much when I stopped there on my way in. A Food Lion, a Dollar General, a vape shop, a cell phone repair place. Apparently a BJJ studio, too. Asheville, the closest city, is about an hour and a half drive on the back roads.

I know it'll take some getting used to. My parents

certainly tried to talk me out of moving into the house; Mom would get this sour, pinched expression whenever I talked about my plans for moving.

Are you sure you want to live out there? she said when I first told her I wasn't going to sell. *It's a summer home, Chloe. It's not a place you live.*

Summer homes are absurd, I shot back. *Why have a house if you're not going to live in it?*

She and my dad both had a two-pronged attack to try to get me to stay in Boston, the two of them alternating calling me over the last few months. Mom wanted me to sell the house to my Aunt Lydia: *It'll stay in the family that way,* she said. *And you can visit when you like.* Dad tried to convince me to sign up for one of those short-term rental sites.

But I didn't want to do either. When my grandma left the house to me, she left a message, too: *Think of it as a place to call your own.*

And I have every intention of doing just that.

It takes me the better part of the afternoon to finish unpacking my things, and when I'm done, it's nearly dinner time. Fortunately, I'm prepared with some frozen butter chicken from the Food Lion. It's not exactly the sambar I used to get from the south Indian takeout place by my apartment, but it still fills my kitchen with the earthy, fragrant scent of coriander and turmeric. I dump it in one of the nice ceramic bowls that were stacked in the cupboard, pour myself a glass of Riesling, and go out on the patio to eat.

The house, like all the houses in the subdivision, juts right up against the lake, with the big wooden patio narrowing to a short pier that stretches over the water. I walk down to the edge and sit there, my feet dangling off the side so the cold, steely water splashes around my ankles as I eat. It's golden hour, the sun just starting to sink into the treeline, and the lake looks like something off a postcard. I can almost picture

Visit Scenic North Carolina! hanging above the golden-glimmering waterline in the same cheery red font that was on the Verity Hollow welcome sign. On the other side of the lake is a wild tangle of trees and overgrowth that suggests we're more isolated than we are.

Because I may be in the middle of nowhere, but my house isn't exactly isolated. There are mirrored piers on either side of me; the one to the left, the one that belongs to the Jenkins family, is only about fifty feet away. There's a little wooden boat tied to the pier, and it bobs on the water and clacks against the post, soft and rhythmic. Didn't Oliver say something about wanting to be out on his boat? I can't imagine letting a ten-year-old row around on the lake by himself.

The thought gives me a tightness in my chest, remembering how his mom talked about him. *You don't have to do that. He can hear just fine.*

I tell myself it's none of my business. He's not my kid. The idea of having kids at all actually fills me with a vague sense of existential terror. All that responsibility on your shoulders, to make sure they turn out decent.

I put the thought of kids out of my mind and focus on the lake, the golden sunlight, the pretty scenery. Still, though, as I finish my meal and the wind picks up, blowing through the uninviting thicket of pine trees on the opposite side of the lake, the boat bangs harder against the pier, and a tight, chilly uneasiness creeps over my skin.

2

THEO

There's someone new in Veritas.

Well, not Veritas anymore. I still think of it that way, even though it's been twenty years since that shithole town dried up for good. It didn't take much. That transcendent blood-soaked killing spree in '65, after I revived for the first time, and then three smaller ones over the next four decades. Four times the killing moon called me across the lake, and each time, Veritas got a little bit smaller. It wasn't just because I was killing off the population, either. It was the fear I sowed, and it grew like the forest, choking out any humans I left alive. More houses emptied. Old Frank's grocery store boarded up. Then the post office closed, sometime after the turn of the millennium, and everything went quiet.

Veritas was finally dead. I was free.

That freedom has lasted for seventeen years, just me and the woods and my cabin. When hikers come through, I kill them, and that's enough to sustain me. I don't even have to die, like I did whenever the killing moon called me into Veritas. Small kills, simple kills. They're enough.

Even though the houses have come back.

I watch them being built through the trees. They're going up one by one, even though they all look the same: big, glittering houses with walls of windows like eyes that look out at the lake. I realized quickly enough that it's not a town. Just a single row of houses, so unlike any of the houses I'm used to seeing this high up in the mountains. Vacation homes.

I can sense the humans moving around them, though. I can sense their comings and goings, all their unique, human scents on the wind. I've mostly been able to ignore them. They're strangers, and they aren't trespassers, since they all stay on their side of the lake. Most importantly, they aren't Veritas, and it was Veritas that killed me. It was Veritas that killed my mother.

It's a particular scent that alerts me to the newcomer. I'm making my rounds along the edge of my territory, looking for signs of hikers or campers or other would-be explorers—anyone I might need to watch out for over the next few days. I don't find anything, but when I make my way toward the eastern side of the lake, the wind gusts, and it brings a scent like a rose garden. Sweet and honeyed, with an underlying storminess like freshly fallen rain.

I stop, sniffing the air, and turn toward the lake. I'm still safely hidden in the woods, but I can see glimmers of the water through the trees.

The wind gusts against, bringing another wash of that oddly appealing scent. This second time, I sense the humanity within it. Someone new is out on the lakeshore, over in the place that's no longer Veritas.

Although I shouldn't—it's still daylight—I creep forward and stop just at the edge of the treeline, scanning the horizon to see if I can find the scent's origin. The other side is far enough away that it's hard even for me to see, despite my excellent vision—vision made for predation, as my father told me when I finally found him. Not in Ohio, like my mother's letter said, but farther north, in New York. That was a long, long time ago.

Still, my excellent predator's vision sweeps along the glossy toy houses and then settles on my target.

A woman.

At first, I think she's sitting on the pier of my young friend Oliver, who lives across the lake with his family and is the only human I let roam around on my territory. But then I realize, no, she's next door. She has her feet in the water, and her head tilted back, like she's looking at the clouds striating across the sky. The wind blows her brown hair away from her shoulders, and when it moves into the light, it flames copper, like sunset on the water. I suck in a breath.

She's beautiful.

When was the last time I considered a human beautiful? Not since I was a human, or thought I was one. Not since a beautiful human girl smiled at me and told me there was a party and then laughed as I slid into the darkness.

My skin tightens. This woman—who is not Maggie Stone, who in fact looks and feels nothing like Maggie Stone —pushes herself up to standing but keeps squinting out at the water. Her legs are long and shapely, leading up into lush, curved hips. I feel something ache in the back of my jaw. I don't know how to put a name to it.

The woman turns away, ducking down to pick something up from the pier. Trash, it looks like. A bottle of something. Then she walks back down the pier to the house it's attached to. This house has been empty for a while, as I remember. To be honest, I don't pay that much attention to which human lives in which house. I only know that they're there, the houses and the humans. And I only care that they stay on their side of the lake, away from me.

Still, I feel something like longing as the woman walks

away, hips swaying a little, bare legs gleaming in the soft-falling sunlight.

For the first time in decades, I want to know a human's name.

THEO

I don't see the woman again, not as night falls, and not the next morning, either. I don't have to sleep much—none of my kind do—and I don't bother going back to my cabin. The night is warm enough and the moon is small enough, just a sliver of a fingernail against the sky, that I'm able to take advantage of the cloak of darkness and risk being out on the open beach.

The pier that I used when I was a boy has long since rotted into the lake, and the boat I keep in the basement of the cabin, along with a pair of polished oars, to use when the killing moon calls my name. Since I rarely have need to cross the water, I rarely go down to the beach. *Beach* was always my mother's word for it—really, it's just a narrow strip of dirt where the lake laps against the shore, barely a foot wide. But the trees don't grow there, and it puts me out in the open. It's important that I stay invisible.

But I want to watch the woman's house. Those big picture windows the houses all have show everything when people turn their lights on after dark—and they do, constantly, night after night. They think they're alone out here, save for each other.

The new woman is no exception. Her house is lit up like a campfire, and it seems to me that it glows brighter than the other houses along the shore. It has a particularly large window on the first floor, one that's practically the entire width of the house, and I can see the silhouettes of furniture against the backdrop of light. Occasionally, I see movement, too. Her? That, I can't tell. I also can't tell if she's alone or not, although I don't catch any other new scents on the wind.

I watch her by watching the light. First, all of downstairs is illuminated. Then it dims into a soft, neon glow. She must be watching TV. Then it flicks off entirely, and the light goes on upstairs, and my breath quickens, because there's a big window up there, too, with a balcony that I can only assume leads into her bedroom. She passes in front of it four times— I count each one, certain it's her—but I don't see much more than that. She has the curtains drawn. Her silhouette is clear. Nothing else is.

Then that light goes off, and the house fades into the night.

I keep vigil, though. That's most of what I do these days, anyway. Keep vigil in the forbidden woods across the lake. Make sure to keep the stories up. The ghost of Theo Shorn haunts these woods, after all, seeking vengeance for his murder. If you want to go hiking, stay on the eastern side of the lake, and definitely don't cross onto the narrow peninsula that cuts into the water like a knife. Those *Keep Out* signs are nailed to the trees for a reason.

It's rare for me to keep vigil like *this*, though. To watch someone specific. At least, someone I don't intend to kill.

What if she crosses the lake? whispers a dark, raspy voice in the back of my head. *Would you kill her then?*

I mutter wordlessly in the back of my throat, the closest I

get to vocal speech, and the sound of my frustration is swallowed up by the waves washing against the dirt my mother called a beach. I kill all trespassers.

Well, except for Oliver, when he showed up a few months ago, crashing through the underbrush. But in the sixty years since my first revival, he's been the only exception.

I stay out on the shore until the light shifts into the cobwebby grey of dawn, and then I slip back into the safety of the woods. My stomach growls, reminding me I need to eat. I was so caught up in my vigil that I hadn't noticed my hunger. It's not the first time it's happened, and I know it won't be the last.

So I go home. Breakfast is a venison steak fried up with garlic from the far western side of my territory and a cup of coffee. The coffee is from the last camper I killed, about a month ago, and I'm almost out. I've been rationing it, saving it for special occasions. And glimpsing that woman, catching her scent, felt special enough.

After I eat, I go out on the porch to finish my coffee. I'm hoping I might catch the trail of her scent again, even though my cabin is set far enough back from the lake that I often don't sense the humans out here. Still, I like being outside more than I like being inside. It's been long enough that the cabin doesn't remind me of my mother, of what my life was like before I died for the first time. But I still feel constrained by it. Enclosed.

The wind stirs the leaves around; I catch whiffs of the animals out in the woods. A raccoon burying into the underbrush. A pair of deer grazing off to the north. The opossums that live in the crawl space under my house, no doubt sleeping now that the sun has come up.

And then a human scent twines through. Not hers, not the woman's. And not a hiker's, either.

Oliver's back.

I settle down on the old porch swing to wait for him; he knows his way through my territory well enough to make it from the beach to the cabin.

Maybe it's hypocritical of me, letting a little human boy wander around my territory when I have a reputation to maintain. But for all my bloodlust, I'm not predisposed to killing children—they don't provide enough of a challenge, for one. For another, they haven't had the years necessary to accumulate any real sins. I assume anyone old enough has done something worthy of death, and I figure children ought to have the opportunity to transgress before I snuff their life out.

Oliver was the first child to ever step foot on my territory, though. It's rough terrain, so the hikers and campers leave the kiddies at home. When Veritas was still around, gasping for breath, the few kids in town knew not to cross the lake. But no one ever told Oliver, and a little over six months ago, I intercepted him near the graveyard after tracking him for about half an hour, nervous about what a small boy was doing out here by himself. When he saw me, he didn't react with fear, only curiosity. Then he made words with his hands. Words I recognized, because my mother had taught me that same way of speaking when I was a child, and it became clear I needed an alternative to my voice.

The second I saw him say, *My name is Oliver! What's yours?* I knew I couldn't kill him, and not just because he was a child. He reminded me too much of the first version of myself, the version that wasn't a killer.

His small, pattering footsteps echo through the trees. I lean forward, watching for him, and a few seconds later, he emerges, looking a great deal like he did that first day, with a brown leaf tangled in his hair and his little blue-and-green dinosaur backpack. He blinks up at the porch, then waves excitedly at me. I gesture for him to come on up.

"You're here early," I say, setting my mostly-empty coffee cup aside to talk.

He shrugs. "Mom was yelling again." Then he sits down on the swing beside me. Even after six months, I'm not totally used to how fearless he is around me. It's like he can't sense that I'm a predator.

I don't mind, though. As much as I shouldn't admit it, it is nice to have the company.

Oliver sets his backpack on his lap, unzips it, and hands me a stack of paper. I know what they are. More of his drawings.

At our second or third meeting, I made the mistake of telling Oliver that I did not cross the lake. I told him this because he wanted me to come over to his house and see his collection of rocks, which I gather is very impressive, and I, of course, don't cross the lake unless it's to kill. I didn't tell him that last part. When he asked, I said I wasn't allowed to leave and then, because I didn't know what else to do, strongly implied that I'm a ghost.

Ever since then, Oliver has been bringing me drawings of what he calls the outside world. At first, they were things around his house: his rock collection, an expensive-looking television set, an odd boxy thing he explained was something called a video game console that belonged to his brother. Eventually, he expanded his subjects to include items from the woods across the lake, and then from Pinella, which had been little more than a post office when I was a boy but has apparently grown to replace Veritas.

The top drawing today shows a row of kids in what look like pajamas, their hands in fists near their faces. Oliver taps my shoulders so I look up at him. "My BJJ classes," he says, and then rolls his eyes.

"You should take these seriously," I tell him. "It's good to be able to defend yourself." As I can personally attest. I know what it is to be the strange boy who doesn't speak with his voice.

"You sound like Dad. He says I need to stop whining and toughen up."

"You don't need to be tougher," I tell him, which is also true. Toughness is wasted on humans. It gets them killed by people like me. "You just need to know what to do if someone tries to hurt you." Another human, I mean, although I don't say that.

Oliver rolls his eyes again, then pushes the page aside. This one shows a table with an ice cream sundae, the ice cream colored in rainbow markers and topped with a dollop of whipped cream and, of course, a fire-engine red cherry. "The ice cream shop in Pinella," Oliver says excitedly. "My mom dropped me off there while she was messing around with something for Owen."

I smile at that. Oliver first started mentioning the ice cream shop a month ago, along with the fact that his mother had forbidden him from trying it. Apparently, he managed to find a way around the ban. "Was it good?"

"The best!" He gives me a huge grin. I flip to the next page.

It's a woman. Just her face, with a dark fall of hair, although there's something sweet in her expression. Oliver is good with portraits. Better than a ten-year-old has any right to be.

"Who's this?" I ask him, studying his face as I sign. I think I already know, even though I couldn't get a good look at her face, not from this distance.

"My new neighbor," he signs back.

My heart pounds in my chest, and I look back down at the portrait. She's lovely. Oliver didn't add much color to this one; just the dark brown of her hair and the lighter brown of her eyes. It's sketchy, perhaps a bit rushed, but I can clearly see the woman in the messy lines on the paper.

Oliver taps on my hand, getting me to look at him again. "She moved in yesterday," he signs, brimming with excitement. "Her name is Chloe!" He signs the name out, letter by letter, and I suck in a sharp breath. Her name. I wanted her name, and now I have it.

"And she knows ASL!" he continues. "Maybe we can all be friends?"

My pulse thunders. Is that why I was so drawn to her, this Chloe, sitting with her legs dangling into the water? Did I sense it, somehow? That she wouldn't laugh at me, like the girls in Veritas did? That she would speak to me, and be able to see me speak, too?

Oliver's staring up at me expectantly, waiting for my response. I swallow. It doesn't matter if she knows ASL; I can't bring a grown woman across the lake. She'll know what I am the second she sees me. A predator, a monster. Women see it much more easily than men, and certainly more easily than children.

"Maybe," I sign. Oliver frowns, and I add, "I'm not sure she'll understand."

"Understand what?"

I grit my jaw. "That I'm a ghost," I finally say, even though I don't like lying to him. Then, on a whim, I add. "Like your mother wouldn't understand."

That was the wrong thing to say, of course. Oliver shakes his head furiously, and his hands and arms fly out. "No, she's not like her at all! She's nice!"

Something pangs in my chest. Sympathy, I suppose. I don't feel it often—certainly not for humans—but it's easy to feel it for Oliver. Oliver's mother is not like my mother, from what he's told me. She's not kind. She's the sort of mother who, in my day, would have shipped a boy like us off to a boarding school so she wouldn't have to deal with him. That sort of thing was more common in the fifties. Not so much now. Now, women like her are expected to raise the children they think are broken.

Still, I can't have this Chloe meet me. I don't want to break Oliver's heart like that, to have him learn that his only friend out here is, in fact, not a ghost but a living murderer.

"Why don't we wait?" I say, forming the words slowly. "Like I told you, I have to be careful who I let on my property. People don't always understand."

"She will," Oliver insists.

He's not usually this stubborn. I sigh. "At least wait a few weeks," I finally say. "Give me a chance to clean up my house."

That finally mollifies him. He sighs and rolls his eyes and huffs a little. "A haunted house doesn't have to be clean!" he signs, stabbing decisively into the air with his small child's fingers. I give him my best approximation of an indulgent smile.

Mostly, though, I hope in two weeks' time, he'll move on to something else.

At least our conversation moves on, this time to a movie Oliver watched a few days ago—he's always telling me about the movies and TV shows he watches. The video games he plays, when he's able to play them. Bringing the world to me. I pay attention, as I always do, but it's harder than usual. My thoughts keep wandering to Oliver's new neighbor.

Chloe, with the long auburn hair and the long legs she splashes in the lake.

I know she won't accept me. I'm nearly 80 years old at this point, even if I still look 30. I know what I am, and what humans are, and what our relationship is. Predator to prey. Killer to victim.

But I think of my father, and the tenderness he had for my mother—enough tenderness to let her live, to send her envelopes of cash every six months, to warn her what her son might turn out to be—and I wonder if maybe I could find that tenderness, too.

4

CHLOE

So it's definitely takes some getting used to, living in the woods like this.

The hardest part is the silence, especially at night. My apartment back in Boston was near the Red Line, and I'd hear the late-night commuter rails go by as I was falling off to sleep. I liked it, the soft whirring racket of the wheels against the tracks. Plus, there were all the other city noises: voices down on the street, honking car horns, the occasional thump of music through my apartment's thin walls.

Out here? Nothing.

For the first week in the house, I'm struck with an overwhelming loneliness. I never hear my neighbors, so they might as well not exist. My coworkers are, as always, user pics on the company's Slack channel and voices in the video-optional meeting we have once a week. I have a single in-person exchange with the teenage cashier at the Food Lion in Pinella, his smile pleasant enough as he hands me my receipt.

My one saving grace is my two best friends, Penelope and Abi, and the video chat we have on my first Friday night at Hanging Lake. We met in college but spread out across the country afterward. Abi went to grad school for a few years and then moved back to Texas afterward to take on her uncle's mortuary business. Of the three of us, she's the most responsible. Penelope is the least, at least on paper. She never stays in one place for too long, and I'm surprised she made it through four years of college, honestly. But she's also the one I'm closest to, the one who took me in when I was spiraling after I realized how much I'm *not* cut out for interpreter work.

We're close enough that I know the real reason for her nomadic tendencies, about the darkness that runs through her family. Even Abi doesn't know that.

Regardless, when Friday rolls around, it's such a relief to see both of their faces and hear their voices, even through a computer screen. Something to fill up the enormous silence of this house.

"How are you holding up out there?" Penelope asks. "I don't know why the two of you both want to live in the middle of nowhere."

Abi rolls her eyes. "I wouldn't say I'm in the middle of nowhere."

"Texas. It's bad enough."

"No, my place is way more isolated." I pick up my laptop and my glass of wine and cart them over to the window. "Check it out."

I turn the computer around so they can see out the glass at the pier, and the orange-red sunset melting into the lake. I get a chorus of oohs and ahhs from Abi and some gentle chiding about environmental degradation from Penelope. Typical for both of them. Later, it's nice watching a movie with them on my computer, pretending for a few hours that I'm not alone.

The weekend rolls into the next week, and I slowly start to find my footing. There's one big consolation: as lonely as the woods are, they are absolutely, breathtakingly beautiful. Even better, my WiFi signal is strong enough that I can take my laptop out to the patio and work by the lake, leaning back in an Adirondack chair as I sift through my company's database. It's probably hell on my wrists, but I like being out in the warm, sunny air, the sound of the lake lapping around me. I can almost pretend I'm on vacation.

It's during one of my work days that I run into Oliver again. Or rather, he runs into me. It's a little after lunch, and I'm scrolling my way through a particularly vexing data discrepancy when I hear a splash out on the lake. I glance up and see a small rowboat on the lake, coming from the direction of the wild peninsula across the water.

Inside the boat is Oliver. Alone. He's also not wearing a life jacket.

I frown over the top of my laptop. The realtor who transferred the house deed into my name told me about the peninsula, a little overhang of land stabbing into the lake proper. Namely, she told me that it was dangerous.

Stick to the eastern side of the lake, she said as I signed papers in her office. *The peninsula's got a bit of a reputation, you know. Hikers have gotten lost out there. Some dangerous wildlife. Ticks and rattlesnakes are probably the least of your worries.*

I've never been one for hiking, so I didn't think much of it. But I do wonder what a ten-year-old is doing wandering around on some apparently dangerous peninsula.

I don't have much time to dwell on it, though. When Oliver sees me, he starts waving one hand furiously around. Then he rows faster, turning the boat toward my pier. I watch him with a sense of alarm rising in my throat; the oars seem too big for his skinny arms, and the boat careens through the water, sending up splashes on either side. It occurs to me that he's going too fast—

And then the boat rams into the pier, sending little shock-waves up to the patio.

"Are you all right?" The words are out of my lips on instinct, and I sign the question a half-second later, as I jump from the chair and bolt down to the boat.

Oliver's grinning, though. He throws a frayed rope around one of the posts on my pier, anchoring the boat in place, then heaves himself out. I can tell he's done this before.

"What are you doing out here?" I ask, signing and saying it at the same time. Oliver adjusts his shirt, slides his back-pack onto his shoulders, and looks up at me.

"Visiting my friend." Then he makes a shape with his hands I've never seen before.

"Sorry," I tell him. "I'm still a bit rusty. I didn't catch that."

Oliver sighs, but then he spells out a name: Theo.

"Oh," I say. "That's your friend's name? Theo?" I spell it out, rather than trying to reproduce the sign for it.

Oliver nods.

I frown and look out at the lake. It's as calm and serene as always, and the trees on the peninsula sway back and forth a little in the wind, like paint brushes moving across the sky. I keep thinking about the realtor, though. *Dangerous wildlife.*

"On the peninsula?" I ask, then point toward the trees. "I didn't think anyone lived over there."

"It's just him," Oliver says, signing quickly. "And he doesn't like people to come see him, except for me. He likes me because I show him what's going on over here. And in town and stuff. Because he can't leave."

Oliver drags his backpack around and starts digging through it. I take a moment to try and register what he's telling me. Maybe the realtor was wrong. Maybe someone lives over there after all.

"Oliver," I say out loud, and he looks up at me, his eyes big and genuine. I sign my next question. "Why doesn't your friend like people to come see him?"

Oliver shrugs and goes back to digging through his backpack. A second later, he extracts a slightly wrinkled sheet of paper and hands it to me. It's a drawing—a really, really good drawing, actually, done in black ink and colored in with pencils. It's a cabin.

"You drew this?" I sign around the drawing.

Oliver nods. "It's Theo's house."

He makes the special sign for Theo's name again, and I store it in my head, along with the spoken version. Both of them seem to thrum in my thoughts. "Does he have a last name?" I finally ask, still not sure what to make of any of this.

"Probably, but he's never told me." Oliver grins again. "He uses ASL, too. Like me."

Something pangs in my heart, and I suddenly wonder if I've been misreading this entire situation. Not once in my admittedly brief interaction with Oliver's mom did I see her use ASL with him. And it occurs to me, as I look down at the drawing of the cabin, that maybe no one lives over there on the peninsula at all. That maybe Oliver just… wants someone to live over there. Someone who can talk to him the way he wants to talk.

"This is a very good drawing," I finally say, the page fluttering a little as I sign.

Oliver beams. "Theo likes my drawings, too."

Discomfort twists in my belly. I glance over at the treeline again. They're dense over there, and there's no pier or anything. No sign of habitation.

I try to hand the drawing back to Oliver, but he shakes his head. "You keep it," he says. "Since Theo doesn't want anyone coming to his territory, I thought I could show it to you the way I show all this stuff over here to him."

My discomfort tightens.

"Thank you for the drawing," I say, and I mean it. I tuck it down beneath my laptop and then turn back to Oliver, who's staring at me expectantly. Half a dozen questions flit through my head, and I finally settle on, "Does your Mom know about Theo?"

Immediately, Theo's gaze flicks away. He nods yes. I wait. He doesn't elaborate.

I try again. "Why doesn't Theo want anyone to come visit him?"

I thought Oliver might have been avoiding the question, but this time, when I ask it, he actually does answer. "He doesn't like living people," Oliver says, as if this is the most natural thing in the world. "He doesn't want them on his property. He doesn't mind me, though, because I bring him drawings."

"I see." I lift my gaze past Oliver, this time to his pier and then up to his house. I'm not sure what to think. *Living people.* What the hell does that mean? Maybe I misunderstood him. I'm still a bit out of practice on my ASL, after all.

Then Oliver taps my arm and signs, "I don't really like people, either. But I like you."

I blink, surprised. This is the first time a kid has ever told me they like me. The truth is, I've never been around children much. I never babysat when I was younger. I don't have any siblings, and my two cousins are my age and haven't seen fit to reproduce yet.

"Well, thank you," I finally say. "I like you, too, Oliver." It seems the least I can say. And honestly, it's true.

Oliver gives me a big, beaming grin.

And then he tears off down my pier, running back to his house, leaving me his boat and the drawing of the cabin. I look down at it, at the sketchy, rough lines. And even though the sun is warm, I get that prickling sense of unease again.

It seems to come from the peninsula.

5

CHLOE

I can't get Oliver's story out of my head. I tell myself it's not my business, that I don't actually know him or his family, but a thin snake of worry keeps wriggling around in my belly. He's ten years old and nonverbal. *Surely* it's not a good idea for him to be traipsing around on the peninsula—the very same peninsula my realtor told me was dangerous? Where hikers routinely get lost?

I don't even know what that means. It's not even that big a patch of land. So how are hikers getting lost?

What if there really is someone living out there?

By the time I finish dinner, I feel like I ought to do something, although I'm not sure what. Eventually, I do what I always do when I'm feeling uncertain: I text Abi and Penelope about it. Penelope gets back to me first, which isn't surprising. Abi's been distracted lately.

Penelope's response is also not terribly surprising.

Go check it out yourself.

I sigh, frowning down at my phone. Of course she'd say

that, growing up the way she did. With the sister and mother she has.

And do what exactly?

I drop the phone on the counter and fix myself a bowl of strawberries and cream for dessert. There was a farm stand selling the strawberries when I drove into town the other day, with a hand-painted sign reading *Last of the season!* How could I resist that?

My phone dings.

Just check it out. See what's out there. If it seems sketch, you can take it to the kid's parents.

I roll my eyes. This is typical of Penelope. She likes putting herself in danger because, from what I gather, her whole childhood and adolescence always existed at the edge of danger. Now, she channels that energy into protesting. She's the sort of person who knows about anti-surveillance makeup and how to get pepper spray out of your eyes and what to do if you get arrested.

And if there is some dude out there? What then?

If the kid's not scared of him, then he can't be that dangerous.

I scowl. Penelope's conception of what is and isn't dangerous is wildly different from mine.

I shove my phone in my pocket and carry my strawberries out to the pier to consider my options. There's still plenty of light left, all of it soft and hazy and golden-tinged, the kind of light that gives everything a halo. The lake throws up sparks as it laps against Oliver's boat, still tied to my pier.

I stare down at the boat. I think about Penelope's message. *Go check it out yourself.*

I take a big bite of my strawberries.

It wouldn't be too hard to row over there once I'm finished. Poke around. Just to see. Then I could even take the boat back over to Oliver's pier when I'm done.

I could look at it as an adventure, I suppose. Same as the adventure of moving to this lake house.

I pull out my phone and find that Abi's chimed in.

ABI

Um, isn't this kind of dangerous?

PENELOPE

Again, if the kid's not scared, Chloe will be fine THIS ONE TIME. Enough to decide if it's sketch or not. Better to take action than do nothing at all.

I fire off a reply before I can stop myself.

I'm doing it. Will let you know when I've landed.

Both of them start typing at once. I pocket my phone and polish off the rest of the strawberries. I wanted to sit out in the golden light and relish them, but what are some fresh strawberries compared to a bit of danger?

I leave my bowl and spoon sitting on the pier and then lower myself down into the boat. It's a lot more rickety than it looks, and it sinks beneath my weight, making the water splash around the sides. In my pocket, my phone buzzes a couple of times, but I don't check to see what either of them has to say. I'm already in the boat. I'm going.

I untie the rope and push off, the boat slicing sideways through the water like it wants to move along the shore. It takes me a few minutes to figure out how to use the oars, and they feel awkward and clumsy as I dip them into the surface. The boat spins sideways, and I slap the water around until I manage to at least point myself in the right direction.

Then I row.

Well, I attempt to row. For a few minutes, it feels like I'm not even moving, like I'm stuck in some swirling eddy and I'm never getting out. I can not fathom how a ten-year-old could do this. But then I heave with as much of my meager upper body strength as I can manage, and the boat shoves forward, toward the peninsula.

Once I get the hang of rowing, though, I find I actually kind of like it. I like the rhythmic slap of the oars against the lake, and the warm rush of the wind as it pushes my hair back away from my face.

It's pleasant, at least until the hull grinds up against the shore of the peninsula.

I jolt forward, startled by how quickly I ran ashore. For a minute, I just sit there and look up at the dense crush of poplar trees forming a wall in front of me. The sun may be warm and golden out here on the water, but the trees seem to swallow up all the light.

Maybe this wasn't such a great idea.

I force myself to stand up, though, thinking about Penelope's last message, how it's better to take action than do nothing. She isn't wrong. Besides, the distance between the peninsula and my pier isn't far at all. I could swim it easily. But I still feel like I just breached into some other world.

I slide my phone out and skim through the torrent of messages from Abi and Penelope. I ignore all of them as I type out my own.

Just landed.

That sets off a new flurry, of course.

ABI

Be fucking careful omg!

PENELOPE

Keep your phone out of sight. If you see anyone, play it cool and then get the fuck out as quickly as you can.

I decide to take Penelope's advice to heart, slipping my phone back down into my pocket. Then I take a few hesitant steps forward, the boat rocking precariously underfoot. There's one terrifying moment when I think the whole thing is going to tip over and dump me in the shallow, muddy water, but I manage to leap out and land on the shore with a huff.

"Last adventure for you," I mutter to myself, then drag the boat further up on the shore so it doesn't get loose on the lake.

I look up at the trees again.

They rustle in the wind, that soft, persistent rushing sound that I'm still getting used to. Plus, there's all the usual insect sounds over here, too: the constant buzzing rattle of grasshoppers, the occasional whir of a cicada.

I swallow and do what I'm certain Penelope would tell me is a stupid idea, but which, in this moment, feels right.

"Hello?" I call out, my voice getting swept up on the wind. "Hi, I live across the lake!"

There's no answer, just the rustle of the trees. I creep sideways along the narrow strip of dirt, the air heavy and damp and hot. The only respite comes from the breeze blowing over the water. The growth is so dense and tangled that I can't imagine anyone lives out here.

But then I see it. A place in the underbrush that's been stomped down, where the underbrush isn't quite so thick. It's not a *path*, per se, but I can tell that someone's walked there more than once, forming a narrow, dark tunnel that goes deeper into the woods.

My heart hammers. I glance back at the houses again. Not just my house. All of them, with their big picture windows catching the golden light of the sun. I'm not actually isolated. I'm swimming distance from at least four other families.

I pat my phone, reassuring myself that it's still in my pocket. Then I step into the woods.

It's hot and still in here, and the thick, leafy branches stretch out to claw at my skin. *Stick to the eastern side of the lake.* I keep hearing the realtor say, shaking her head ruefully. *The peninsula's got a bit of a reputation, you know. If you like hiking, there are more well-maintained trails over in Nantahala National Forest.*

Yeah, this definitely isn't well-maintained. I keep swiping at my bare arms, certain I feel ticks crawling on me, although it's probably just beads of sweat. The trees seem to bow down under the weight of the hot air, and my skin is already damp and sticky.

This is looking more like a path, though. I can just barely make it out through the dense undergrowth, but there are enough trampled ferns and bare patches of dirt that it's clear someone has walked here, even if it was just Oliver. Although I don't think Oliver's footsteps are heavy enough to crush down the greenery like this.

Which is a thought that makes my heartbeat quicken. Because that means someone *does* live out here.

"Hello?" I call out again. "I'm just a—" I'm not sure how to classify my relationship to Oliver. "Oliver's babysitter," I finally finish.

The forest ripples around me. Somewhere, birds cry out. I keep creeping forward, following the path until I step, suddenly and unexpectedly, into a clearing.

I stop, sweeping my gaze around. The light here is dim and dappled, like early twilight, but I can see that the space is large. Larger than you'd expect for a natural clearing, although it's also quite overgrown, and the trees are tall enough that their branches still form a spiderwebbed roof overhead. Long, pale grasses grow out of the fallen leaves and mulch, along with a few dots of white flowers, pretty and unexpected.

Then the wind gusts, making the trees groan and the grass ripple. And I realize this isn't a clearing, but a graveyard.

Not a new one, certainly. The glimpses of gravestones I see are old and cracked. I would have taken them for rocks, honestly, except that the one closest to me is still fully intact, even if it's covered with a fine, velvety pelt of moss.

I crouch down, sweeping the grass aside. The name carved into the stone has faded, but even in the dim light I can read it:

THEODORE SHORN

1943 - 1960

"Theodore Shorn," I say out loud, and then, a second later, make the connection: Theo. Oliver said his friend's name was Theo.

Any lingering trepidation melts away, replaced with a rush of pity. The realtor was right. No one lives out here. Oliver probably just followed the same path I did and saw the gravestone. What did he say about Theo? That he didn't like living people and couldn't leave his territory?

"Sounds like a ghost to me," I say as I stand up. Not that I believe in ghosts, of course. But a sweet, lonely ten-year-old would. He might see a name on a sixty-year-old gravestone and give it to an imaginary friend. A ghost who can't leave the confines of these overgrown woods.

Another gust of wind. More groans and creaks from the trees. More soft rustling.

And then a loud, sudden *snap.*

I freeze, my adrenaline spiking, even though I know it could be anything. A squirrel, a deer, a dead tree branch finally succumbing to its rot.

Still, I call out a shaky, "Hello?"

Nothing. No movement, no sounds but the insects and the wind.

"I'm leaving now," I say, just in case, and then I flee.

6

———

THEO

Someone has come into my territory.

That's all I know at first; I'm weeding the little vegetable patch I have out back when I catch a whiff of the citrusy scent of human fear. It's startling; the hikers who come out usually don't smell of fear, not anymore. There's enough cell service, even on my peninsula, that no one's ever truly lost.

But then the wind shifts, and I catch something under that fear. Something sweet and familiar.

Chloe. The trowel drops out of my hands and lands with a thump in the dirt. *Oliver*, I think, my heart hardening. But when I sniff the air, I don't smell him at all. Just her.

The scent's coming from the lake, and I have a momentary sense of panic. Am I supposed to kill her? That's what I've always done when someone comes into my territory. The urge to do it is as overwhelming as rage. But I don't feel either now. In fact, the idea of killing her makes me vaguely queasy.

However, I absolutely do not want her finding my cabin,

44

or my garden, or any other evidence that I exist. I'm supposed to be a ghost.

Her scent rushes through the air again, and I bolt, moving quickly around the side of my cabin and darting into the thick tangle of trees, where I can at least crouch in the shadows and decide what to do next. Maybe I can scare her off, somehow.

But then I hear her voice for the first time.

"Hello?"

Just one word. It makes my heart jump around in my chest.

"Hi, I live across the lake!"

She's definitely still down by the beach. I can tell by how her voice carries on the wind. But more than that, I'm struck by the sound of her voice itself—the soft, musical lilt of it. I'm struck in place, her scent wrapping around me. I don't want to kill her. I don't want to scare her, either.

I don't know what I want to do.

Footsteps, faint and rustling. She's moving into the trees.

I follow the sound trail she leaves behind. Like all the humans who stumble into my territory, she's wildly noisy, and it's easy to track her through the dappled light of the forest. She's on the old footpath that Mom and I would use, the one that linked the cabin to the cemetery and then to the pier. The pier's long gone. The cemetery isn't.

I see Chloe's trail before I see *her*, a ripple through the dense underlayer in the forest. Her steps skitter over the fallen leaves, creating a riot of sound. I hide myself among the brush, my breath tight in my chest. Her fear has lessened into a kind of mild trepidation. It occurs to me, given the way the blood pounds in my temples, that maybe I'm the one who's afraid now.

Which is absurd. How can a monster like me be afraid of a human woman?

"I'm Oliver's babysitter!"

I jolt at her voice, at how loud it is. I was so distracted by her presence that I didn't realize how close that presence was.

Acting on a surge of panic, I melt further back into the trees, just as she pushes past where I'm standing. And I see her. A glimpse of her, anyway: her long, thick hair, falling around her shoulders, and her bare arms with their golden sheen from being out in the sun. She ducks beneath a long, spindly branch, then glances around.

For a split second, I see the flash of her eyes, and I feel like I've been skinned alive, like she's staring straight through me.

But then she looks away and keeps going. I let out a low, quiet breath, but I swear my heart is louder.

I should kill her. I should burst through this brush and wrap my fingers around her throat and squeeze the air out of them. Or slam the back of her head against one of the nearby tulip trees over and over until the grey of the bark turns red with her blood.

It's an image that turns my breath shuddery. That makes my cock grow in my pants. And I still don't want to fucking act on it.

Her footsteps stop. She must have found the cemetery.

I take a deep breath, trying to calm myself down. It's fine for her to find the cemetery. There's no real sign of my presence there. But I need her to turn back, to go back to her side of the lake, before I do the thing I'm made to do.

I slip through the trees, gliding closer to the clearing. I duck beneath a shrub of azalea and, my breath thick in my lungs, peer through the gap in the leaves.

And there she is.

Seeing her like this, up close, is so much better than seeing her from across the lake. Her features are delicate and pretty, her lips full, her hair slightly mussed from the wind.

Oliver's portrait of her, the one I currently have tacked to the wall above my bed, really is an excellent likeness.

Chloe, I think, and my chest feels strange again. Overly tight.

Chloe tilts her head and steps into the cemetery's overgrown grass. She's looking at something.

And when she pulls the grass away, I know it's my grave.

I feel like my soul is growing to crawl out of my skin. Chloe crouches down, runs her hands over the stone.

"Theodore Shorn," she says.

Hearing my name in her soft, sultry voice makes my heart pound and my cock stiffen even more, enough that it's uncomfortable, all that hard length between my legs. The early-evening light spilling through the trees overhead gives her skin a soft, golden glow, and I want to know what it would feel like beneath my hand. I want to feel the warmth of her blood pumping through her veins and the dampness of her breath on my cheek. I imagine myself killing her again, this time settling on the intimacy of choking. That's not usually how I kill. I want the blood. I want to see the inside of a body strewn across the floor.

But there's no touching when you kill like that. The blade does all that work. And god, do I want to touch her.

I step forward, delirious with lust. And I step on a branch like one of my fucking human victims. The crack is thunderous.

Chloe gasps and jerks up, her eyes wide as she whips her head around. Her fear scent slams over me, and I have to bite back a groan.

"Hello?" she rasps. I squeeze my hands into fists, trying to stop myself from stepping out of the trees and killing her because I don't know any other fucking way to show her that she's beautiful.

"I'm leaving now," Chloe says, her voice shaky.

Then she runs, the sound thunderous as she dives back onto the path.

I breathe, trying to get ahold of myself. I don't follow her, just listen to her retreating footsteps. It's only when it sounds like she's nearly to the beach that I follow, my own steps slow and cautious. I tell myself it's because I want to make sure she's fled, and not because I want to see her again before she does.

By the time I make it to the treeline, she's already pushed out on the water. I recognize the boat as Oliver's, and I feel a little skip in my heart. Did he send her out here? It seems strange that he would send her alone, though. He knows I don't like trespassers.

Is she a trespasser?

I stand among the poplars, watching Chloe row back toward her house, with its huge windows reflecting the setting sun. The boat turns sideways a little, and for a moment, she's haloed by golden light. Heat surges through me, flooding into my cock again.

Normally, killing is more than enough. What need does a monster like me have for sex? For companionship? The few years I spent with my father showed me how treacherous that can be, especially if a human is involved. The killing urge is always there, bubbling under the surface.

I can feel it now, even, hot and pulsing. I could chase her, I suppose. Splash out into the water and drag her into the darkness, killing her the same way I died that first time. I'd go under with her, though. I'd make sure she wasn't alone as the light slipped out of her eyes.

But I don't move from my spot in the trees, just reach down and unbuckle my fly so I can ease my cock out. Jerking off is never as good as killing, although it's a close enough approximation, and the pressure of my hand around my length makes me suck my breath in. A new image flits into my mind, of me and Chloe. But this time. I'm not killing her. I'm fucking her.

I imagine fucking her on top of my grave, burying myself to the hilt as she groans beneath me, her cunt as hot as the friction of my palm. I stroke myself faster, rocking my cock into my fist, watching Chloe row into the golden light. Pressure builds tight in my body, and she's not even halfway across the lake when a pulsing, unfamiliar pleasure courses through me. I groan, dropping my head back, as cum spurts between my fingers, splattering across the dead leaves on the ground.

Dizziness washes over me. An orgasm, and I didn't even have to kill someone to get it.

I drop my softening cock and wipe my hands on my jeans, not sure what to think. Across the lake, Chloe bumps up against her pier and scrambles out of the boat. Her movements are quick and a little panicked, although she's downwind now, and I can't smell it, that sweet, pungent scent of her fear.

She stops, standing there on the edge of the pier. Then she turns back toward my peninsula. I stiffen and drop my hands down to my still-bare cock, feeling suddenly perceived even though there's no way she can see me, not from that distance and not with me hidden by the trees.

But she watches, the wind blowing her hair around her face. And just for a second, I think I know what it would feel like for her gaze to touch my skin.

7

CHLOE

I don't feel truly safe until I'm back in my house, the deadbolt lodged firmly in place and the curtains on those big living room windows drawn tightly shut. I'm not sure what I'm afraid of, exactly. A snap in the woods? I know, intellectually, that doesn't mean someone was watching me.

Still, the whole boat ride across the lake, my skin prickled like that's exactly what was happening.

It's better inside, though. Safe as houses, as they say. I check in with Abi and Penelope.

> Didn't see anything. Just found a cool old graveyard, though.

PENELOPE

> Oooh, you're just like Abi. Living next door to a graveyard!

ABI

There's still some leftover adrenaline surging through me. I'm not sure how to put it into words, though, even though it's got me feeling spiky and uncertain. I can't stop thinking about that gravestone. Theodore Shorn, dead in 1960. He had just been a teenager. I wonder if that's why Oliver latched onto the name.

I type it into Google on a lark. Predictably, nothing comes up but those questionable people locator sites. I sigh, scrolling through the first few pages of returns.

Then, on another whim, I type *Theodore Shorn Hanging Lake 1960*. And this time, I get something.

An old archived newspaper article, it looks like, one that's been digitized from something called the *Veritas Evening Reporter*. It dates from 1960, and when it comes up, there's a scanned black-and-white picture of a teenage boy. A portrait, his light hair slicked back, his eyes sunken, his expression unsmiling.

The Hanging Lake County sheriff has ruled the recent drowning death of Veritas local boy, Theodore Shorn, an accidental death.

The death occurred nearly a week ago, and the boy's mother, Ruth Shorn, has accused four local teenagers of unlawful activities. The four teenagers were present for the boy's death but have maintained that Shorn slipped and fell on a wet patch of pier.

"This is a terrible tragedy," Sheriff Mandle says. "But it was not the result of wrongdoing. I hope we as a community can put this accident behind us."

Miss Shorn was not available for comment.

I frown, click back to look at the other hits, starting with a ghost investigators forum from the early 2010s.

rbd1979: Anyone ever check out the western peninsula on Hanging Lake? I heard it's hella haunted and I'm gonna be in the area in a few weeks.

demon_hunter_69: Don't fucking do it, man. I grew up around there. People straight up die if they go on the peninsula. Everybody knows you stay away.

rbd1979: Seriously? What's the story there?

There's no response. The conversation shifts to something else.

I try another search: *Hanging Lake ghost stories.* And this, it seems, is the jackpot. There's a whole litany of YouTube videos dedicated to the subject, all with headlines like, *Is a ghost killing people on Hanging Lake?* And *Is this lake HAUNTED by a SERIAL KILLER?*

A serial killer?

I click on the video, trying to connect the dots here. What does a serial killer have to do with a boy who was killed in the 1960s? How many fucking ghost stories are there about this place?

It does explain Oliver's story, though. He probably heard bits and pieces about it. Then, when he went exploring on the peninsula, he saw the name on the gravestone and ran with it. It's certainly the most logical explanation.

The video isn't long, just fifteen minutes of a pleasant

man's voice speaking over a stock video of a tree-lined lake that looks almost but not quite like the lake outside my back door. "It all happened here," the voiceover says. "In the small town of Veritas, North Carolina, on the shores of Hanging Lake. Theo Shorn, a mute teenage boy—"

I freeze, press my finger down on the video to pause it. *A mute teenage boy.*

Nonverbal, he means. Like Oliver.

I glance over at my window, although of course I don't see anything, not with the curtains drawn. What did Oliver say? *He uses ASL, too. Like me.*

I start the video again.

"—was drowned off one of the town's piers. It was ruled an accident, a terrible tragedy. But his mother, Ruth Shorn, maintained that he had been murdered by a group of four local teenagers."

Their faces flash on the screen, portrait photos like the one I saw of Theo himself. Black and white. Old-fashioned. Three boys and a girl.

"Ruth's pleas to investigate her son's death went unheard, and she eventually disappeared. Because the Shorn family had been outcasts, living in an isolated cabin on a small peninsula that juts into the belly of the lake, no one checked up on her. It was assumed by many that she had left town.

"Until 1965."

The screen flashes with a scan of a newspaper headline: the Veritas Reporter, the same newsletter I had seen earlier. But this is the front page, and the headline reads, SEVEN DEAD IN MASS SLAYING.

My heart leaps up in my chest. An old, icy fear surges through my body.

"It was August," the voiceover says, the image fading to a stock photo of a man wearing a balaclava, some cheesy photographer's idea of a killer. "A masked attacker came into Veritas and slaughtered seven people with an ax. Four of the victims were the same four people whom Ruth Shorn had accused of killing her son, Theo." Their photos flash on the screen, only this time they're a little older, and they aren't portraits but photographs. The woman's photograph is from her wedding, and a man smiles pleasantly beside her. "Maggie Putnam's husband, Ralph, was also found among the dead, although their eight-month-old daughter was left alive, screaming for her parents." More pictures, blurry and black-and-white. "The other deaths were the sheriff, Walter Mandle, and a sheriff's deputy, Joe Seager.

"The killer was never caught," the voiceover continues. "Although rumors spread. The most common was that it was Ruth—at least, until they searched her cabin." A long, dramatic pause. "There, they found her body laid out on her bed: a skeleton, long since dead."

My blood pounds in my ears. I'm afraid of what I'm going to hear next.

"But that wasn't the end of it." Another image of the Veritas newspaper, this one from 1971. "There was another spree six years later that left five people dead. Three dismembered, one who was bludgeoned to death, and one who was drowned in the lake." The image on screen fades to a ghostly forest. "Just like Theo Hartshorn, nine years earlier.

"There were two more attacks in the following years that followed similar patterns, the most recent in 2001. They would occur at night, always on a full moon. Survivors would report seeing a large figure stalking through the street. Theo Shorn's father, who has never been identified? Or perhaps, Theo Shorn himself, come from the dead to enact revenge on the living?"

This last question is punctuated with Theo Shorn's portrait, his pale eyes looming heavily on my phone. For a moment, it feels like his image is staring up at me, watching me from sixty-five years ago.

"Fuck," I whisper, closing out the app before the video can finish and then tossing my phone onto the coffee table. I sink back into the couch, staring at the darkened TV hanging above the big fireplace. I've heard a story like this before, but not about Theo Shorn.

About Penelope's mother.

A Hunter, that's what Penelope called her. *My sister's one, too.* Killers who can't die. But she assured me they were rare. *You'll probably never meet another one in your life,* Penelope said the night I found out, my skin slicked with cold sweat.

I look over at my closed curtains, hiding the dark crush of the woods. The last attack happened over twenty years ago. There's no reason to think a Hunter, or anyone, lives out there. After all, I made it out unscathed. So has Oliver.

It's just a ghost story, I tell myself. Oliver's just a weird, lonely kid with an overactive imagination. He heard a ghost story about a nonverbal teenager who used to live across the lake.

I keep telling myself this, but I can't shake the feeling that I'm wrong.

"I'm sorry. What is this about, exactly?"

Blaire Jenkins frowns at me from where she's leaning against the frame of her front door, her expression one of bored annoyance.

I had a hard time sleeping last night. That stupid YouTube video kept playing in my head, and I composed and deleted about a dozen messages to Penelope asking if her family knows someone named Theo Shorn. When I learned about it five years ago, she swore me to secrecy, her eyes dark and glinting. *Don't tell anyone*, she said, the two of us huddled in the bathroom of her sister Callie's apartment in Miami after a man attacked us outside a nightclub, and I saw something I absolutely wasn't supposed to see. *Not even Abi. Swear it to me, then just—forget everything I told you. Okay?*

I didn't forget, of course. How could I? But I've never brought it up since, and I can't bring myself to do it now. It feels crazy, especially in the light of morning.

Of course, that didn't stop my brain from spiraling out in anxiety about Oliver going over to the peninsula alone. Even if there isn't a killer lurking in the woods, that place was wild. Certainly too dangerous for a kid on his own. So eventually, I bucked up my courage and walked next door. If nothing else, I wanted to know that his parents had gone over there with him, that they knew it was safe.

Now, though, I'm starting to regret my decision.

"I just wanted you to know about the story," I say. "It's awfully gruesome, and—"

"And what?" Blaire counters. "So Oliver read a ghost story? You never read ghost stories as a kid?"

She glares at me from under her fringe of blonde hair.

"He spoke about Theo Shorn as if he were, you know, alive." The morning sun beats down on my shoulders, hot enough to make the oatmeal I had for breakfast churn around in my stomach. "And I just worried, what if someone's actually out there?"

"And what? They'll steal Oliver away?" Blaire laughs cruelly, and for a second, I see the teenage mean girl she almost certainly was. "I don't know if you realize this, but Oliver isn't normal. So I don't think he holds much of an appeal to kidnappers."

I gape at her, too stunned to speak. From deep inside the house, a male voice calls out her name.

"Is that all?" she asks sharply. "My husband needs me."

"Have you been over there?" I blurt out. "To make sure it's safe?"

Blaire stares at me coolly. "No one lives out there," she says. "And I can't believe you interrupted my breakfast to tell me my son has an imaginary friend."

I swallow, my throat dry. I didn't think this through. "But Theo Shorn really existed."

It's a stupid thing to say, and I'm immediately met with another cruel laugh. "So?" Blaire rolls her eyes. "I'm supposed to get worked up over the Hanging Lake boogeyman? It's a *story*. Hikers get lost. Some serial killer came through here fifty years ago. So what? I still don't understand why you're on my front porch."

I worry the hem of my shirt. I ought to just leave. I know that. It's not like I can explain that Theodore Shorn might be an unkillable murderer—that'll just make me sound even crazier. But I feel like I'm bolted down to this spot.

"My realtor told me there were dangerous animals out there," I finally say, because there's this awkward, heavy silence between us, and because part of me wants some sign that Blaire actually does care about her son. "Like rattlesnakes."

Blaire sniffs. Behind her, a man stomps in the hallway, looking as clean-cut as a pastor. I can only assume it's Mr. Jenkins. "What in the world is going on here?" he barks.

"It's the neighbor," Blaire says, looking at me. "She's worried about Oliver going over to the peninsula. He told her about his little imaginary friend."

The man scoffs at that. "We don't need any do-gooders hanging around telling us how to raise that boy."

They both stare at me, like they're daring me to argue. I squeeze my hands into fists. "I just wanted to make sure you knew it was safe."

"Mind your own business," Blaire says icily, before stepping back into the cool dark of her house and slamming the door shut, the bang like a punctuation mark.

And all I can do is blink at the door for a few seconds, my heart thumping. That did not exactly go how I had pictured.

Not that I was even sure what I wanted to accomplish. I don't have proof of anything. Just that prickling sense of unease.

I should probably suck it up and call Penelope about it.

I step off the porch, feeling guilty and shaken up all at once, and cut across the lawn, back toward my house. I've just crossed over the property line when I feel something brush against my hand. A second later, Oliver himself jumps in front of me and blinks through the tousled bangs of his hair.

"Oliver," I say, too surprised to remember to sign. Oliver just grins and nods, then signs a quick, "Hello!"

"Did you hear me talking with your mom?" I ask, forming the words slowly.

He nods, and my heart twists around in my chest.

But then his fingers start flying, fast enough that I struggle to keep up. "I wanted to tell you not to worry," he says, his expression earnest. "I know Theo seems scary, but he's actually very nice. Did you meet him?"

It takes me a second to register that last question. "Theo?" I spell the name out. I still haven't gotten the hang of the personalized sign Oliver uses for him.

Oliver nods. "You said you went to his territory! Even though I told you he doesn't like visitors. But I think he would like you, because you're nice, too. So I was wondering if you met."

Oliver drops his hands to his side and stares up at me expectantly. I wish I knew *something* about kids.

Finally, I do a quick, jerky, "No."

"You didn't see him at all? Did you go to his cabin?"

I shake my head, unease settling in my stomach again. "I found a cemetery," I finally say, stumbling over the word for *cemetery*. I'm really going to have to amp up my vocabulary, living next door to this kid. "And a gravestone. With Theo's name on it."

I'm not sure what I expect to happen, sharing this information. I almost feel kind of bad about it, like I'm trapping Oliver in a lie. But he just grins.

"That's his gravestone," Oliver sighs, emphasizing the *his* with a dramatic surge of his shoulders. "Didn't I tell you? He's a ghost."

I breathe out. A ghost. An imaginary friend. Not a murderer.

"You didn't mention that," I say.

"Oh, sorry." Oliver shrugs. "Well, he is. And he was probably watching you, even if you couldn't see him. He can make himself invisible."

I smile at that, and some of the worry lifts off my shoulders. This is definitely getting into imaginary friend territory.

"That's a pretty cool trick," I say

"Yeah, it is." Oliver studies me for a moment longer, squinting into the bright morning sunlight. "I hope you'll meet him soon, though." He signs more fervently. "He's just shy. But just wait 'til I introduce you. I know the three of us will be best friends."

THEO

I can not stop thinking about her.

It doesn't help that her scent seems to be everywhere, as strong as if she bled all over the woods. I tell myself it has to be my imagination. There's no way it could linger this long, and there's no sign of her out on the pier. But it follows me as I make my rounds, even when I'm on the far side of the peninsula, away from the lake houses. It's like she's attached herself to me somehow.

This obsession reminds me, a little, of the killing moon—that terrible, nagging urge that lights my blood on fire. I think maybe that's what it is, the start of a killing moon, even though this does feel different. But it's been so long since the last one that maybe I've just forgotten.

Still, when I finish with my rounds, I go back to the cabin and pull out my box of blades from its place in the old, cracked fireplace. I take them out one by one and arrange them in a neat row on the kitchen table: my axe, my machete, my butcher's cleaver. In the past, when the killing moon would call out to me, the first thing I did was select a weapon. But none of them are singing to me. They glint in the lemony sunlight drifting in through the dirty window above the sink, and I think about all the blood they've spilled and all the lives they've ended, but I don't feel any terrible urge to kill

It's something else.

I pace around my cabin, feeling antsy and agitated. My thoughts, of course, keep returning to *her*. Chloe. They keep returning to an undeniable but no less alarming truth:

I liked having her in my territory. I liked smelling her on the wind, and I liked watching her through the trees. I think I'm agitated because I want her to come back.

It's an absurd thought. She's human. I kill humans who come onto my land—well, adult humans anyway. But yesterday, I didn't feel that hot spark of rage like I do when others come onto my peninsula. It was almost like—

Like she belongs here.

So I put the weapons away. I find myself sniffing the air, even though I doubt she'll return. Oliver might. And then I can—what? Tell him I do want to meet her after all?

Foolish. Just because I don't want to harm her doesn't mean she won't immediately sense what I am.

There is a way I can watch her, though. My mother had a telescope that she got from her grandfather. When I was a boy, she used to take me out to our pier so we could look at the stars up close. The moon, too.

I haven't thought about that telescope in decades, but I'm certain it's still up in the little attic storage space where she kept it, along with the other items that belonged to her family.

Excitement spurs in my chest, and I dart into the hallway to drag down the attic steps. They creak as they slam to the scuffed wooden floor, expelling clouds of dust. I don't care. I climb up into the storage space, which looks like how I remember from my childhood: Dusty. Cramped. The scent is so much stronger now, though. All the oils of my family's skin—my mother's, her parents', her grandparents'—left to bake in the heat.

The telescope is exactly where it always was, right next to the storage space entrance. I hug it to my chest and step back down, heart hammering. I leave the attic yawning open as I step outside and make my way to the beach. There, I unlatch the storage case and carefully set up the stand and then the telescope proper. I'm surprised I still remember how, and while it's true that my killer's hands feel oversized and clumsy as I tighten the screws and insert the eyepiece, I get it done. Within a few minutes, my mother's telescope is settled in a patch of sandy dirt, pointed at Chloe's house.

My breath is tight as I peer through the viewfinder. For a moment, the image is blurred and bright, but I adjust it into sharpness.

Her big picture windows fill my vision, and then—her. Chloe.

She's upside down. Everything is upside down through the telescope.

Still, it lets me see through the big window and into her tidy living room, where she's sitting on her couch, a computer resting in her lap. She stares at the screen, frowning a little, fingers skittering across the keyboard. Her hair is loose around her shoulders. Her legs bare.

I suck in my breath. Yes, the entire scene is upside down, so she looks a little like a spider hanging from a web. But it's better than nothing. Certainly better than what I can see with my naked eye, even if my vision is superior to a human's.

Chloe pauses her typing and looks up. I don't know at what; it's out of the range of my view. She tilts her head a little and goes back to her computer. And stays like that, for a while. I can't tear my gaze away from her, though. There's a comfort to it, and the magnification almost makes me feel like I'm with her, like we're breathing the same air.

When she stands up, setting her laptop aside, my breath catches in my chest. She stretches, lifting her arms overhead, and her shirt rises enough to reveal a flash of her pale, soft belly. I bite down on my lip, shift my hips around. My cock is growing.

Chloe walks around the width of the sofa and then, to my excitement, stands in front of her window. She puts her hands on the glass and gazes outward, and I study her face, memorizing the lines of her cheekbones and the fullness of her lips. Even upside-down, magnified through glass and light, she's so beautiful.

If I were another type of killer, the kind that leaves the flesh of their victims unblemished, maybe then I could share in the intimacy of her death. I could kiss her as she breathed her last breath and find some way to preserve her so she could stay with me in my cabin until the end of my very long and very unnatural life.

But I'm not that kind of killer. I rend and destroy. If I were to kill Chloe, she would be nothing but meat. The pleasure of her hot blood on my hands would be temporary. A single moment of ecstasy that would not be worth the annihilation of her beauty.

So I watch her, my breath ragged. I watch as she turns away from the window, as she settles back on the couch, as she takes a long drink from a water bottle.

That's all I can do. Watch.

OLIVER COMES to visit me a few days after I pull out the telescope. Thankfully, he doesn't time his visit while I'm watching Chloe, so I don't have to explain myself to him.

Instead, I smell him while I'm making my rounds. Although nearly all of my free time has been swallowed up by watching Chloe through the telescope, following her movements through the back half of her house and along the pier, I do maintain that one crucial aspect of my routine. I save it for when she disappears from my view, though.

Normally, when Oliver visits during my patrols, I let him wait at the cabin. He knows not to go snuffling around in the woods. There are other dangerous things on this peninsula, rattlesnakes and black widow spiders chief among them. I don't want to take the blame for their violence.

But today, when I sense him, I cut my rounds short and intercept him while he's still on the trail to my cabin.

He yelps when I step into his path, then laughs. "You scared me," he signs.

"Sorry," I respond. I'm not sure what to say next. Should I ask about her? Or should I let him bring her up?

Fortunately, Oliver is usually the one to drive the conversation, and today's no exception. "Sorry I haven't been by in a few days." He doesn't elaborate, and I sense something from him, a kind of quiet fear. It's always there when I haven't seen him for a while, and I don't know what it means. It's certainly not like the fear I instill in humans, the fear I'm used to. When I tried to ask him about it once, he put his hands in his lap and didn't move until I changed the subject.

"Got you some good pictures, though." He takes off down the path toward my cabin, and I follow behind him. Once we're there, he plops down on the porch swing, as usual, and pulls a new set of drawings out of his backpack and hands them to me. I flip through them, the way I always do. He brought me comic book characters this time, and some of them I even recognize from my own childhood, although I watch attentively while he explains who they are.

The only one that isn't from a comic book is Chloe.

It's not just her face but a sketch of her from the knees up, one hand on her hip, with her pretty features furrowed in concern.

I stop here. I can't stop myself. The likeness is so good, and it's nice to see her right side up. And the expression Oliver captured, with that faint trace of fear—

My body heats.

When Oliver taps my knee, I nearly jump out of my skin. "That's Chloe," he signs.

My heart hammers. "Your friend?" I respond, afraid my face gives everything away. "Who can sign?" As if I didn't immediately recognize her.

Oliver nods. "She said she came over here the other day, but she didn't see you."

Blood pulses in my temple. "I didn't see her," I lie, barely able to keep my hands from shaking. "I was probably on the other side of the peninsula."

Oliver shrugs, unbothered. "That's okay. She saw your gravestone, though, so she knows you're a ghost. I think she's scared of you."

My blood sparks. "Did she say that?"

"No, I can just tell. I told her you were nice, but I guess she thinks ghosts are scary." Oliver sets his hands down in his lap and looks out at the little patch of my front yard. The wind pushes his hair away from his eyes. "That's why I think you should meet her." He signs it without looking at me. "So she knows you're real, and that you're nice."

Panic flares up in me. I see her, just for a moment, hanging upside down in my head the way she's always hanging upside down in my telescope. And I wish I *could* meet her. I wish I really were just the ghost Oliver thinks I am. But if Chloe is already frightened by the threat of me, then it's hopeless. She almost certainly read about my previous killing moons.

That's why it'll never work. I know what I am. A Hunter, my father calls us, and I came up with a name that I can say with my hands. We're predators. Humans sense it, that we're dangerous to them. The only reason Oliver doesn't is because he's a child, because he doesn't understand the ways of the world.

"Please? Can I introduce you?" He signs this emphatically and actually looks me in the eye, and I feel his hopefulness jolt through me. For a second, I feel the way I do right before I end someone's life. They always look at me with hope when they're pleading for their survival.

"No." I sign it and shake my head. Oliver's face falls, but I prefer it to that look of hope. I don't want to think about killing around him.

"Not yet," I add, just because I feel some creep of empathy at his disappointment. "Maybe in a few weeks."

"To clean your house?" Oliver scowls. "You told me that last time."

"I know. It's still true." I force myself to smile, even though Oliver's still sulking at me. "Thank you for the pictures. I always like them."

"She won't be afraid of you if she meets you," Oliver says. "I know that's what you're scared of, that she'll think you're weird. But she's not like normal people. She's nice to me."

His face is so earnest as he signs, his eyes blazing, and I wish it really were that simple.

9

THEO

Oliver comes and goes, but I still can't get Chloe out of my thoughts. She really is like the killing moon: constant, urgent, obsessive.

I hang the new picture of her beside the old one, on the wall beside my bed. Then I go into my closet and pry back the floorboard in the left-hand corner to get at my metal lockbox. The lock is broken, but that doesn't matter, not with the hiding place. That's where I set the rest of the drawings, adding them to the collection that Oliver has brought me.

I'm not sure why I started doing this. For the last sixty years, the only things I've kept in that lockbox are newspaper clippings about my four killing moons and their aftermath. They're still there, buried underneath the drawings, but I've read them so many times over the years they've become stale. The drawings are new and therefore interesting. I like to look at them sometimes, studying how the world outside my peninsula has changed. When the killing moon hits again, I want to be prepared.

I hope it doesn't call me anytime soon, though. Not with Chloe's sweetness calling me instead.

That night, I lie in bed and stare up at the ceiling. Like my father, I don't sleep much, although I can sometimes will myself to drift off when my cold, obsessive thoughts become too much.

It doesn't work tonight, though. This new obsession with Chloe is so different from what I'm used to. Where the killing moon is the ice of death, Chloe is the fire of freshly spilled blood. She makes me feel agitated and out of sorts, but in a way that I don't ever want to end. The thought of her face makes my cock hard, and I have to touch myself to relieve the pressure. Before her, I only ever came when I was killing someone, and these orgasms feel strange and half-completed. They don't slake the fire or the ice. They just leave me restless.

By midnight, I give up trying to sleep. I know from previous experience there's no point in watching her house through the telescope, not this late. She usually goes to bed by eleven, so I'll have nothing to look at but a dark, empty window. Unlike me, she's asleep.

The thought stirs something in me. A wisp of an idea.

She's asleep.

I've killed people who were asleep before. I've broken their locks and crept through the dark hallways of their houses, and I've watched them, lying in bed, their breaths slow and steady. Most of the time, they don't even wake up until my blade is lodged in their throat.

I could watch her.

I could be near her.

I shove myself out of my bed. Yes, this is what I need to do. Chloe draws my attention across the water like the killing moon, and what is it I do when there's a killing moon? I go across the lake and slake my urges. It's true that my urge for Chloe is expansive and ill-defined. It's just a need to smell her, to be close to her. But if that's what it will take to clear my thoughts—

I spring into action. Obviously, I leave my weapons behind, save for a slim little switchblade, which I can use to pick the lock on her door. My rowboat I drag out of its place under my cabin and down to the lakeshore. Heavy work that makes my muscles ache, yes, but it feels good. It feels right.

The lake is dark and still. The moon itself is only half-full, not a killing moon at all, but it casts just enough thin, hazy light to make the water glimmer as it laps against the sides of my boat. I row quickly across the water, keeping my gaze fixed on the houses along the shore. They're all dark and shut up tight for the night, but this is my first time in years that I'm crossing the lake with the possibility of a real audience. Even Veritas, when it still existed, was a little further back, and the lake shore was overgrown.

I don't sense any humans, though. Not really. They're all tucked in their houses, safe and sound. And they'll stay safe and sound tonight. I only have one target in mind.

I maneuver underneath Chloe's pier, into the murk with the cobwebs and spiders and other crawling things. Then I let the water wash me up into the tangle of reeds growing along the shoreline, where my boat lodges in a wedge of mud. It's not a perfect hiding spot, but it's good enough. I'll be gone before the sun rises anyway.

I slither up onto the pier and then stop, breathing hard. Chloe's house rises in front of me, the huge window reflecting the moonlight but revealing nothing else, because she has the curtains pulled.

It feels strange, standing here on this side of the lake without the pull of the killing moon compelling me forward. For a moment, I'm not even sure what to do, and I just stand there, staring at her house, the warm, damp wind whispering along the back of my neck. My hand slips into my pocket of its own accord, almost, and pulls out my switch blade. I flip it open, let it catch the moonlight for a moment.

I look back up at Chloe's house, considering the back door on the porch or the French doors on her balcony. The back door will be much easier.

My heart is racing. It never races. Not when I'm killing, anyway.

I move forward, stepping onto her porch. It's strange, standing on it instead of watching it from afar. There's the blue Adirondack chair where she works in the mornings sometimes. There's the hummingbird feeder she hung a few days ago, the sugar water nearly empty. And there's the door that will lead me to her.

I've picked dozens of locks in my long life. Hundreds, probably. But this is the first time my hands have shaken so badly. It takes me three tries to wedge the knife into place, and I stop and let out a long breath and force myself to focus. Not just on the lock but on her. I can sense her on the other side of this window. Her steady, sleeping breath and slow heartbeat.

My cock jolts. I wriggle the knife around until the lock gives.

Then I turn the knob, and I ease the door open.

Her scent washes over me. The other day, when she was in my territory, it blended too much with the scent of the woods. But here, it's concentrated. It's pure. I can pick out each individual element: lilacs, like the ones that carpet the forest floor in the spring. Cedar. Fresh oranges. It all makes the back of my jaw ache.

I step into the living room and pull the door shut behind me. It's quieter in here, all the outside world muffled by the house's walls, and that makes it easier to focus on Chloe. She's upstairs, and it feels for a moment like she's floating above me. I can tell she's still asleep.

I snap my knife shut and slip it in my pocket. Then I go to her, keeping my steps as light as I can in my big work boots. Her floor is covered in a thick, lush carpet, though, and I have a predator's gait. I don't make a sound as I weave through the cavernous living room and up the staircase and into the dark, narrow hallway, where the sound of her body is thunderous. Living humans are so noisy. She's louder than most, but it's not noise, the way it usually is. Her body sounds more like music.

Her bedroom door is cracked open, and I nudge it with my toe, releasing more of that music. But then I stop in the doorway, feeling paralyzed because, honestly, I don't know what to do next.

So I just watch her. The bed is huge, and she sleeps in the center of it like a queen, curled up on her side with the blanket tucked under her chin. Her hair curls on the pillow beside her and glimmers copper in the moonbeam shining in through a crack in the curtains that cover the balcony doors.

Every other time I've been in this situation, I've had a weapon in my hand. An axe or a hunting knife. A chainsaw, on one memorable occasion. But right now, my hands are empty, and the switchblade in my pocket feels as dangerous as a cheap ballpoint pen.

I risk stepping into the bedroom, keeping myself tucked away in the inky shadows. Chloe's breath remains steady and even, which gives me enough confidence to move closer to the bed, although I stay out of that beam of silver moonlight. I inhale deeply, drawing her scent into my lungs, and then I close my eyes so the soft music of her body washes over me.

My cock pulses, filling with blood. I let my eyes flutter open and adjust myself, biting down on my lip at the pressure of my hand on my erection. Still, a noise of pleasure manages to escape my throat. A single, soft grunt.

I freeze, dropping my hand to my side. Chloe moans and

mutters something, then rolls over, burying her face into her pillow. My heart thuds furiously against my ribcage. I can't move. I *should* move, I know that. I should turn and go out the way I came, through her living room and down her pier and across the lake, back to where I belong.

But I don't. I want to be in the same room as her for as long as I can manage.

She shifts again, rolling onto her back. I press my spine against the wall and admire the curves of her body underneath the thin comforter. Maybe I can pull it away. Not to touch. I just want to look.

I step forward again, my breath soft and shuddery, my eyes fixed on the pale hollow of Chloe's throat. Her pulse is a soft, whispery rhythm in the background. I don't know how many times I've stood in the shadows and listened to the sound of someone's sleeping pulse. But this is the first time I don't want to silence it. If anything, I wish I could record it and take it home with me and let it play anytime I try to sleep.

I'm so caught up in this fantasy, this idea that I could have even a small part of Chloe in my cabin, that I don't realize the pulse's steady beat is quickening. It's not until there's a sudden, rushing roar in the sound of her breath that I realize I've stayed too long.

She's waking up.

Panic seizes me. I stumble backward, arms flailing out. My shoes feel too heavy for the carpet, and they make my movements clumsy. I should have taken them off. I shouldn't have come here at all. I should have—

Chloe's eyes slide open. Just for a moment, they seem to glow in the moonlight. Just for a moment, I think it's too dark for her to see me.

And then she starts to scream.

10

CHLOE

There's a man in my room. A tall, hulking man with huge shoulders and big, muscular arms. That's all I can see of him in the dark. This enormous, dark silhouette towering over my bed.

A million thoughts slam through my head, one right after another. I'm dreaming. I'm hallucinating. I hung a towel over the back of the closet door, and that's what this is. Someone broke in. I'm being robbed. I'm being killed? Maybe it's one of my relatives, angry that I got the house and they didn't. Maybe it's Oliver.

All this cascades through me in the span of a second. Then my vision solidifies, and it's definitely not a towel or a pile of clothes or a relative.

It's a huge, terrifying man.

I scream, the sound splitting the night in two. Then I heave myself out of the bed, the sheets tangling up around my bare legs. I'm in my fucking underwear, just a pair of plain black cotton undies and a flimsy little spaghetti strap top, and I can't believe I'm even thinking something as asinine as *I need to cover up* because there's a fucking man in my bedroom.

I shriek as I try to untangle my legs and wind up landing hard on my hands and knees on the floor. Then I scramble myself up to standing and bolt toward the door. "Help!" I scream. "Someone's he—"

A hand slaps around my mouth, a warm, rough palm sealing my nose shut. For a second, I smell pine trees.

Then he drags me backward until I slam up against his broad, solid chest. His arm wraps around me, holding me in place. His breath is ragged in my ear.

"Please!" I shriek into his palm. He doesn't let go. If anything, he squeezes me tighter. I squirm against him, flailing my arms around, but I can't get any leverage. His strength is like a metal vise holding me in place.

He pulls me backward. At first, I think he's taking me to the bed, and a sick, horrifying panic surges in my belly, and I try to fight him again, more desperately this time. But then he keeps going, past the bed. There's a whir of dizzying movement, and the next thing I know, he's spun me around and shoved me against the wall, his hand still tight across my mouth to hold me in place.

The difference is, this time, I can see him. He stares down at me through a tangle of straggly, dirty-blond hair, his pale eyes gleaming with a coldness that reminds me of moonlight. His mouth is set in a firm line, and I breathe against his hand, squirming against the wall.

He lifts his other hand. His forearm is enormous, corded with muscle, and his fingers are thick and rough-looking.

And then he signs at me.

O, he spells out. *L. I. V. E. R.*

I go slack, my gaze crawling over his face. His long, unwashed hair. His bright eyes. I shake my head against his hand.

I was so fucking stupid. Oliver doesn't have an imaginary friend. There really is a man living on the peninsula.

And what if he really is a Hunter?

The man makes a low grunting noise in the back of his throat and flicks his free hand at me. It takes me a second to realize he's saying, "Don't scream."

I stare at him, my breath tight and constricting in my lungs. His eyes bore into mine. For a moment, I think they're silver, but then he shifts his head a little, and I realize that they're actually a very pale blue, the same color as ice.

Why the fuck am I noticing his eyes?

"Don't scream," he signs again, right before he takes his hand away from my mouth.

"Who are you?" I ask, my hands shaking so badly I'm not sure he'll even understand me.

"I can hear you," he says, forming the words slowly, his eyes boring into mine. "I just don't speak. Like Oliver."

Like Oliver. "You're him," I whisper, slumping against the wall. The man doesn't move, just keeps staring at me. The intensity in his gaze sends an overwhelming heat to the center of my chest. It's not exactly fear. It's more like he has me trapped without even touching me. "The friend," I say, signing the word as I speak. The man's eyes don't leave my face. "He has a name for you," I speak, trying to approximate it with my fingers. "I don't exactly remember—"

He makes the sign, and my heart thuds around. "My name," he signs. Then, he spells it out: *T. H. E. O.*

Blood pounds in my ears. I think of the gravestone, the name carved on the stone.

"Who are you?" I ask, speaking and signing at the same time. "Really?"

Theo tilts his head a little, still staring at me. His hands stay at his side.

"Why are you here?"

That gets a reaction. A small one. His expression flickers a little, and for the first time, his eyes dart away from me. That dread coils more tightly around in my belly.

"Is it about Oliver?" The question comes out strangled, and I don't bother signing it. My fear has my thoughts so clouded that I can't even remember half the words anyway. "Are you—you've been meeting with him, haven't you? Why? Do you live out there? On the peninsula?" It feels like a dam's been unlocked, and the questions spill out of me, one after another. Theo just watches me through the tangle of his hair, not moving. "Is your name really Theo?"

That question, out of all of them, gets a response. He nods his head once, a sharp jerk of his chin.

"Theo Shorn?" I whisper, staring up at him.

He doesn't move. Terror spikes through my blood.

"Are you going to hurt me?"

This gets a response, too. He shakes his head with that same sharp, jerky motion, his hair falling into his eyes. He reaches up, distractedly, and pushes it away, sweeping it back so I can see his face clearly for the first time.

I nearly throw up.

It *is* him. Theo Shorn. I recognize him from that grainy, black-and-white photograph I saw on my phone. He has the same heavy-browed eyes, the same full mouth and high cheekbones. His hair's different, obviously. And he's bigger and fully grown. But I can see the impression of that boy in his features.

I plaster my spine to the wall, my heart hammering. Theo's brow furrows, and he studies me with that same dark intensity.

Then he says, "Don't be afraid."

"You broke into my house!" I shriek, even though that's not why I'm afraid. If he's a Hunter, then he's a killer. And I don't want to die tonight.

"I wanted to see you," he signs.

"Why?"

It comes out as a shout, and he jolts a little and lunges toward me, which makes my fear spike again. But he just puts his hand on the wall beside my head and leans in close. I smell pine needles again, and something steely, like petrichor. His hair may be lank, but he doesn't smell dirty. He smells like the lake. Like something wild.

He leans closer to me. I don't move. I'm afraid that if I move, he'll kill me.

His lips part. His eyes gleam. His tongue flashes, a brief spark of pink.

Then his rough fingers brush my cheek, and my breath explodes out of me in a soft, pathetic little whimper. His jaw tightens when he hears it, but all he does is brush my hair behind my ear. Then he trails his fingers down the side of my neck. It feels—

Good, honestly. It feels fucking good as he traces his hand over my collarbone. There's something tentative and exploratory in his touch, like he can't quite believe I'm real.

His hand stops on my upper arm, and I force myself to look up at him.

He's staring at me with an expression I've never seen on a man. Hunger. Restraint. Fire. I don't know what to make of it, except—

Except it sends heat flushing between my thighs.

"Please," I whisper. "Please don't kil—"

I don't get the plea out, though. Because Theo Shorn kisses me.

Well, he presses his mouth against my mouth. I freeze, not knowing what to do. It's not forceful, the way he does it. It's just his mouth on mine, soft and gentle.

I can't remember the last time a man kissed me. A year. Two years? Men never have what I need. I learned that quickly enough, how fucked up my fantasies are. It's easier to be alone.

But he'll have it. A Hunter will have it.

The thought is sudden and treacherous. But it's also why I part my lips. Or maybe it's because he smells like pine sap, like mountain air. Maybe it's the slightly forceful grip he has on my forearm. Maybe I've lost my mind.

But I open my mouth to him.

It's just a small movement, but he makes a surprised noise in the back of his throat, and then a kind of low growl that rumbles through my belly. Then he tilts his head and slides his tongue over mine and pushes one hand up in my hair, his fingers tight against my scalp.

The way he kisses is slow, almost tentative, but I can feel a power pulsing behind it. When he shifts his body against mine, pinning me to the wall, a hard ridge digs into my thigh, and my clit flares to life. A soft moan hums in my throat.

I don't want him to stop kissing me. Which is crazy. I know it's crazy. But I can feel myself melting into him. His warm, exploratory mouth. His rough hands on my arm and in my hair. The strong heat of his body sandwiching me against the wall.

When the kiss ends, he's the one to end it. He pulls away, staring down at me with those icy-blue eyes, and I see it again. The boy in the photograph, all grown up.

"Are you really the Theo Shorn from the ghost story?" I whisper. "The one who died when he was seventeen?"

The man nods.

Fear tears through me again, evaporating any lingering heat from his kiss. I jerk away, squirming out of his grip. He lets me go, I'll give him that, although his icy gaze follows me as I stumble away from him.

"You don't look dead," I say, trying to keep my voice light.

"I'm not." He turns his body toward me, and I'm struck

again by how huge he is. Tall and broad-shouldered beneath his dark shirt.

"So you're eighty years old?" I whisper, my voice shaking. He doesn't look it, of course. He looks to be in his mid-thirties at most. But the Hunters don't age. Penelope told me that, even though she wasn't supposed to.

Theo frowns. "What I am is complicated." His eyes flash. "But you already know that, don't you?"

I tremble, my chest too tight for me to speak. I'm able to sign, though, even though my hands shake. "What do you want with Oliver?"

Theo tilts his head, and I swear, just for a second, that his expression softens. "I don't want to harm him." A pause, and then, with a simple flick of his hands. "Or you."

My heart pounds. My room spins around. "But you do harm people."

Theo's eyes burn straight through me. I take another couple of stumbling steps back and hit the side of my bed. "You kill people," I sign.

Theo nods his head yes.

I whimper and slump down on the bed.

"But I'm not going to kill you," he says quickly. "Or Oliver. Truly."

We stare at each other, the moonlight flooding around us. "I know what you are," I finally whisper, my heart racing. "I know you aren't human."

Something flickers across Theo's face. I think it might be surprise.

Then he makes a sign I've never seen before. He presses his fists together, then swipes his palm out like a blade. There's something about it, about the harsh, curving shape of his fingers, that makes me shudder.

"I don't know what that means," I breathe out.

"A killer," he signs, and my heart constricts, "whose only purpose is to kill."

I whimper, jerking away from him. Tears blur my vision.

"But not you," he says, signing quickly. "Not Oliver."

"Why not?" I manage to sign it, even though my entire body is shaking. "What makes us different?"

Theo stares at me for a long, long time.

"Oliver is like me before I knew what I am," he finally says. "Lonely and different. And you—"

His expression changes, darkening into that expression from earlier, the one that made me relent to his kiss. Heat. Hunger. Lust.

Through the cloud of my fear, I feel my own bloom of arousal, and I hate myself for it.

"You are very beautiful," he says.

It's the last thing I expect. For a minute, I think I've misunderstood him. But I don't get a chance to ask any more questions, because he whips around and bolts out of the bedroom.

11

THEO

My body feels the way it does right before a kill, like all my atoms are rioting, threatening to obliterate me. I race down the stairs and into Chloe's living room and then erupt out into the warm, humid night, the frog song overwhelming. I don't stop running until I get to the end of the pier, where I jump into the lake with a splash, sinking down in the murk.

For a moment, I consider staying down there, letting the water flood my lungs like it did sixty years ago, until everything goes black. At this point in my life, a drowning won't take long for me to revive. Certainly not the five years it did the first time. A month or two, maybe. The longer you're alive, the easier reviving becomes. Especially a relatively simple death like drowning.

But when my lungs start burning, I don't have the willpower to stay in the dark. I shoot myself up to the surface, gasping as I drink in the humid air. Then I whip around to look at Chloe's house.

The light is on in her bedroom. At first, that's all I can see, the soft pinkish glow through the curtains covering her windows. My chest heaves in the water, and my skin buzzes.

I know what you are. I know you aren't human.

Is *this* why I felt so drawn to her the moment I saw her in the fading sunlight? She's not one of my kind. Not a Hunter. But she didn't seem surprised when I told her my name, that I was the boy who died sixty years ago. Maybe that's why I showed her the sign for what I am, the killer-whose-purpose-is-to-kill.

I breathe out, eyes fixed on the window. A shadow moves past it, and she has something lifted to the side of her head. She's holding a phone.

My stomach bottoms out with something like betrayal. Did she call the police?

It was one of my father's first lessons to me, after I finally found him in that little clapboard house outside Schenectady. *Don't tell humans what you are,* he said, the two of us sitting on his screened-in back porch, a corn field rolling toward the horizon. He was smoking a cigarette, I remember, and not really looking at me. *Not even to scare 'em. Our strength is hiding in plain sight.*

You told Mom, I wrote out on a notepad, the hurt of her death still fresh.

He stiffened. I remember it even now, sitting in the cold, black water. He stiffened and looked at me through the veil of cigarette smoke trailing from behind his fingers.

That was different, he said darkly, although he didn't, at the time, tell me why. Later, though, I realized it was because he loved her. Well, as much as we can love anyone.

The living room light comes on in Chloe's house, and a few seconds later, she appears in the window. I was right; she is on the phone, and she stands in the window and peers out at the lake. Not that she'll be able to see anything with all the lights on in her house like that.

Still, I instinctively sink a little lower into the lake, submerging myself in the cold, inky water. My boots keep wanting to drag me under, but I'm strong enough to keep myself afloat. Perk of being what I am, I guess.

Inside the house, Chloe paces back and forth, the phone still pressed to her ear. My stomach twists around, and I don't know if I do feel betrayed or not that she called the police. I don't blame her, particularly, even if it's about to make my life a hell of a lot more complicated.

In fact, I shouldn't be here at all. I should be dragging my boat out from under her pier and making my way back to my cabin to prepare for the cops' inevitable arrival. But she's still watching, and that much movement, so close to her house, she'll absolutely notice.

She stops pacing and stands with the phone to her ear, nodding every few seconds. I wonder what they're telling her. In the bright light of her living room, she looks pale. Afraid.

Of me. I know that. I usually love soaking up humans' fear. But with Chloe, it feels stale and sour.

Chloe draws herself up. I keep waiting for her to switch off the light and pull the curtains shut so I can fetch my boat.

But she doesn't.

Instead, she walks over to the back door and pushes it open.

I reflexively jerk back, my heavy legs kicking out beneath the water. What the hell is she doing? Why would the cops tell her to come outside? Idiots. They know how many people go missing around here, even if it's been a good twenty years since the last killing moon.

Chloe switches on the porch light, and it makes her seem to glow as she steps onto the pier. I slide lower into the water, my heart hammering, and push backward, as slow and careful as I can. I don't want to make too loud a splash.

"Um, hello?"

The quiver of fear in her voice chimes in my head. Part of me desperately wants to answer her, to go swimming back to the pier and heave myself out like some swamp monster. The other part of me knows damn well this has to be a trap.

"Theo?" She says my name a little louder, although the wind catches it and blows it away. "I, um, I was hoping maybe we could talk?"

My entire body goes into high alert: all my muscles tense up, and my blood surges the way it does before a kill. At the same time, some unfamiliar warmth in my chest tries to pull me toward her.

Chloe says something into the phone, too soft for me to hear at this distance, especially over the lapping of the waves. Then she looks out at the lake again.

"Are you there?" she calls out.

God, I want to go to her. She looks lovely there in the yellow porch light, her hair glistening around her pale, terrified face. I'm sure her fear would be delicious when she sees me for the first time, gliding through the water like a shark.

But I don't know *why* she's doing it. I worry it's a trap, even though what scares me about that isn't the threat of getting caught, but of what I would do to avoid it. Who I would kill.

An image of the police flashes through my head, as clear as the image of Chloe on her porch, never once straying from the sphere of light, as if it's a shield that will protect her from danger. I imagine them swarming her house, the red and blue lights flashing, shouting dumb commands at me. I've had standoffs with the police before. Back in '87, I even let them shoot me. But it's not a killing moon tonight, and I don't want to die. So if this is some scheme to put me off my guard, to keep me on this side of the lake until the cops arrive, I know what'll happen: I'll fight. I'll kill.

And I might even kill Chloe.

The idea makes me sick to my stomach. I push back in the water again, a slow and steady butterfly kick. Chloe's talking to whoever it is on the phone, her voice low and slightly panicked. Probably begging the cops to let her go back inside. I hope they fucking do.

I take a deep breath and drop under the water, spiraling around so I'm facing my peninsula. The cops'll find my boat and oars, but they won't find any traces of *me*. They might find hairs or flakes of skin or fingerprints, sure, but it won't lead them to me. I'm not human. I'm untraceable, like all of my kind.

So the boat can be a sacrifice. I don't believe in God or the devil, not anymore, but something gave me the strength to kiss Chloe there in her room, her big frightened eyes gazing up at me. And something, just for a few brief seconds, told her to kiss back.

So the boat will be a sacrifice to that, whatever it is. It'll lead them to my territory, but that's okay. I can act fast. Clear everything out of my cabin that gives even the faintest suggestion that I exist. I've done it before.

I glide through the water, sliding up only to catch a few gulps of air before ducking back under. And as I slip deep into the darkness, I leave Chloe behind me, shrouded in the light.

CHLOE

I sit frozen on my bed, listening to Theo's heavy footsteps as he thumps down the stairs. My body is drawn tight between terror and something dangerously close to arousal. A sign of my own sick desires, the ones I've always tried to keep buried.

My first movement is to tentatively lick my lips, like I might find some lingering taste of him. My first kiss in what? Two years? The dating apps are a fucking nightmare, and I learned early on that most guys are not worth the trouble, especially with my tastes. My vibrator, a good-sized dildo, and my collection of questionable porn have been more than adequate in keeping me happy.

Until this absolute madman, this murdered-boy-turned-Hunter, fucking unraveled me.

Downstairs, the back door clicks shut. I wonder if he really left or if this is some ruse, that he'll hide in a closet or one of the unnecessary bathrooms until I've let my guard down so he can jump out at me to finish the job.

I never should have told him I know what he is.

I stand up, still feeling numb. Grab my phone from off the

bedside table. Turn on the bedroom light. It's brighter than I'm expecting.

I swipe my phone open and stare down at the keypad. A normal person would call 911. But then the cops will come out here, and everyone on the street will see, including Oliver. And it's not like Theo hurt me. He just—

Kissed me.

Looked at me like he wanted to consume me.

Made my clit inflame because there's something deeply wrong with my sense of desire.

So instead, I pull up Penelope's number, my skin clammy with fear. She answers on the second ring.

"Are you okay?" Her voice is slurred a little, like she was asleep. But Penelope sleeps like a grizzled assassin from a fantasy novel. With one eye open.

"I don't know." I walk over to the bedroom window and peer out at the lake from around the curtain. I don't see much beyond some glimmers of light on the water and my own reflection in the glass. "Something weird just happened."

"Talk to me." Penelope already sounds awake. "And seriously. Are you okay?"

"I think so." I pull away from the window and pace across the carpet in my bare feet, my heart still pounding. "There was a man here. He—" I don't know how to say it, this thing Penelope told me I was better off forgetting. "I think he might be—there's this ghost story around here, right? That this boy died and then came back and—"

"Chloe." Penelope's voice is strong and firm and motherly. "I don't know what the fuck you're talking about. If this man is still in the house, say *good night*."

I let out a faintly hysterical laugh. "He's not in the house," I say. "Or I mean, he's not holding me hostage or anything. What I'm trying to say is—" I say the next part as fast as I can, like pulling off a Bandaid. "Ithinkhemightbelikeyoursister."

The phone crackles in my ear, and I stop my pacing a few steps away from the doorway. He left it hanging open when he fled.

"Why do you say that?" Penelope finally asks, more calmly than I expect.

I take a deep breath, tightening my fingers around my phone.

"Chloe," Penelope says sharply. "I'm not fucking around. This is serious. What did he say to you?"

"He said he wasn't going to hurt me," I say quickly. "But that he's killed people—"

Penelope sucks in her breath.

"And that he's eighty years old."

I don't tell her about the sign he made, or how he explained it afterward. *A killer whose only purpose is to kill.*

More silence. Not just on the phone. In the house. I think he really is gone.

"He also—" I swallow. "He kissed me. And I kissed him back."

"What the fuck?" Penelope shrieks. "He broke into your house, and you just made out with him?"

"It's complicated!" I shout back, although I really don't want to get into the details of my sexual preferences right now. "What the hell should I do? I don't want to call the police."

"Yeah, fuck that." Penelope takes another deep breath. "I'm gonna get Callie, okay? Are you sure this guy's not gonna hurt you?" She pauses. "Do you even know his name?"

"Theo," I say. "Theo Shorn."

Penelope mutters the name to herself. I step out into the hallway, peering into the dark. The house certainly *feels* empty.

"Okay, here's what I want you to do," Penelope says. "You sure he's not going to hurt you?"

No, I'm not, but I still say, "Reasonably sure, yeah."

Penelope sighs at that. "I'm guessing your grandparents didn't leave you a gun along with the house?"

"No, of course not."

"You should fix that. Anyway, see if he's still… around. I'm going to get Callie on the line, and I want you to make him talk to her." I can hear the edge of panic in Penelope's voice, and I can't say I blame her. But while I do feel scared—my heart fluttering, my palms clammy—I wouldn't say I'm *panicked*. I really don't think he's going to kill me. I mean, he hasn't killed Oliver.

"I'm going downstairs now," I say.

"I'm pulling Callie onto the call," Penelope says. "I'll just be gone for one second."

The phone clicks over. I step into the hallway, switching the lights on as I go, until I'm in the living room. The curtains on the picture window are pushed open, revealing the lake. The back door is shut, though.

Shut, but the lock is broken.

"I'm back," Penelope says breathlessly. "Callie's here, too."

"Hello."

Callie's voice sends a little chill over my skin, the way it always does.

"Is he with you?" Callie asks. "Theo Shorn?"

"I don't see him." I press my face closer to the glass, trying to get a view of the lake. I don't want to turn the light off, even though I know it's stupid. It just makes me feel safer. "I'm going to go outside, okay?"

"Be careful," Penelope says. Callie doesn't say anything.

I push the door open and step out onto the porch, flicking on the light. The night feels like velvet on my skin as I tilt the phone away from my mouth and call out, "Hello?" I definitely don't sound certain of myself.

The wind seems to swallow up my voice, and I strain for

some sign of him: footsteps or a soft rush of breath. Anything. All I hear is the lapping of the lake.

"Theo?" I try again. "I, um, I was hoping maybe we could talk?"

"Anything?" Penelope says.

"No."

"Just because you don't see him doesn't mean he isn't there," Callie says coolly. "I know the name. Theo Shorn. The little ghost story he hides behind."

My stomach twists around. The little ghost story that I bought into until he stepped into my bedroom. I realize now I was only buying into it because I didn't want the alternative to be true.

"Try again," Penelope says tightly. "Callie's going to tell him to leave you the fuck alone."

My skin prickles. Do I want that, though? Really?

"Are you there?" I call out again. The lake swallows up my question.

"I don't think he's here," I say into the phone.

Someone sighs; I'm not sure if it's Penelope or Callie. I scan the darkness, but I can't see anything. Just shadows and stars.

"Go back inside," Callie says. "Bar yourself in your room and keep your phone on you. If he shows back up, call me."

"I'll text you the number," Penelope adds.

"Okay," I say distractedly, still staring out at the dark lake. Fear quivers around in my belly, but it doesn't quite seem to match Callie and Penelope's worry.

I don't want to hurt you, he said, and I think I believe him.

13

CHLOE

Theo Shorn doesn't come back. I wake up the next morning to warm sunlight falling across my face, my office chair jammed up under my bedroom door knob. Something tells me that wouldn't have actually kept him out, but it's undisturbed, regardless.

I send a quick text over to Penelope.

> Just checking in. I'm fine. No sign of him.

Then I leave my phone sitting on my bedside table and go downstairs to investigate.

The house feels like it did last night: quiet and empty. I forgot to close the curtains when I came back inside, and the living room is flooded with hot sunlight. Through the glass, the lake ripples with miniature waves, and the sky is an endless, cloudless blue. It looks nothing like it did last night, when it was all just empty darkness.

I fix a quick breakfast, granola and yogurt and slices of the plump, juicy peaches I picked up from the little farm stand that sits on the highway between here and Pinella.

Brew a cup of coffee. And then, because it's what I've done most mornings since I moved in, I take it out on my patio to eat.

It's nice out. The sun is warm on my skin, but the breeze blowing over the lake is cool. As I eat, I watch the thick wall of trees across the water. The wind makes their leaves shimmer in the sunlight, but there's no sign of Theo Shorn. Or of anyone.

There *is* a strange, hollow knocking sound, though. I hear it occasionally, and I think it's an animal at first, maybe a squirrel hunting for nuts in one of the oak trees growing on my property. But when the wind gusts, it gets louder. And it isn't coming from the direction of my yard, either.

It seems to be coming from the lake.

My breath quickens, although I wouldn't say I feel afraid, exactly. I reach instinctively for my phone, only to remember I left it upstairs.

"Hello?" I call out softly. No answer.

I get up from the table and take a few steps forward, trying to follow the sound. There's a distinctive pattern to it: the wind gusts, and the knocking echoes a couple of times, then fades. Wood on wood, that's what it sounds like.

And it sounds like it's beneath my pier.

I jump off my patio, into the damp, marshy grass that rolls into the lake. I've never been down here, and I know it's stupid, what I'm doing. At the very least, I should have Penelope on the phone with me. Or her sister.

But I keep creeping forward, hand out on the pier for balance. There's another particularly strong gust of wind, another round of knocking. And this time, I see what it is.

A boat.

There's a boat tied to my pier.

It's not Oliver's boat. This boat looks a lot older, the red paint so worn down it's almost pink. When the wind blows, the rippling waves push it up against the pier post.

I suck in a breath of air and lift my gaze to the crowd of oak trees growing up around my yard. Is he still here, lurking somewhere? Watching me right now?

I swallow, but it's hard to be scared in the bright light of morning. Especially when I wasn't all that scared last night.

An idea hits me, then. Probably a stupid one. But if he's over here, on this side of the lake—

What's stopping me from taking this boat to *his* side of the lake?

My heart pounds against my ribcage. If he's watching me, he might try to stop me from taking the boat. Then I can get him on the phone with Penelope and Callie. But if he isn't here, if he isn't paying attention, it's a chance for me to snoop around. To learn more about him.

It's stupid, I know. But I'm going to do it anyway.

I slide down to the waterline and drag the boat out into the open, then step inside. The whole time, my skin prickles, and I glance over my shoulder, expecting him to emerge out of the shadows like he did last night, staring at me through his long, pale hair. But he doesn't. The trees watch me. There's no sign of anyone else.

I settle down on the bench and pluck at the rope until it comes loose. Then I push myself off with one of the oars, hard enough that a wave catches me and drags me out to the water. I row toward the peninsula, the oars rising and falling. I glance over my shoulder again, but there's no sign of him. There's no sign of anyone.

Even though this boat is older and bigger and heavier than Oliver's, I have a better sense of how to work the oars now, and I make good time to the peninsula. When I slide up into the shallows, I step into the water and drag the boat up onto the shore, grateful that I threw on flip flops instead of real shoes when I came outside this morning. That gratefulness is short-lived, though, as I turn toward the trees.

"Fuck," I murmur, walking sideways along the treeline. Everything is so dense and overgrown, and I think back to what my realtor told me. Ticks. Rattlesnakes.

Unkillable murderers.

I don't turn back, though. I mean, I'm here now, and some dark, throbbing curiosity pushes me forward until I find that barely-there path to the cemetery. I figure that's a good place to start. Oliver said Theo lived in a cabin, and it would make sense that this old trail would lead there.

Still, it's not easy getting to the cemetery again. My flip flops snag on the overgrowth, and I keep feeling the forest whisper across my skin. But I push on, and when I catch sight of the clearing and the rough, overgrown graveyard, I breathe a sigh of relief.

I pick my way through the grass until I find Theo Shorn's grave. The name is there, clear in the dappled sunlight. So are the dates: 1943-1960. I do the math backward in my head. He would actually be 82 this year.

My skin prickles again, and I run my fingers over the rough stone, my chest tight. Penelope did explain a little bit of it to me, what Callie is. How she's not really human, how she can die and come back to life, something she's already done once. *A perfect predator,* Penelope told me the night of the attack, holding me while I sobbed and shook in the apartment bathtub. *You don't have to be scared of her. But there are others out there. And you should stay far, far away from them.*

Clearly, I'm not good at following instructions.

I rise up to standing and spin around slowly. Then I see it. A small gap in the trees. Another path, this one a little clearer than the one that brought me here.

It may be more defined, but it's darker, the way it weaves into the woods. The trees are thicker overhead and block out any of the warming light of the sun I felt in the cemetery. But since it's easier to walk, I move more quickly, ducking under wayward branches and pushing aside loops of ropy vines.

Then I feel something. A presence.

I stop, my heart hammering. The woods ripple around me, but I don't hear anything. No footsteps. No breaths. Well, aside from my own.

It can't be him. I took his boat.

Can't it?

I push forward, more slowly this time. My footsteps sound like thunder. And I still feel it, that presence. That prickling on the back of my neck like someone's watching.

"Hello?" I call out, my voice low and tremulous. "Theo?"

I stop in the middle of the trail and listen. Tree branches blow around overhead, getting entangled with each other. Warning signals go off in my body: *this is stupid why did you steal his boat you didn't even bring your phone you fucking idiot you need to get out of here*

I whirl around to go back the way I came—

And there he is, his huge form blocking the path.

I shriek and stumble backward and slam into a nearby tree. Theo watches me with his icy blue eyes. He's swept his hair back into a ponytail at the base of his neck, which just highlights the sharp lines of his cheekbones.

"I'm s-sorry," I stammer. "I was—I just—"

His eyes burn into me.

"I brought your boat back," I say. Then, remembering myself, I sign it too.

Theo studies me for a second longer. Then he lifts his hands and signs, "You didn't call the police."

I drop my mouth open, not sure how to answer. My first thought is not understanding how he could know that, followed by another thought reminding me that if he is like Callie, then he's not human. Maybe he can sense things.

I shake my head no.

"Why not?"

I take a deep breath. This deep into the forest, there's no wind, even though I can hear it, blowing across the tops of the trees. Theo stares at me, waiting. He's changed his clothes, I notice stupidly. A fresh grey T-shirt that stretches across this thick chest. Dark jeans. Heavy black boots.

"You were on the phone last night," he says. "Who?"

The damp, stifling heat makes me feel swoony. "A friend," I sign. "I think she's like you." I can't remember the sign he made, although I try my best, clapping my wrists together and swiping my fingers through the air.

It's good enough, though. I see it in Theo's face, the way his expression hardens. "She calls herself a Hunter," I say out loud.

Theo takes a step toward me, his steps heavy but quiet, even in the underbrush. I press against the tree, the bark rough through my shirt.

"You're not a Hunter." He uses his sign for it. "You're human."

"Yes," I whisper.

He stops a few inches from me, and I think of last night, how his mouth felt on my mine.

"How do you know her?" he asks.

"I'm friends with her sister." This time, when I talk to him, my hands don't shake so much. "She's human."

Theo tilts his head a little, as if to say, *Interesting.* I breathe out.

"Why did you come here?" he asks.

Sweat beads on my forehead. Drips down my neck.

"I wanted to know about you." But that's not the truth, not really. When I pushed his boat into the water, part of me had hoped he would come after me. Drag me into the grass and kiss me again. Touch me in that rough way I've always dreamed about.

Shame floods into my cheeks, but Theo only stares at me. I wonder just how much he can sense what I'm feeling. It's an unsettling thought.

So just to be safe, I tell the truth.

"I wanted to see you," I sign, my breath too shuddery in my throat to speak anyway.

Up until this moment, his face had been unreadable, even in the soft, dappled sunlight. But now, it changes. Surprise brightens in his eyes. His lips part. His hands lift and hover there, like he doesn't know what to say.

"And now I've found you," I sign. "So maybe we can talk?"

14

THEO

Chloe looks like some creature of the forest with all those leaves and twigs caught in her hair. Like the fairies my mother believed in enough that she would leave out saucers of cream and tell me not to step into mushroom circles.

But unlike those fairies, Chloe is real.

And she's staring at me like she's not *that* afraid of me. Even though I was right, and she did see what I am the second she met me.

Not that it's gone how I expected. She knows the word *Hunter*. A human shouldn't know that word, not as it applies to me.

"What do you want to talk about?"

She looks up at me with her big doe eyes, and I feel something trembling inside me. That urge that feels like the killing moon but isn't. It's warm, so warm that the heat of the woods is almost intolerable.

I want to kiss her again. Somehow, though, I manage to restrain myself.

Chloe lifts her hands, her brow furrowed. She shapes a

single word— *hurt*—and then shakes her head. "Is it okay if I speak?" she signs instead.

I nod.

"Thank you." There's her voice again, soft and musical. The blood thrums in my veins. "I'm sorry, this is very—it's easier for me. I'm still out of practice with ASL and—" She hitches her shoulders. "This is a weird situation, you know?" Then she laughs nervously, shaking her head. "That's an understatement, isn't it?"

"I agree."

Chloe looks up at me. Her cheeks are flushed, and I can smell the blood beneath her skin. My cock stirs.

"That this is strange," I add. "I've been very isolated."

She breathes out. "Why don't you want to hurt me?" she asks. "You said that last night. You didn't want to hurt me—"

"And I told you," I interrupt, my hands fluttering. "Because you're beautiful."

The blush in her cheeks deepened. "That doesn't seem like a very good reason," she mutters.

I wish I could explain it better. That it's not so much that she's beautiful but that she stirs all these feelings up inside me. That she's like my killing moon, but instead of being cold and pale, she's as bright as the sun. She's the light that went missing the night I drowned in Hanging Lake.

"You are different," I finally say instead, which isn't much better, and it just makes her face knot up with more confusion. "I don't like trespassers, but you're not a trespasser. I don't mind you being here." No, that's not right. I correct myself. "I like you being here. In my territory."

Chloe sucks in her breath, presses herself against the trees. "Your territory," she murmurs. "That's why this place is dangerous, isn't it? You.. Hurt people who..." Her voice trails off.

"I kill trespassers," I say, and when the red drains out of

Chloe's face, turning it ashy and pale, I feel some guilt at enjoying it. Her fear is sweet to me, but not in the way fear usually is. "And I kill people who hurt me."

That's the easiest way to explain the killing moon, for now.

"I see," Chloe says, and there's a breathiness in her voice that's like the tremble in her hands when she was signing last night. That same sweet fear.

"Would you like to see my cabin?" I ask. I don't know why; the question just comes to me, and it feels right. Maybe because she's a guest and not a trespasser. Or maybe I want her to leave a trace of her scent in my home.

Fear flickers through her eyes, but she plasters on a brave smile. I like that. "Do I have a choice?"

I frown at that. Then nod. Then sign, "Always."

Her breath hitches, a sound like a tree branch cracking in the woods. She didn't actually say yes to seeing my cabin, but I pretend she did, stepping past her to lead her to my home. My father would chide me, having a human at my back, but it feels the polite thing to do in this situation. Besides, I doubt she has a gun. There was no sign of it in those tight jean shorts she's wearing.

When we get to my cabin, Chloe steps up beside me and stares at it. For a moment, I feel a shudder of embarrassment; compared to her house, it looks condemned. The roof is sagging and missing shingles. The windows are dirty. At least the porch is swept, and the inside is clean. Too clean, I realize now. Clean enough that if she had called the cops, they would have known someone lived there, despite my efforts last night to hide the traces of my presence.

But she didn't call the cops.

"I can make you something to drink," I sign to her, and then I step up on the porch. I half expect her to turn and run, but she doesn't. She follows me.

I can feel her emotions wafting up behind me: more of that sweet fear, but also confusion. Surprise, when she walks through the door.

"It's nice in here," she says, and I hear the surprise in her voice, too. Once again, I see my cabin through her eyes: plain, with little furniture. But tidy. Mom would have hated it if I had let the inside fall into disrepair, even if I don't tend to the exterior as I should.

I nod at her, not sure how else to acknowledge the compliment. "I can make you coffee," I sign. There's still enough for both of us, even though I hid it away in the back of the old pantry. "Or there's well water."

"Water's fine," she says. "It's, um, it's too hot for coffee."

I nod and slip into the kitchen. I did draw water from the well this morning when the cops didn't show up last night, and I dig out two glasses from where I hid them and fill them with it. When I carry them back into the living room, Chloe is perched on the edge of my old sofa, her hands in her lap.

It's so strange, having her in my home, the way she seems to light up all the dusty, cobwebbed darkness. When she lifts her eyes to meet mine, I have to squeeze the glasses together to keep from dropping them. I'm not used to being seen this much.

"Thanks," she signs. "I was thirsty from rowing over here. I really did bring back your boat, by the way." She pauses. "I assume it was your boat."

I hand her the glass and sit down on the sofa beside her. She's so close—close enough that I feel her blood pumping in her veins and the breath exhaling through her lips—but she doesn't pull away from me. I set my own water glass aside so I can sign.

"Was it under your pier?"

She nods before taking a sip of the water. There's something about that first drink that sends fire scorching through my body. It's so *trusting*. She knows what I am, knows at least some of the horror I'm capable of, and she still took a sip of that water.

"Then it was mine," I finish.

We stare at each other.

Her scent is overpowering. I'm used to smelling her from afar, so that it's washed out by the scent of the lake. But now, she's inches from me, and I can catch all the complexity of it. Both the scent of her body and the scent of her blood, but also those emotions churning beneath it. The fear's mostly gone. There's something else, though. Something that reminds me of fear, and of excitement, and of—

For a second, I slam backward into time. Several years ago, before the lake houses were built. I was stalking some trespassers who had set up a campsite on the beach, a tent and a small fire that trailed smoke up to the starry night sky.

They were fucking.

They were fucking, and the scent of their arousal led me straight to them. I felt nothing from it; my blood was up for killing, not sex. But I do remember that scent. Rich and lush and earthy, like soil after a thunderstorm.

And I smell it now, wafting off Chloe.

I smelled it last night, too, when her mouth was against mine, but I had been so distracted by the whole situation that I hadn't dwelt on it.

Chloe shifts on the couch, sips from the water again. Her eyes watch me over the edge of her glass. I don't know how to read what I see in them—the only human emotion I ever *really* recognize is terror. But there's something there. A small ember of a fire.

"How did you get back here?" She speaks the question, and the sound of her voice goes straight to my cock, which is already hard from being near her.

"Last night," she adds.

It takes me a second to realize what she's saying. "I swam," I sign.

"Oh."

The air feels thick. I move closer to her, the way I do unsuspecting prey. Is she unsuspecting? I don't know.

She doesn't pull away, just watches me, the glass pressed to her lips. She's not drinking, though.

Something surges in me. Perhaps we don't have real self-control, us Hunters. But I wrap my hand around hers and pull the glass away. Her eyes widen a little.

And then I kiss her again.

This time, there's no pause. She returns the kiss, and her arousal blooms brighter than the rest of her scent, and it works on me like blood does. My whole body erupts, and I push her roughly down onto the sofa. Distantly, I hear the water glass fall to the wooden floorboard slats, but I don't care. I keep kissing her, plunging my tongue into her mouth, and she does the same

I press my weight into her, pinning her down. Now, there's a trace of fear working through her arousal. Heightening it, though, not drowning it out.

All the movements come to me easily, the way they do when I'm killing. I haven't fucked much. Certainly not since I've been back on my peninsula. Even before then, it was rare for me to even be interested. But with Chloe—

All I want to do is plunge inside her.

I break the kiss, and Chloe sucks down a deep gasp of air, her face flushed. "Don't stop," she whispers, and I sense something like shame. Maybe it should make me feel bad, but it doesn't. I know what I am.

So I attack her. Well, I attack her clothes, flaying them off her body like strips of skin. Chloe moans, bucking her hips, and the sound reverberates through my chest.

I claw at her bra, shoving it up around her throat so I can

get at her breasts, which tremble from the rough, gasping breaths she's taking. Her nipples are sharp even in the drowsy heat, and I drag one into my mouth, swirling it with my tongue so I can taste her skin. This makes her groan and roll her hips, still half-covered in her pesky jean shorts and, presumably, another layer of underwear. I kiss down her belly, dragging myself away from her so I can flay those off, too.

"Don't stop," Chloe whispers. "I like—like it like this."

I don't really understand what she means, but I take her at her word, that she doesn't want me to stop. I yank her shorts down over her knees, everything getting tangled up in her long, smooth legs. By the time they're free, I don't want to bother doing the same with the underwear. My treasure is laid out in front of me, almost completely unwrapped, and I have no fucking patience.

I growl softly, a sound I only ever make when I'm in the middle of a kill, when my body's already drenched in blood. Then I grab Chloe's flimsy panties with both hands and rip them in half.

She shrieks and jolts against the sofa, but her arousal explodes, too, like I just crushed a rose bloom in my hand. And then all I can look at is her cunt: the dark, downy triangle of hair falling over the faint impression of her slit.

"Theo," she breathes, and the sound of my name in that beautiful, musical voice is the only thing that could drag my gaze away from her pussy.

It's worth it, though, because I see her face. Flushed, lips parted in ecstasy, eyes shining with trepidation.

I want to split her open. I want to scoop her blood out with my hands and smear it on my face, want to crawl inside her body and curl up there, nestled among her organs. But I also don't want to kill her.

She's staring at me, and there's something pleading in her

expression, the way people will look at me right before I kill them. *Please,* they say. *Please don't.*

Chloe's mouth parts, showing me her pink tongue.

Then she reaches down between our bodies and grazes her fingers across the top of my jeans.

"Please," she whispers. "Please."

No *don't.*

And so I do.

15

CHLOE

I think I'm dreaming. It feels like a dream. This decaying cabin that's somehow swept and tidy on the inside, the dim light from the faded, floral curtains covering the window. The glass of water, which tasted faintly steelish, like the lake.

A fucking murderer ripping my clothes off me like a hunting dog trying to get to its prey.

It's exactly how I've always wanted to be fucked. Violently.

Now I'm naked on his sofa, the fabric rough against my bare back. My clit is throbbing to be touched, but Theo just stares down at me. He's still fully dressed, still in that T-shirt and jeans, and I'm completely vulnerable. Completely at his mercy.

The idea makes my clit throb.

I think of all the terrible hook-ups I've had in my life, chasing a moment like this and never finding it.

"Please," I whisper, hardly aware of my lips moving. Or my hand, for that matter, reaching to get at his cock. "Please."

I still can't bring myself to say it, though. I've never been able to. *Please fuck me so hard it hurts.* But I think he understands, because his eyes darken, and he shoves his fly down and reaches inside, rearranging things. Then he pulls out his cock.

It's big. Big, and so hard that the skin seems to shine as it stretches around his thick girth. He's almost as big as my dildo, the one that looks cartoonishly huge but is the only thing that's ever come close to giving me what I crave.

I whimper softly, imagining how beautifully that cock is going to hurt. Even better, I think Theo likes it, because he smiles: a devilish, evil-looking grin. I wonder if he grins like that before he kills people.

I wonder, fleetingly, if he's going to kill me. And to my shame, lust floods into my clit.

Theo growls and grabs his cock at its base and slides it between my folds, running his head up and down, gathering up the moisture seeping out from between my legs. He's going too slow, although when he brushes my clit, I cry out and arch my back, and he stays there, grinding his cock down on me. I moan, my eyes rolling back, legs trembling, waiting for him to shove himself inside me.

But he doesn't. He strokes my clit with his cockhead, moving in quick, swiping motions. Heat builds in my belly, hot and molten, and I lift my gaze to him again. He watches me intently, those icy blue eyes bearing into me as he starts to slap my clit with cock. My body jolts.

This is what I need.

"H-harder," I pant, digging my nails into the couch.

He smiles again, dark and wicked. Then he quickens his pace, smacking his cock down over and over against my inflamed clit. I shriek, bucking into the pain of it, the pleasure building fast.

He's going to make me come, I think in a daze. I wonder if he can sense that, too.

"Use your hand," I whisper, hardly believing myself. I never ask for what I want. It's never worth it.

But Theo's eyes blaze with hunger, and then he strikes my pussy hard with his palm. I groan and arch my back, spreading my legs wider and rocking my hips, and he keeps striking me, the soft smack of his skin against my wet cunt echoing through the room.

My orgasm hits fast, almost out of nowhere. I scream out, half in surprise and half in pleasure. It wasn't just the pain but the threat of him, of all he could do to me, that got me soaking. I thrash against the couch, and Theo pins me down at the shoulder. He growls again, a sound far more animal than human, as he rubs his cock against me, plying my walls open

I pant, my vision dotted as the last waves of orgasm pulse through my body. Theo's eyes burn into me.

Then he thrusts himself inside my cunt.

It hurts. It doesn't matter that I'm drenched or even that I'm still coming a little. He's so big, and he stabs me with his cock like he's stabbing me with a knife, and it hurts.

But fuck me, I like it. I like how Theo's eyes flutter closed, and his fingers tighten on my shoulder, digging into my skin, like a threat of more violence. I like how he moans word-lessly, how my pussy can barely stretch to accommodate him. I like how he buries himself inside my trembling body and then looks at me and bares his teeth, his breath fast and heavy, matching mine.

As he ruts into me, I reach up and cup his face, spreading my fingers over his cheek. I don't know why; it just feels right, like he's the beast and I'm the beauty who can soothe him. As soon as I touch him, his eyes widen, and he makes a rough, frightening sound in the back of his throat, and he fucks me harder.

I moan, sliding my hand up until my fingers are tangled in his hair, and drop my head back, baring my throat to him as I languish in the painful pleasure of his thrusts. He bows his head over me, kissing my face and then my neck, which makes me spark with a fear that pulses straight into my clit. It's not long before his kisses turn to sharp, nipping bites that leave bright spots of pain all the way down to my breasts. When he drags one of my nipples into his mouth again, my body clenches around his dick. Again. I'm going to come again.

"Don't stop," I pant, tugging on his hair. "Don't fucking stop. I'm so close."

He grunts into me, rolling into my pussy in a way that means his big, painful cock is sliding very not-painfully against my G-spot. My body shakes. I dig my fingers into his shoulder and hook my legs around his hips, dragging him down to me, holding him in place. Then his teeth clench around my nipple, and I howl and then I come, the hot pleasure pouring through my limbs as the pain in my breast explodes outward.

He releases me and buries his nose between my breasts and makes more of those throaty, desperate sounds as he keeps stroking me through my orgasm, like he's trying to drag it out as long as possible. I've never felt anything like this before; this constant, rhythmic surging, as steady as the lake waves lapping against the shore, not even when I fuck myself. I've never come so hard that it hurts, like I'm doing now. But god, it's the best kind of hurt, like the hurt of his cock and the hurt of his teeth.

His thrusts quicken, turning erratic, and his face is still buried between my tits so that his breath is warm and damp on my skin as he pants. I roll my eyes up to the ceiling, the exposed wooden beams crossing overhead. A loose veil of cobweb flaps back and forth, catching the lemony light of the sun, mesmerizing me as I come down from the burning intensity of my orgasm.

Suddenly, Theo roars, and I don't care about spiderwebs. He tosses his head back, his hips shuddering against mine, and I know he came inside me. I don't care.

I like it, even.

Theo breathes heavily, his chest pressed against mine, the fabric of his T-shirt damp with both of our sweat.

I don't know what to say. Or do, for that matter. I honestly just want to stay like this, his cock softening inside me, his firm, heavy body crushing me into the couch. I think I would give anything to be crushed by him for real.

Eventually, though, Theo lifts his head until our eyes meet. They're as pale and icy as ever. I think of the photograph of Theo Shorn in the newspaper. Of him, decades ago.

Penelope's going to kill me when she finds out what I've done.

"Is everything okay?" I ask, my voice shaky.

Theo tilts his head, studying me. Then he pulls back. Pulls out of me, his cock slapping wetly against the inside of my thigh.

"I thought you wanted to do that," he says. There's a long pause, his hands lifted but unmoving. Then: "I sensed it."

My heart flutters. So he does feel it. My arousal. My desire.

"I did want it," I whisper back, and it feels vaguely shameful to say it out loud.

Theo keeps gazing down at me, like I'm a puzzle he's trying to take apart. He drops one hand to my cheek, brushing it with the back of his knuckle. I tilt my head into the touch. I wanted it. I wanted *him*, and I still fucking do.

It's the way he looks at me, I think. Men don't look at me like that. All that Hunter's intensity, directed right at me.

But Theo jumps off the couch, his eyes fixed on the door.

"What's wrong?" I sit up, my heart pounding.

"Get dressed," Theo signs. "Oliver's here."

A new panic slices through me. I scramble off the couch, grabbing my clothes as I can find them. Theo hurled them all over the room. My panties, of course, are little more than rags.

He leaves me alone, the door slamming behind him as he steps out on the front porch. As I get dressed, I try to work out what exactly I'm going to say to Oliver. Obviously, I can say I was here to return the boat, but how do I explain getting the boat in the first place? How do you explain stalking to a ten-year-old?

I pull my shirt on over my head, rake my fingers through my hair, and step out onto the porch just as Theo and Oliver step out of the woods.

Oliver's eyes get huge when he sees me, and he waves his hand around excitedly and runs up to the porch. Behind him, Theo catches my eye. There's a soft expression on his face. He's almost smiling.

"What are you doing here?" Oliver asks. "Theo said he met you yesterday. I told you he's nice!"

Heat rises into my cheeks, and I glance back at Theo, watching us from where he's standing beneath the low-hanging branches of one of the trees. "Yes, Theo introduced himself yesterday," I say carefully, speaking the words because it's easier. Less chance of me messing up. "But he left his boat, and I had to return it."

Oliver laughs and whips around to look at Theo. He signs something, although I can't see all of it, despite how animated Oliver is. But Theo peels himself away from the tree and answers in a slow, laconic sort of way. "I got scared," he says. "I don't like strangers seeing me. So I swam home." He lifts his eyes to mine, and they flash like diamonds. "Chloe was very kind to bring the boat back."

"I'm so glad you're here!" Oliver whips around to face me again. "Now we can all be friends. Right?"

Oliver's eyes brim with excitement. Hopefulness, too. My heart pangs. He's lonely. I knew that already, but this just seems to bring in such stark relief. He's lonely. Probably neglected, which gives me another pang.

But he's still staring up at me, clearly expecting an answer. "Yes," I sign. "Yes, we can all be friends."

Oliver beams, then pushes past me and flings himself on the old porch swing and starts digging through his backpack. Theo crosses the lawn. His eyes never leave me, like he's waiting for me to do something. To say something to Oliver, maybe.

But then he lifts his hands and says, "I hope you mean that. About us being friends."

His eyes sear through me, making my breath catch. I think of his rough hands on my body, his mouth on my mouth, his violent and shuddering thrusts.

"You want to be friends?" I sign back.

Theo steps onto the porch and stops near me, blocking the warm stream of sunlight. Behind me, Oliver rustles papers around, clearly impatient.

"I would like that very much," Theo says. "I would like to see you again."

Oliver stomps his foot on the wooden slats of the porch, trying to get our attention. But Theo's gaze never leaves mine, and I feel like I'm on fire. I don't dare ask if he means what I think he means. Not with Oliver here.

Still, it doesn't change my answer.

"I'd like that, too."

16

CHLOE

I hitch a ride home with Oliver, who initially insists on doing the rowing himself. Of course, he tires out about halfway across the lake, and I have to take over, pushing us through the calm waters. I don't have a sense of what time it is, although the sun feels higher overhead than I expected. Thank god it's the weekend.

Penelope's probably freaking out, though.

"I'm glad you came by," I tell Oliver. He's staring down at his backpack and jerks his gaze up at the sound of my voice. "Otherwise, I would have had to swim home like Theo did last night."

Oliver laughs, his eyes crinkling up. "Theo's strong," he signs. "He doesn't mind swimming."

Yes. Theo *is* strong. Dangerous, too. I know he said he doesn't want to hurt Oliver, and honestly, after seeing the two of them interact on the porch—I believe him. He was calm and patient and complimented Oliver on the drawings he brought over. I know what Theo is, but in those moments, the two of them sitting side by side on the swing, I couldn't see it in him. I would have thought he was just a man.

Not like when he was fucking me. The thought hits me hard, and the oars flop crookedly in the water. Oliver frowns at me.

"Sorry," I say. "Caught an eddy there."

"Don't flip us over!" Oliver pats his backpack. "Mom and Dad would kill me if I came home wet. The last time I went swimming, I dripped water on the kitchen, and I got grounded for two weeks."

There's that pang in my chest again. "Two weeks?" I say lightly. "That's a long time."

Too long, really. Just for getting lake water in the house? But I keep my mouth shut.

Oliver shrugs, though, and then hunches over his backpack so that his hair falls into his eyes. I frown, concern tightening in my belly.

"Hey," I say, and when Oliver looks up at me, his expression nearly breaks my heart. No kid should look that fucking sad. I swallow down that concern, though, and force my voice to be as bright and cheery as I can. "If you ever want to go swimming, you can come dry off at my place before you head home, okay?"

Immediately, Oliver beams and nods his head furiously.

A few minutes later, the boat bumps up against Oliver's pier, and he jumps out, leaving me to tie it off. "I have to go," he signs. "I have to help Dad clean out the garage. Owen was supposed to do it—" He cuts himself off, curling his hands into little fists. "He never has to do chores."

Discomfort settles in my chest again. "Well, if you want to come over afterward, we can split a Coke."

Oliver grins. "Mom never lets me have Cokes. Or candy. Or chips. Or anything good."

"Well, it'll be our secret."

Oliver waves goodbye, slides on his backpack, and takes off down the pier. For a moment, I just sit in the boat, watching as he runs up to the back door and flings it open and disappears inside. There's a half-second where I hear a raised woman's voice, just before it slams shut.

I think of the way Theo is with him—the patience, the gentleness. No matter what kind of monster Theo might be, I can kind of understand why Oliver would rather spend time with him.

Eventually, I pull out of the boat, taking the oars with me. I lay them in the grass of Oliver's yard, figuring that's the safest place for them, even though his mother seems like the type who would complain. Well, let her.

The first thing I do when I get back home is check my phone. It's nearly noon—almost four hours have passed since I went to the peninsula. There are also a few texts from Penelope, growing increasingly more worried.

> **PENELOPE**
>
> You around?
>
> Call me please. Callie has an idea for talking to this guy.
>
> Dude, don't do this to me. ANSWER YOUR DAMN PHONE.

Guilt twists around in my stomach. We went through this about a month ago with Abi—she flipped out and went dark during one of our movie nights, and Penelope and I texted furiously back and forth before she finally responded and said she was fine. But I remember that sick feeling of worry in my stomach.

When I call Penelope, she answers on the first ring.

"Are you okay?" she says instead of hello.

"Definitely okay." I take a deep breath. Should I tell her? I have to tell her. She's my best friend. "I went over to the peninsula, where Theo Shorn lives."

"What the fuck!" Penelope shrieks, which I expected. "And you didn't take your phone? Jesus Christ, Chloe, what the hell were you thinking?"

"He didn't do anything." Well, that's not entirely true, is it? "I mean, he didn't do anything… bad."

Silence fills the line.

"So what exactly did he… do?" Penelope says in a low voice.

Heat floods into my cheeks, and I walk over to my window and pull back the curtains to look out at the lake. At the woods, hiding Theo's cabin.

"He kissed you again, didn't he?" Penelope's voice is flat. "Chloe, I know you think you understand what's going on here, but he's dangerous. I don't care what he says to you, what he does, he's—"

"I fucked him."

The words roll out of me before I can stop them, but it feels better, having them out there instead of choking me up from the inside.

Penelope gives me one second of peace before screaming, "You did *what?*"

"I fucked him." It feels even better saying it the second time. "And he made me come. Twice."

"I didn't need to know that!" Penelope shouts. "Oh my god, Chloe, you don't—I'm coming out there, okay? And I'm bringing Callie. You can't stay there."

"Why not?" I fling myself on my bed and stare up at the ceiling fan, spinning in slow, lazy circles. "Look, Penelope, I know he's dangerous, okay? I'm not stupid. But he's—" I fumble around for the right word and eventually settle on Oliver's. "He's nice."

"Hunters are not *nice,*" Penelope hisses. "My sister, I love her, but she's not *nice.*"

"She saved us from that creep back in Miami." I sit up, my heart racing. "And, like, you stay with her all the time. You're staying with her right now. And she's never hurt you—"

"But she could," Penelope snaps.

My chest tightens.

"I can't talk about this shit over the phone," Penelope says. "But if she doesn't—doesn't *work out* regularly, then she'll go crazy. I wouldn't be safe then."

My skin prickles, suddenly cold with fear. Even the warmth of the sun doesn't seem like enough. "What do you mean?"

"I mean she would lose control," Penelope says. "And I'm her *sister.* She actually does care about me. But I would still be in danger. This fucking dude—you don't know him. For all you know, him fucking you is part of his, uh, workout plan."

The fear spikes, quickening my heartbeat. I think of Theo staring at me in the woods, all his attention fixed straight on me, like I was the most important thing in the world. Then I think of the way he fucked me. Like he was stabbing me.

Which is also exactly how I've always wanted to be fucked. Like I'm being killed.

"He broke into your house," Penelope says. "You'd never seen him before, and he still—"

"He knew about me," I say. "From this kid next door. Oliver. Oliver's friends with him."

"Jesus fuck, Chloe."

"He definitely wouldn't hurt Oliver." Saying it out, I believe it, too. "I saw them together this morning. He treats Oliver better than Oliver's parents treat him, I'm pretty sure. Big dad energy."

"Big *dad* energy?" Penelope sputters. "Do you hear yourself right now?"

"Yeah. He's protective." I shrug. "Look, I'm not gonna deny that this might be—dangerous for me. But not for Oliver. I feel pretty sure about that."

"Pretty sure?"

"Very sure." I take a deep breath to steady myself. "I know it sounds crazy, okay? And I'm not saying I'm not scared of him—"

"No, because that's his whole god damn appeal, isn't it?"

I open my mouth, wanting to deny it. But I can't. She's right.

"Knew it." Penelope sighs. "He's a predator, Chloe. Like, literally. Like the way a wolf is a predator. He's not—" Her voice tightens. "He's not human," she says softly. "And he sees you as prey. That's the appeal of *you* to *him*."

I know damn well Penelope's trying to scare me, but everything she's saying just quickens my blood a little bit more. The stings of pain around my breasts, on my throat, on the places where Theo bit me, suddenly start to throb like my still-aching clit. Prey. What's prey but a focused target? All my life, I've gotten passed over by men. In high school, I never got dates to dances. My first year of college, before I met Abi and Penelope, I'd go out clubbing with my dorm mate and some of her friends, and I'd always get left sitting alone in the booth, sipping on a Coke because I didn't even have a fake ID to get a real drink. All for what? To maybe go home with some guy who couldn't even give me what I needed?

But when Theo Shorn found me on his property, he looked at me like nothing else in the world mattered.

So yeah. Maybe I like being prey.

Not that I can say any of this to Penelope. I'm not sure I want to say it to anyone.

"Chloe?" Penelope's voice drags me back to my sunny bedroom. "Are you listening to me?"

"Yeah, yeah. He's a wolf, I'm little red riding hood."

"This isn't a joke." Her voice is dead serious. "I really think Callie and I need to come visit. Keep you safe."

"What does Callie think about that?"

Penelope doesn't say anything.

"I'm fine. Really." I sit up, take a deep breath. "Look, if it makes you feel better—I won't go over there again, okay? I'll stay on my side of the lake. If he comes back, you'll be the first to know."

Penelope breathes softly. "He really is a wolf," she says quietly. "The man-eating kind. They all are."

And our ancestors tamed wolves, didn't they?

But I don't say that out loud.

17

THEO

I'm late making my rounds, but I don't care. My whole body feels like a lightning storm, and Chloe's scent is everywhere. Not just on the air. On *me*. On my hands. On my clothes. Every time I breathe in, I smell her—not just her, but her desire. Her pleasure. The scent of her orgasms. It was intoxicating, the way her body came alive for me, all her muscles clenching and rippling against mine. It was like the seconds before someone dies, how there's this big rush of blood and adrenaline that comes spilling out of them. But instead of death, I gave her pleasure.

And I want to do it again and again and again.

I stomp through the woods and force myself to concentrate. It's easier on the other side of my territory, near the little strip of land that connects my peninsula to the mainland. There's a big DANGER: KEEP OUT sign posted there. Not by me. It showed up about ten years back, after I killed a quartet of hikers and left their bodies hanging from the trees not far from here. That was my idea of a warning.

People ignore the sign, of course, although not often. Over the last decade, I've had fewer and fewer trespassers.

Whether it's from the sign, from the ghost stories, from some other warning put out by the state of North Carolina, I don't know. But it's keeping me isolated out here, the way I like it.

I walk up to the sign, which is currently overgrown with honeysuckle vines. No flowers, not this time of year: just lush, dense greenery. I suck in a deep breath of air. No sign of humans. Not in my territory, and not on the winding hiking trails over on the other side of the lake, either. I can vaguely sense the humans in their lake houses, though. I've grown more or less accustomed to them over the last few years, enough so that usually their scents fade into the background and become part of the woods, like the scents of all the animals that live out here, the squirrels and opossums and raccoons and deer.

This afternoon, though, something kind of cracks inside me. I breathe again, taking in the scents. The crack widens.

A quiver of fear works down my spine.

I freeze, wondering if I really felt it. The last time I felt real fear was during my last killing moon, twenty years ago. One of my would-be victims had a shotgun pointed at my head, and I looked at her through the blood dripping into my eyes and dropped my knife. That's always how it has to end, during a killing moon. With my death.

And no matter how many times I do it, I always feel fear in the seconds before I die. I felt it then, a little tremble of terror, right before she pulled the trigger.

It had taken me longer than usual to wake up from that death. Half my brain had been blown out, and although my kind don't really die the way humans do, that was the closest I'd ever come to a real death. Usually, I can sense the world around me while I'm in that half-living state, all its comings and goings. That time, though, everything sank into shadows. I don't even remember, even now, how I managed to burrow myself into the dirt the way my father had taught me. *Underground is better*, he said. *You'll heal faster.*

A faint headache throbs in my temple, like a distant memory of that death. Jesus, why am I even thinking about it? Why am I remembering that fear?

The crack shudders inside me.

I whirl away from the KEEP OUT sign and stalk into the woods proper. It feels better in there, being hidden away. Out of sight of the sky.

The empty sky.

There was hardly any moon last night, while I was rowing across the lake. We're close to a new moon, which means a new lunar cycle. In another two weeks, the moon will be full.

The thought makes my jaw tighten. My belly squirms around.

A killing moon.

The thought hits me hard. Like a punch. Like a shotgun blast, actually. I slump against one of the nearby poplar trees and suck in a sharp breath. "No," I mutter, tilting my gaze up to the sky. Not that I can see it beneath the canopy of tree leaves. "No. Not now."

The forest answers with its rustles and insect song. I close my eyes and try to concentrate. If this is the start of a killing moon, it doesn't feel the way it usually does. But I've been all mixed up since I caught my first glimpse of Chloe. Wanting to be near her feels so much like the killing moon that maybe that's why I didn't sense the real thing lurking underneath.

"No!" I shout, slamming my fist into the tree trunk. The tree shakes, and a few birds erupt out, making leaves rain down around me. Over twenty years since the last one. And how long since my last kill? A year? Year and a half?

Don't go too long without killing, my father told me. *You'll lose yourself in the bloodlust. You need that control to function, son.*

He never did tell me how long was too long, though. Just said it depends. Just said, *You'll know.*

I tear away from the tree and stalk toward my cabin. I don't feel like I'm losing myself. I know who I am. Where I am. *What* I am. I know I only want to kill trespassers unless the killing moon tells me otherwise, and it isn't quite whispering to me yet. There's just an empty hollow feeling in my chest.

I know I don't want to kill Chloe.

That thought gives me some comfort, and I hold on to it as I tear through the woods, not caring about moving silently. I keep walking through the underbrush until I make it to the beach, with its view of the lake houses. They rise like teeth, windows gleaming in the sun.

I can smell her, that warm, heady scent drifting above the others. She's inside, tucked away safely. She's not afraid.

Oliver's unhappy, though. His scent is fainter, although I'm close enough to pick up a thin waft of misery. I sense that from him now and then, this quiet, resigned sadness. Always when he's at home, though. Usually, he shows up on my front porch not long after. He doesn't say anything about it, and I don't ask. But he's not sad when he's with me.

An idea starts to roll around in my head. I told Chloe she's not a trespasser. Neither's Oliver, of course. They're *guests*. But I want to make them feel more permanent, like they're part of the forest. Part of my territory. That way, if this crack widens, if I start to rankle with the need to kill, they'll be safe. They'll belong here, and I won't—break, the way my father said. I won't hurt them, just like I promised.

An overnight trip, I think suddenly. Oliver has never stayed more than a few hours, and he always leaves well before sunset. But if they spend the night and wake up to the morning sun—and they will, of course—that will mark them as special. Not like the other trespassers.

My thoughts whir excitedly. We'll camp out, like the hikers who try to pass through here. I'll invite them as guests, and I can set up a tent outside somewhere. Maybe down near the lakeshore, over on the other side of the peninsula. It'll be just like the campers do before I kill them. A tent and a fire and marshmallows on a stick. But since I'll be there, I'll be part of it, and they'll be welcome.

I stalk through the woods, rolling the idea around and trying to look at it from all angles. All possibilities. To my relief, the crack from earlier seems to shrink up a little, especially at the thought of Chloe being here overnight, her body warm and soft next to mine. *Especially* at the thought of other things we could do after Oliver's asleep, deep in the woods where he won't hear.

Yes, I think this will work.

I look at the lake houses again. I put out my senses until I find them both. Chloe and Oliver: the only humans who matter. The only ones I would do anything to protect.

THERE PROVES to be one snag in my plan: telling Oliver and Chloe about it.

I expected Oliver to visit, especially when I sensed that sadness from across the lake. I figured I would invite him and tell him to invite Chloe.

But I never see him. A few days pass with no sign of him. I don't even see him when I set out my telescope to watch Chloe, who continues on her usual routine: working on her laptop during the day, occasionally bringing food out to her patio to eat, watching TV in the evenings with the curtains drawn shut. But Oliver is elusive. I see his brother on occasion, running around the pier with some other teenage boys. His parents, both the mother and the father. I don't like them

—or the older brother, for that matter. They remind me of my four killers from when I was seventeen.

But there's no sign of Oliver aside from the faint trace of his sadness.

I'm not sure what to think. This is not the longest I've gone without seeing him, in fairness. But I'm anxious to carry out my little sleepover. Each night, the moon gets a little bigger, and each night, I feel it more, the ice of moonlight on my skin. Watching Chloe is the only thing that warms me up.

After four days, I consider going across the water. I don't dare go into Oliver's house, but I could go into Chloe's again. Invite her and tell her to bring the boy.

Something stops me, though. I fling open the doors to my basement and stare down into the musty dark, but I don't drag out the rowboat. It feels—

Dangerous, I suppose is the word. Not for me. But I look into the basement, and I think of my father telling me about the madness that takes hold if we don't kill. *You'll feel it in your body*, he said, eyes fixed on mine. *Deep in the pit of your stomach.*

I heave the basement door shut, letting it clang against the frame. I'm not sure if that's what I'm feeling, this tightness in my belly. But I don't think I should go across the water.

The moon gets bigger. It sings out to me, although it's faint, and I mostly ignore it. I take out my knives and clean them again, even if they don't need it. I sharpen them, too, one by one, telling myself I need to do something with my hands.

But I know. Deep down, I know. The killing moon is going to rise soon. Maybe not this month. Maybe not even the next. But soon. And I need Chloe and Theo to do this one thing, to spend the night, to become part of my—

My family, I guess is the word for it.

There's one morning when I'm making my rounds that the killing moon is louder than usual. I swear I hear it in the trilling of cicadas and grasshoppers, a pulsing, rhythmic cry to get ready. I shriek and pound my fists into the trees until they bleed, and that quiets it down. A little.

Then I catch something on the wind. A soft, familiar scent. Oliver.

Relief floods through me, and I tear off into the woods, crashing through the underbrush until I meet him on the path to my cabin. At the graveyard, specifically. He jumps when he sees me, which is unusual.

Something's wrong, though. I don't know what, only that he seems paler than the last time I saw him, his eyes sunken in. He blinks up at me through his messy hair, squeezing the straps of his backpack.

We stare at each other. I don't know what to say.

"I brought you some drawings," he signs to me. Then, a beat later: "How long can I stay?"

My chest tightens. "How long would you like to stay?"

Oliver hesitates. The overgrown grass of the graveyard ripples around him. "Can I spend the night?"

Immediately, the killing moon goes silent. The insects are still singing, but that's expected here in the woods. I don't feel cold. Everything's back to normal

If ever there was proof that I need Oliver and Chloe to survive the night, this is it.

"Yes," I say, and there's another immediate change, this time in Oliver's mood. He brightens from the inside out, a smile cracking across his worn face. "But I have one request."

Oliver blinks, doubt creeping in.

"I want you to invite Chloe to join us."

18

CHLOE

It's been a week since I've heard from Theo. Or from Oliver, for that matter. I thought he would show up at my house after his chores that day he intercepted me on the peninsula, but he never did. There's been no sign of him since then, either. I'm not sure if I should be worried or not.

Theo, I have fewer expectations for. He might be a Hunter, but he's still a man, and men have always been a source of disappointment. That doesn't stop me from waking up in the middle of the night, hoping that it was his footsteps that woke me. Never is.

"You're fucking lucky," Penelope told me after three days of silence from him. "All he wanted to do was fuck you."

I scowled down at her face on the laptop. It was just me and her on the Zoom call. Abi's been distracted by something. An investigation, she said in her text, which apparently didn't warrant more explanation.

"You don't have to say it like that," I snapped, because I certainly don't feel lucky. I feel rejected. I couldn't tell Penelope that, though.

"Whatever," she said. "Hopefully, he'll stay away. Otherwise, I'm coming down there."

I'm not talking to Penelope *or* Abi tonight, though. The sun's just starting to set, and I'm watching TV, although my attention really isn't focused on it. I keep thinking about Theo. Replaying the last time I saw him until my body feels hot and distracted.

That's when I hear tapping on my back window.

I sit up, my heart leaping in my chest, even though I doubt it's Theo. I already know he doesn't knock.

The tapping continues, soft and insistent. When I push back the curtain, Oliver's standing on my porch, wearing his blue-and-green dinosaur backpack and, more unusually, carrying a sleeping bag tucked under his arm. Worry blooms in my chest.

"Oliver?" I sign at him through the glass. "Is everything okay?"

He nods and signs, "Can I come inside?"

I push open the door. Oliver promptly marches into my living room, sets down his sleeping bag, and digs through his backpack. I watch him, frowning. I'm fine with him being here, I really am. I just don't understand what's going on. Or why he has a sleeping bag.

He pulls something out of his backpack. I think at first it's one of his drawings, but when he hands it to me, I see it's a yellowed envelope with my name written across the front in big, block letters. Not a child's hand, although Oliver is such a good artist, I imagine his penmanship is probably pretty good.

"What's this?" I ask, looking up at him. He smiles deviously at me, his eyes glittering a little. "Is it going to explain why you have your sleeping bag?"

"Open it!"

I do. The envelope's paper feels old, as does the stationery inside, which is festooned with a swirling, feminine flower print. There's not much written on it, although it's in the same blocky hand as my name.

Chloe,

I have invited Oliver to camp in my territory tonight. I would like you to do the same.

-Theo Shorn

I jerk my gaze up at Oliver, and he bursts into a huge, gleaming smile. "Will you come?" he signs furiously, hands flying. "Please! Theo says we can build a fire and he says if you have marshmallows you can bring them but he'll cook breakfast for us. Please, please, please!"

I blink, my brain struggling to parse the onslaught. Oliver keeps signing *please* over and over.

"Why is there a letter?" I ask.

Oliver sighs dramatically. "He wanted me to ask you but I said what if you didn't believe me and so I told him to write you an invitation and so he did."

It takes me another two seconds to register everything Oliver has just signed to me. As I'm staring at him, he says, "Go get your stuff!"

"Your mom is okay with this?" I ask.

Oliver goes still, hands hanging in midair. Then he says, "She doesn't care."

She doesn't know, I think suddenly, although I'm not sure how Oliver managed to sneak out of his house with his backpack and his sleeping bag.

"Please, please, please!" Oliver sighs.

I bite my bottom lip. I know the responsible adult thing to do would be to march Oliver back over to his house and tell his parents about this impromptu camping trip. But I think about the few interactions I've had with them. The distant shouting I heard the other day, after I brought Oliver home from the peninsula. How dejected he seemed.

He's not dejected now. Now, he's bouncing up and down on his heels, beaming at me with excitement. He's also still signing the word *please*.

"Stop," I say. "You're going to wear your fingers out."

Oliver rolls his eyes and keeps signing.

I sigh. "When did Theo ask you about this?"

"This afternoon," Oliver says. "Please, Chloe? Theo *really* wants you to come, too! He said I could only spend the night if you were there!"

It's a trap, says a voice in my head that sounds suspiciously like Penelope. But I don't actually believe it. I—

Want to see Theo again.

I can feel my will wearing down, if for no other reason than Oliver's big, earnest eyes would break my heart if I told him no.

"Fine. I'll go."

I tell myself that I'm only agreeing to this because of Oliver. I don't think that's the whole reason, even though I'm trying to deny my foolish excitement at seeing a man who isn't even human.

Oliver jumps up in the air. "Hurry!" he signs. "Get everything you need. Do you have marshmallows?"

I smile at him. I actually do, an impulse buy from the day I moved in. I haven't even cracked the bag open yet. "Why don't you check the cupboard while I pack my things?"

Oliver scurries off into the kitchen, and I take a deep breath. My body brims with electricity. Is this a bad idea? Absolutely.

Am I going to do it anyway? Also, absolutely.

I switch off the TV and head into my room to pack, the

sound of Oliver ransacking my kitchen following behind me. I throw a few things in my own backpack: fresh clothes, a hairbrush, a change of clothes.

When I slide my phone into the bag, I think about Penelope telling me to get a gun. A knife will have to do.

When I come back into the living room, Oliver has gathered a pile of snacks in addition to the marshmallows, seemingly at random—a handful of granola bars, a bag of oranges, and three cans of Coke. "Your snacks are as lame as what we have at home," he tells me.

"Hey, you don't have Cokes or marshmallows." I slip into the kitchen with my backpack, drag open my cutlery drawer, and extract my big butcher's knife. Oliver's still in the living room, not paying any attention to me. It doesn't take long for me to wrap it in a towel and add it to my things. Just to be on the safe side.

"Are you ready?" I rejoin him in the living room, shouldering my backpack. Oliver found a grocery bag from the stash I keep beneath the sink and managed to pack up all my lame snacks that way.

"Yes!" he signs. "I'm so excited. Theo was worried you would say no, but I told him I'd make sure you didn't."

My heart clenches at that. "He wanted me to say yes?" I ask as we file out of the living room and onto my back porch. I glance over at the Jenkins house. It's shut up for the night, the living room window dark. Seems early for that, so I crane my neck, looking for his parents' Range Rover.

Gone.

Something like sadness washes over me. Maybe Oliver didn't have to sneak out at all. Maybe they just left him alone.

I don't ask. Oliver's already halfway down the pier anyway, and in the falling light, I can make out his boat bobbing in the water.

"I can row," I tell him. "It's getting dark."

He just shrugs at that, seemingly unbothered. Or maybe he's just excited about this prospective camping trip. I watch as he carefully arranges his backpack and sleeping bag and the bag of snacks in the back of the boat. Then he holds out his hands for my backpack. I give it to him. It feels like he knows exactly what to do.

Still, I think it's better for me to row; the boat is definitely heavier than what he's used to. I push off into the dark lake, my thoughts churning around.

"I didn't see your parents' car in the drive," I say when we're about halfway across. Night's falling fast; I can just barely make out the peninsula, and that's only because of the thin, orangey-pink line of sunlight limning across the trees.

"My brother had a game," Oliver signs. I have to squint to see his hand movements in the dark.

"And you didn't want to go?"

Oliver doesn't answer, just stares out at the lake. His early excitement seems to have dampened a bit, and I don't want to pry. I'm going to have to come up with a story, I realize. Something to explain why I stole their son away for the night. Something that doesn't involve an undead killer.

I let the boat run aground on the shore with a thump. The trees crowd up close, dark and foreboding, and I hear Penelope's voice again. *He's dangerous. You can't trust him.*

"Do you have a flashlight?" I turn toward Oliver, but he's already catapulting himself off the boat, landing in the waves with a splash. He waves his arms around wildly, then turns to me and signs, "Shout at him that we're here."

"Um, okay." I swallow and stand up, the boat rocking beneath the waves. "We're here!" I call out, the wind swallowing up my voice. It makes me think of the night Theo first kissed me, how I called out to him from my patio.

This time, though, I get a response. A few yards down the shore, there's a soft rustle in the underbrush. A second later,

Theo steps out, looking very much like the monster in a ghost story. Big and dark and foreboding. Wreathed in shadow.

Oliver doesn't care, though. He takes off running down the beach and then, somewhat to my surprise, flings his arms around Theo's waist. It seems to surprise Theo, too. Even in the gloomy dusklight, I can see him startle a little, and he lifts his arms awkwardly, like he doesn't know where to put them. Then he pats Theo softly on the back.

I shoulder my backpack and grab what I can of Oliver's supplies, then carefully step out of the boat. A light blinks off down the beach; Theo, it seems, has a lantern, and it casts a small yellow circle around him and Oliver. He lifts a single hand in greeting, the other still pressed on Oliver's back, since Oliver's still squeezing his hips like he doesn't want to let go.

God, I hope this isn't a huge fucking mistake.

19

THEO

I sit on an old log, watching Chloe and Oliver through the flicker of firelight. My heart feels light and fluttery and strange, but at least any traces of the killing moon have vanished. All I feel is… excitement.

Yes. I think that's what it is.

Oliver took longer than I expected to collect Chloe, even with the invitation he made me write for her. It worked out, though, because it gave me time to set up our camping site: two big tents that I collected from victims, both clean of any blood. Sleeping bags, too, although Oliver did tell me he didn't need one. And the fire, currently crackling in a circle of big grey stones.

Both of them are happy. I sense it, but I can see it, too. Oliver is beaming, his mouth sticky from melted marshmallows. Chloe smiles down at him, the firelight making her skin seem to glow in the darkness. She's roasting the marshmallows for Oliver because he kept burning them, turning them into blackened, smoking coals. "See?" she says, pulling her stick out of the fire. "This is what they're supposed to look like."

She has three on the stick, all a perfect golden-brown. Oliver grabs for one. "Careful," she says gently. "You don't want to burn yourself."

Oliver snatches the marshmallow anyway, hissing before he pops the whole thing in his mouth. Then he moans and falls on his back and kicks his legs around, which just makes Chloe laugh, that sweet twinkling sound that chimes like the stars.

I'm on the opposite side of the fire from them, and the flames feel like a wall separating us. Even so, I'm much closer than I usually am in these kinds of situations. Usually, when I watch people roast marshmallows and laugh, I'm in the trees, and I'm planning how to kill them.

I don't feel that now, though. If anything, I want to freeze this moment so I can look at it for the rest of my long and violent life.

"Do you want one?" Chloe asks. I think at first she's talking to Oliver, but then I feel her eyes on me in the dark. She stands up, the flames illuminating her bare legs, and holds out the stick. "I made three." A shy, faltering smile. "One for each of us."

She's happy, but she's also scared. Well, *scared* is perhaps too strong a word. It's certainly not the terror I'm used to feeling from humans. But there's some trepidation in the way she looks at me, along with a kind of hopefulness. Like she's happy, and she's worried I'm going to make her not-happy.

I don't want her to be not-happy.

I nod yes, and Chloe walks around the fire, crossing that boundary I thought of as impassable. Then she sits down on the log I'm using as a chair and offers me the stick.

I pull off the marshmallow and take a bite. Suddenly, I understand why Oliver reacted the way he did.

"It's good," I sign, my fingers flashing in the firelight. "Very well toasted." I don't know what else to say.

Chloe smiles. "Thanks." God, I love it when she speaks instead of signs. I do appreciate that she can talk to me in that way. But her voice makes my blood spark.

I watch as she bites into the last marshmallow on the stick, her teeth flashing in the firelight. There's a moment where I imagine her tearing into flesh, where the melty sugar turns to white sinew, and the firelight almost looks like blood on her face.

I suck in my breath, heat flooding through my body.

Chloe finishes the marshmallow and peers up at me through the uneven light, and I feel a faint shift in her emotions. Arousal and confusion and that quivering trepidation, all wound together.

"Why'd you invite us camping?" she asks.

I freeze. How the hell am I going to explain the killing moon to her?

I'm saved, though. Over on the other side of the fire, Oliver yelps and yanks his marshmallow stick out of the fire, the end burning like a torch.

"Drop it in the fire!" Chloe shouts, jumping to her feet. Oliver wings the stick forward into the flames, and it sparks and sputters. She breathes out, and I try not to enjoy the spike of fear and adrenaline it caused in her.

"Why can't I do this?" Oliver signs, his scowl clear in the firelight.

Chloe laughs. "You can't put the marshmallow *in* the fire, silly. Here, let me show you again." She glances over at me, and I feel it, that tug toward me. But it's only for a second, because then she's on her feet, walking to the other side of the fire. The human side, I think numbly.

At least I got out of answering her question.

I settle back on my log and watch her with Oliver. Watch her thread the marshmallow on a fresh stick and place it in his hand, then show him how to hold it a few centimeters from the fire until the heat makes its surface crack with gold. Oliver grins, and their happiness is as warm and undeniable as the heat of the fire. It's such a rare human emotion for me to experience. Usually, the only time I feel it is those seconds before I snatch it away.

But not tonight. The call of the killing moon has finally quieted, and I don't see either of them as trespassers. Not with me here with them, out in the open, the firelight looping us together.

It's all working exactly as I hoped.

It's a little before midnight by the time Oliver falls asleep, crawling sleepily into his tent. Chloe zips it shut for him and then stands with her arms crossed over her chest, watching the entrance like she thinks he might burst out, screaming, the way campers here usually do.

The wind blows across the lake, making the fire gutter, and she turns toward me. For a minute, we just stare at each other.

Then she signs, "His parents left him alone. Did you know that?"

I tense up again. Then, sensing an opportunity, I nod. "It's why I thought to invite him camping." I'm certain she can see the lie in my hands.

Or maybe not. Her shoulders soften a little, and she walks around the fire and comes to sit beside me on the log, crossing her legs so she can lean forward and look into the flames.

"My friend says I shouldn't trust you." This, she speaks, breathing the words out like smoke.

Her friend is right, of course. Anyone who knows what I am would say the same thing. And yet I still brush my hand against her shoulder to get her attention. As soon as her big, luminous eyes fix on me, I say, "But here you are."

Uncertainty flutters across Chloe's face. "I didn't want to leave Oliver alone."

"I won't hurt him." I pause, watching the shadows move across her skin. "Or you."

Chloe drinks me in. "My friend would say this is a trap."

"Did you tell her about it?"

Chloe gives me a sly, slow smile. "No," she says. "When Oliver showed up, I didn't really think about it all. I just—" She breathes out. "I just wanted to see you again."

For a second, it feels like the world comes to a standstill. This peninsula, these woods, Hanging Lake—they've been my entire world for years. For decades. And she just froze it in time.

"Why?" I ask, the movement small and uncertain.

Chloe trembles. "I don't know."

But I do. I can smell it on her. The arousal. The lust.

"It wasn't because of the other day in my cabin?"

Immediately, all of Chloe's blood rushes to the surface. And I can't help myself. I grin.

"That's why I wanted to see *you* again," I say.

"I've never seen you smile before," Chloe mutters sullenly, which isn't true. I know I smiled at her while I was fucking her.

I don't bother to correct her, though. "I don't usually have a reason to smile."

Not unless I'm killing someone, of course. Plenty of my victims have seen my smile before they died. But this is different.

Chloe breathes out, her breasts rising and falling beneath her shirt. I suddenly want nothing more than to see them again. To shove her shirt up and close my mouth around her pebbled nipple. To taste her sweat on my tongue. To feel her racing heartbeat.

"What's so special about me?" Chloe says. "Why don't you want to hurt us?" This last question, she signs, tilting her head toward the tent.

"Oliver is a kid," I respond. "I don't kill kids. And he reminds me of how I was when I was younger. Before I died."

The wind gusts again, stirring Chloe's hair around.

"Is he a Hunter, too?" she whispers.

I shake my head no.

She breathes out.

"As for you," I say. "I told you the night we met." My heart hammers. "You're beautiful."

Her body responds to the compliment, all that heat and sweet scent perfuming the air. I don't just want to taste it, I realize. I want to hunt it. I want to hunt *her*. Not to kill, though.

I shift closer to her. She doesn't pull away. Her arousal blooms, hot and sweet on the wind.

"Are you going to kiss me again?" she murmurs, so soft I almost think I'm imagining it.

I stare at her for a moment, my breath tight. "No," I sign. "I want to chase you first."

Her fear bursts like fireworks, hot and bright and dazzling before they sparkle back into the darkness. But, like fireworks, it leaves behind a smoky trace of excitement.

"I want to chase you," I say, my hands shaking. "And then I want to fuck you when I catch you."

Chloe sucks in her breath. "What about Oliver?" she signs.

"I can sense if he wakes up," I sign back. "You know that, right? From your friend?"

Chloe's lips part. Her breasts push against her thin shirt.

"I can sense humans," I continue. "If they're awake or asleep. If Oliver wakes up, we'll come back."

"You can sense me, too," she signs, and it's clear to me she doesn't mean it as a question.

All I do is nod.

Blood rushes to Chloe's cheeks. "You can sense what I'm feeling now." Her hands flutter against my chest.

"You want to be chased," I say.

The fire flashes in the darkness, casting long shadows across the campsite. Chloe stares at me for a long time, and I can feel all those emotions warring inside her—lust and fear and excitement. "Yes," she whispers.

I stand up. It does not escape my notice that my cock, already painfully hard, is just inches from her face. But I refrain from doing anything. Not with Oliver here, even if he is asleep in the tent. His slow, steady breathing is more than clear.

I hope he stays like that long enough for me to expel all these demons churning around inside me, hungry for a chase. Long enough that I can sink into Chloe's wet, hot cunt one more time.

Chloe rises too, her movements shaky. I don't take my eyes off her as I pick up the big bucket of lake water I put next to the fire.

"Then run," I sign.

I tilt the bucket over and dump all the water on the flames, extinguishing them in a swell of pale smoke. The darkness melts around us.

Chloe sucks in her breath—

And then she takes off into the pitch-black woods.

CHLOE

I can't believe I'm doing this, racing through the dark, crowded wilderness. I can barely see more than a few inches in front of me, and I swing my arms out, trying to claw the branches away.

But fuck, the way Theo looked at me in the firelight sent heat shooting straight into my pussy. This is exactly the kind of darkness I've always fantasized about. How could I say no?

So I run, my steps loud and crashing as the branches lash out at my bare legs. I'm choosing to trust him about Oliver. Maybe that's stupid of me. But I do know how well Hunters can sense humans, like he said. I saw it with Callie, how she knew from four blocks away that me and Penelope were about to be attacked.

That's also how I know Theo will find me, no matter where I wind up on his peninsula. The idea gives me a strange, delirious thrill.

I burst out of the woods and stumble to a stop, blinking out at the dark, glimmering waves of Hanging Lake. The moon is half-formed, and it, along with the brilliant scatter of stars, provides barely enough light to see by. I honestly have no idea where I am. There are no houses here to serve as a compass.

Something cracks out in the woods. I whip around, my breath tight.

I want to chase you, he said, and I know I've barely given him chase. I've barely given myself chase. When he catches me, I want to be scared, and tired, and desperate.

So I take off running again, this time staying parallel to the lake. I pump my arms and legs, pushing my breath out in sharp, short bursts. Frantic thoughts flicker through my head —*you are a camper here and he kills campers he's going to kill you* —and my fear erupts, sudden and unexpected.

As unexpected as the exposed root branch that catches my foot.

For a moment, I feel snagged. Then I fly forward and land hard on my hands and knees, knocking all the air out of me.

Footsteps off to my left.

I twist around until I'm sitting on my ass and scan the darkness. I can't see anything but the faint suggestion of movement from the wind.

"Fuck," I whisper as I scramble up to standing. I can feel him nearby, the prickle of his eyes on my skin. But I can't see him.

It's terrifying, and it makes heat surge toward my clit.

I jog forward, my shoes pounding against the packed dirt along the shoreline, trying to catch my breath. Trying to see anything in the darkness.

Tree branches. Undead killers. Anything.

More slow, heavy footsteps. I whirl around, my fear blooming again. It's real, my fear, but that just enhances my also-very-real desire. I know there's a chance I can't trust Theo. I know he might very well want to kill me like he does every other intruder on his property.

And as fucked up as it is, that thought just makes me even more excited.

More footsteps. They sound like they're coming from the water, and I whip around and finally catch a glimpse of him: a big, hulking shadow against the glimmer of the starry lake.

Does he have a fucking knife in his hand? No, he doesn't. Which is good, because the knife I brought with me is still in my backpack, which I tossed into the other tent when I arrived. Shows how worried I really am.

I take off running, back into the woods. The tree branches lash out at me, and I duck my head down and throw my hands out to protect myself. Something in the air shifts, and I know Theo's followed me again. I can feel the heaviness of his presence.

And I keep going. Because I fucking *love* it, the way my fear amplifies everything. The way every branch feels like it might be his long, rough fingers reaching out to grab at my hair or scrape across my skin. Every time I feel something scratch me, I screech and throw my hands around, sure I'm going to slam into his sturdy chest.

I don't. It's all trees and vines and feathery ferns. I keep pushing through, ducking low, trying to run as best I can when the forest keeps trying to ensnare me, like it wants to intervene on his behalf.

Then I hear rustling. Not behind me. Off to my left.

I freeze, breathing hard. The rustling continues, soft and whispery. Now it sounds like it's coming from my right.

"Theo?" I whimper, spinning around in place. I can't see a damn thing: not here in the dense woods, away from what little light the lake provides.

A snap of a broken branch. I jerk around, my breath tight and panicky.

He's here.

He stands just a few feet away, nothing more than a

shadow against the darkness. My chest constricts; how did he get there so fast? I don't remember Callie moving like that. But then, that night was years ago, and I had been tipsy from the $5 Mai Tais. Not like tonight, when I'm stone cold sober and know exactly what I'm looking at.

Theo steps toward me, and when he tilts his head, his eyes turn red for a moment, like some predatory animal. I jerk back instinctively, heart hammering, and slam into the broad trunk of a tree.

"Do you want me to keep running?" I ask raggedly. All I want is for him to say yes.

He nods.

I peel away from the tree and duck back into the underbrush. This time, though, he follows after me, his steps heavy and calculated compared to my frantic, panicked running. Branches snap out at me, stinging my cheeks with whips of pain. Roots claw at my ankles, and I stumble but manage to upright myself before I fall.

He's getting closer, and I wonder if this is how all his victims felt, if they ran through the woods in the darkness like this, blind and terrified. I wonder if I'm about to become one of them.

Then I erupt out of the trees. I'm not expecting it; I thought I was running deeper into the woods, toward Theo's cabin. But no. Hanging Lake rolls out in front of me, its black water filled with diamonds. I have a brief flickering thought about how beautiful it is, like the sky fell to the earth.

Then I slip on a loose patch of stones and fall face-first into the water.

It's shockingly cold, especially compared to the damp heat of the night, the damp heat of my skin. I wrench my head back, gasping as the steely taste floods my mouth—

And then a big, rough hand curls around my throat.

I freeze. We both do, just for a second. Then Theo yanks

me up to standing and winds his other arm around my waist, pinning me up against him. I can feel his cock pressing into the small of my back. He breathes softly, warming my skin.

"You caught me," I say weakly, staring out at the water.

He pulls me around to face him. I can't make out much in the darkness, aside from his pale hair, which shines platinum in the moonlight. And his left eye, which shines red again as he drinks me in.

I hold my breath, waiting, my hands curled into fists. There's a part of me that thinks this might be it. I'm going to die. The idea doesn't bother me as much as it should.

Theo presses his hand to the top of my head and forces me down to my knees. I slam into the mud, the lake water lapping around my legs, as he holds me in place with one hand.

The other hand unbuckles his belt. Zips down his fly. Pulls out his cock.

Heat explodes in me. Relief, too. When he bats his big cockhead against my lips, I open them to pull him into my mouth, eager and hungry. Maybe I'm rewarding him for not killing me. I don't know.

I swallow him as best I can, gagging a little around his size. He makes that same rough grunting noise he did when he fucked me in his cabin, and his fingers tighten against my hair, holding me in place as I suck greedily on his cock. Running like that—being chased, thinking I might die—has left me hornier than I've ever felt in my fucking life. Even the salt of him, of his sweat and his precum, almost tastes sweet to me. It sends heat soaring between my legs, and I wrap my hands around his hips to give me leverage to try and draw him deeper into my mouth.

I *am* thanking him. But not for keeping me alive. For giving me the terror that's always been missing from my previous pitiful sexual encounters.

I fuck him with my mouth, my jaw slack so spit pools around my lips and slides out to slick his thick, hot shaft. He grunts, tightening his fingers in my hair, adding a touch of pain that makes me moan.

When it becomes too difficult for me to breathe around his cock, I release him and lick his balls, taut against his body. I draw one into my mouth and then the other, stroking his spit-drenched dick the entire time. My body buzzes with need.

Theo's grunts grow louder. He rocks his hips so his cock slaps wetly against my cheek, and I can't stand it anymore. I slide my free hand down and stroke my pussy over my shorts. It's infuriating, all that fabric. It's not my hand that I want between my legs.

"Fuck me," I whisper against his cock, licking it between each word. "Please, Theo. I need you to fuck me—"

He yanks me by the hair and throws me onto my back. I land with a splash in the soft, lapping waters of Hanging Lake, mud squelching between my thighs. Theo drops down between my legs and yanks my shorts off like he did before, although this time, thankfully, he doesn't shred my panties, just pulls them off in one smooth motion. I hike my hips up, trying to keep my cunt clear of the mud. Not that I need to. Theo hooks his arms into my legs and bends me in half, right before he latches his mouth to my pussy.

I cry out, the sound plaintive and small compared to the enormous rushing of the night wind. Theo's thick, hot tongue swipes the full length of my slit, making my whole body shudder. When his teeth scrape softly against my clit, I scream.

I scream like I really am being murdered out here.

He growls against me, the vibrations not that different from my favorite toy, the little rabbit vibrator that I keep in my bedside drawer. But fuck me, this is so much better. He eats me like he's *eating* me, like he wants to devour me from the pussy up. When I look down, past my bent-in-half torso, all I can see are my pale, mud-streaked legs and his blond hair.

"I'm gonna come," I whisper, dropping my head back into the mud. The lake laps over us, and the cold of the water is a sharp contrast to Theo's hot, killer's tongue. I jolt, but he doesn't even seem to notice, just thrusts his tongue into my cunt and suckles down on my clit. I shriek again, arching into him, and my orgasm is a tight, painful knot in my belly. "I'm gonna come!" I shout again, slamming my fists into the mud, and Theo groans, and then I do, the pleasure is hot and pulsing as it pours through my body.

Immediately, Theo flips me over, forcing me onto my hands and knees. The waves splash around us, the mud sucking at my fingers.

A second later, my killer is inside me.

He pushes his cock into me the way he did in the cabin: suddenly, violently, painfully. I scream again, curling my fingers up like I'm dying. And Theo fucks me like he's killing me. His strokes are fast and hard and brutal, and my whole body shakes with each impact. I slump forward, laying my cheek on the shore, gasping as Hanging Lake splashes over my mouth and my nose, flooding my sinuses with cold, steely lake water.

Theo's stabbing me. He's drowning me. My cunt clenches down on him, begging for more.

Another wave splashes over us. I choke and sputter, sucking down too much dirty lake water. For a moment, I can't breathe, and the world is dark and murky like I'm at the bottom of the lake.

He's killing me, I think numbly.

I come.

The orgasm that tears through me at that moment is

overwhelming, in large part because I didn't expect it. But everything is so perfect: Theo's big, stretching cock, the water splashing into my mouth, the dizzying lack of air.

The idea that I might die like this.

I scream again, sucking in more lake water, enough that my chest burns and the world starts to go dark and light like old film, and I feel a kind of hot, terrible desperation at the edge of my pleasure.

And then there's a pain in my scalp, and this time when I suck in my breath, it's air that fills my lungs, not water. My orgasm is still ripping me apart, my cunt contracting and squeezing around Theo's painful, driving cock.

But his hand is tangled up in my hair, holding my head above the mud and lapping waves.

He didn't kill me at all. In fact, he saved my life.

I scream again, lake water dripping down my chin. Theo jerks me backward until I'm sitting on his cock, his arms squeezing tight around my chest as I bounce up and down on him, impaling myself on his erection as he bites at my neck—small, warning little nips that sting my skin.

He growls into me, his breath hot and shuddery. I squeeze down on his cock, wanting him to come inside me again, wanting to feel his hot seed leak down my thigh. Wanting *him*, this killer who wouldn't let me die even though I was chasing it, finally freeing all those dark, tumultuous desires I've always locked away.

Until him.

He growls and squeezes me so tightly I can't move. Then he roars, bucking his hips into me as he pumps his cum up into my pussy. He doesn't sound human.

He isn't human.

I slump back against his chest, trying to catch my breath. The wind picks up, and the mud and lake water on my skin suddenly feels too cold, too clammy. I shiver, and Theo nuzzles softly against my neck, right before he pulls us both up to our feet, his cock sliding out of me in the process. The waves splash harmlessly around our ankles.

Then he turns me around, and I look up at him in the darkness, my legs wobbling. He signs something, and I have to squint it to make it out.

"You were drowning yourself."

My heart thumps.

"You didn't let me," I counter.

Theo smooths my wet hair back from my cheek. His eyes are human again, hidden by the darkness. No predatory eye shine. I miss it.

Theo lifts his hands close to my face, like he wants to make sure I can see.

"Why would I want you to die?" he asks.

And then he pulls me in for a long, melting kiss.

21

THEO

Chloe is a ruin. Dripping wet hair, mud smeared all over her bare legs. She blinks up at me when I pull away from the kiss, her lips parted, and I swear I can see her heat radiating on the air.

I have a million questions. I felt it, the way she came as the waves splashed around her face. Felt the hot, rippling contractions of her cunt around my dick as surely as I felt her breath shudder and catch in her lungs. It sent a thunderous swell of pleasure into my belly, the idea of her dying while impaled on my cock, but it also gave me a hot, feverish panic. It wasn't until I dragged her up—

Until you saved her life

—That the panic subsided.

I don't know what any of it means. But I also don't want to ask her about it. Not now, in the dark. She can barely see me when I talk to her.

She settles against my chest, dampening my shirt. It's like she feels safe with me, which is a strange realization, and not one I'm used to. But I also don't feel a single whisper of the killing moon, and for that, I'm immensely grateful. She's a kind of magic, I think.

I tug her sideways, guiding her in slow, stumbling steps over into the lake proper. She doesn't resist, especially when I kneel and scoop up big handfuls of water and splash them over her mud-streaked legs, scrubbing the dirt away.

"God, I really got filthy, didn't I?" She speaks it, her voice soft and shaky. I nod, even though I don't think she can see, and keep cleaning her, running my hands along the muscular swell of her calves, the soft bend of her knees, the thick heat of her thighs. Her cunt is still exposed, and the lingering scent of both of our arousal is heavy in the air. It makes the back of my jaw ache.

"Thank you," she says softly when she realizes what I'm doing. I keep working, scrubbing the dirt away from her legs and her plump, gorgeous ass. Every touch sends a kind of electricity up through my fingers, and my thoughts fill with the images of what we just did. It's like when I kill, how all the blood and screams fill my head for days. But this time, it's thoughts of her pleasure.

I stand up, peel my shirt off, and use it to clean the lingering traces of mud away from her face. She lets me, her eyes searching for me in the dark. For the first time in a very long time, I wish I could speak. I don't like how the darkness silences me.

But at the same time, Chloe seems to understand. I don't sense any confusion. I don't sense fear. I do sense shame, I think, dark and simmering just below the surface. A kind of tension, like she's afraid I'm going to ask about the source of that shame. And something else. A steady, glowing warmth, like a good campfire. It's the kind of thing humans feel right before I make myself known.

"How's Oliver?" she asks.

I look at her, wondering how much she can see. "Still asleep," I sign, and Chloe squints a little, then sighs.

"Still asleep?" she asks. "Tap me once for yes or twice for no. I'm sorry, but I can barely see."

I grin at that. My clever girl, finding a way to cut through the darkness keeping me gagged. I tap her once.

Her shoulders soften a little. "Did he ever wake up?" she asks. "While we were…"

Her voice trails off. I tap her once again. Oliver is safe and snug in his tent.

A guest, not a trespasser. Just like her.

When I'm satisfied she's clean enough, I pluck her shorts out from where I tossed them into a bank of river reeds and hand them to her. I feel her blush more than I see it. "Thanks," she mumbles. "This was—this was fun."

I reach over and tap her once.

She laughs, and it's such a pretty sound, like the starlight reflecting on the lake. I want to ask if we can do it again, but I know there's no point. Not in the darkness.

I take her hand in mine, though, relishing the silkiness of her skin. I've never held a woman's hand before, not even in those years in New York, where I experimented with sex for the first time. That she doesn't pull away, that she lets me lead her back to the campsite along the beach, makes my heart feel too big for my rib cage.

We walk without speaking, although my Chloe isn't silent. I can hear her body: her quickened blood, her soft breath, the turmoil of her emotions. Beneath it is the peaceful trail of Oliver's scent, leading us back to camp.

Eventually, I have to lead her into the forest, and I step in front of her to push the branches away. I can smell the tiny cuts on her skin from where the trees lashed her open while she was running from me. That bloody scent—that was how

I was able to follow her in the dark, like I do all my prey. Well, the blood, and her arousal.

We're almost to the camp when Chloe stops, tugging back on my still-damp T-shirt. "Wait," she says. "I want to ask you something. You can just tap your response, okay?"

I turn to her. In the woods, there's no starlight to offer any illumination, and I see her the way I see all things in the dark, in a kind of grey-scale. She looks like a ghost.

She takes a deep breath, loud as a gunshot.

"What we did earlier?" she whispers, her voice soft and rasping. "Can we do it again?"

All the blood pours straight into my cock, an uncomfortable tightness forming in my pants. For a second, I consider taking her again, right here—throwing her down on her hands and knees, yanking down her shorts, burying myself to the hilt. But no. We're too close to the camp. Oliver might hear us and wake up. Besides, she's clean, as clean as I could get her, and I don't want to dirty her again.

I can hear her held breath, though. Her pounding heart. I step up to her and cup her face with my hand, tilting her eyes up to meet mine. Those, I think, she sees.

When I tap her once, her smile lights up all the darkness.

22

CHLOE

I wake up the next morning to the scent of frying meat, my back aching from sleeping on the ground. I've never liked camping, although this experience has certainly been better than my last one.

When I crawl out of my tent, Oliver is already up, watching Theo cook something in a black cast-iron skillet over the fire. I blink out at the early-morning sunlight, and Theo's the first to see me, lifting his gaze from the pan. He waves and gives me a sly, dark smile that makes my breath catch.

Oliver, of course, doesn't register any of that. He whirls around to face me, his hands flying. "Theo's making us breakfast, like he promised. It's—" He hesitates, then looks back at Theo questionably.

"Venison," Theo spells out. "And coffee, if you want some."

"Ah." I stumble forward and slump down on the log to watch the steaks cook and sizzle in the pan. My mouth waters at the scent of them. I didn't have much dinner the night before. "Coffee would be great."

Fortunately, it doesn't take much longer for Theo to get

breakfast together. He lays the venison stakes out on old, chipped plates, along with the oranges Theo brought from my house. The coffee he prepares over the fire, too, in some ancient-looking metal canister. He pours that into matching ceramic coffee mugs, and although we have to drink it black, the caffeine does help me feel more awake after a night of outdoor sleep.

"Did you have fun?" Oliver signs at me between bites of his steak, which he doesn't bother cutting into pieces—he just stabs the whole thing with his fork and gnaws into it.

"Yeah," I tell him. "I had fun."

I can feel Theo staring at me from across the low, warm fire, and when I glance over at him, he's smiling.

"My favorite part was roasting marshmallows," I add.

Oliver nods at that and keeps tearing into his breakfast. I eat mine, too, although not quite enthusiastically. I'm actually not super looking forward to going back over the lake and explaining to his parents why I kidnapped their child for an impromptu camping trip with his imaginary ghost friend.

Maybe they didn't notice he was missing, I think, squinting up at the sky. It's definitely still early, the horizon limned with grey.

Theo watches me, his brow furrowed a little with concern. I guess he can sense it, my worry. I flash him a smile, wondering if he thinks the worry is because of him. Because of what we did last night.

I take a deep breath and look over at Oliver, who's just finishing up his last orange slice. "We should probably get back," I say. "We don't want your parents to be worried."

Oliver freezes, the orange slice still in his hands. When he looks up at me, something snags in my throat. There's a real sadness in his expression. The kind of sadness you don't ever want to see on a kid.

He drops the orange slice onto his plate. "I want to stay."

That tight feeling in my throat pulls even tighter, and I glance over at Theo, who watches us guardedly. "I'm sure Theo has things to do," I say carefully.

Oliver immediately looks over at him. "He has to do his hauntings," Oliver says. "I can help."

I don't know what Oliver means by *hauntings*, and, in fact, I think I might have misunderstood. But Theo says, "Chloe's right. You should check in with your parents. And hauntings will be boring for you."

Oliver stares forlornly down at his uneaten orange slice. Then he throws it into the fire, hard enough to make sparks fly up.

"I want to stay here," he signs.

I sigh. "Let's just check in, okay? Maybe you can come visit this afternoon?"

Oliver doesn't answer.

He also doesn't protest again, though, not even when he tries to help put the tents away and Theo tells him not to worry about it. I suspect Theo has had the same basic thought I had: namely, that the sooner I can get Oliver back to his parents, the less likely they are to call the police.

Still, Oliver is sullen as we hike across the peninsula, his arms crossed over his chest. They stay firmly in place as I throw my backpack in the rowboat and pull it out into the water. Clearly, I'm the one who has to row us back home.

"I had fun," I tell him as we push across the calm, warm waters. "Thanks for having Theo invite me."

Oliver blinks, then looks away from me, out at the lake. I slap the oars into the water and wish I knew what to say. This is part of why I gave up on working as a translator; at the end of the day, I'm just not that good with people.

Same as Theo, I think wryly.

I row the boat over to Oliver's pier, and I'm relieved that the house still looks closed up, like it did last night. I half expect Blaire or his sullen father to burst out of the back door, screaming at us, but nothing happens. I tie the boat off.

"Are you gonna have to sneak in?" I ask, knowing that I'm being a terrible role model.

Oliver looks up at me with that heartbreakingly sad expression. He climbs out of the boat without answering, and the worry in my throat tightens again.

Something's wrong. Even I can tell that.

I jog after him, put my hand on his shoulder. "I can take the blame," I say, "If you're worried you're going to get in trouble."

He stops and looks up at me, the wind blowing his hair into his eyes. Then, finally, he says something.

"I'm not going to get in trouble."

He doesn't exactly seem happy about it, though.

He turns from me and keeps walking up the pier. My worry deepens, and I keep looking to the back door of his house, to the white vertical blinds blocking the view of the living room. I dig out my phone and check the time: almost eight-thirty. Surely someone would be awake by now?

Oliver jumps off the pier and walks around the side of the house. I follow after him—

And that's when I see it. His parents' big Range Rover is still gone.

The worry turns into a dark, sick feeling in the pit of my stomach, especially as I watch Oliver flip over a rock in the flower bed—a rock that I see quickly enough is one of those decorative key hiders. He pulls the key out and squeezes it in his little palm.

"Your parents left you alone?" I cry out. "Overnight?"

Oliver looks over at me, his eyes shadowed.

"You can tell me." I rush over to him and kneel so we're eye level. He keeps staring at me. "They shouldn't have done that."

He breathes out. "They'll be back on Sunday night," he says.

I gape at him. "That's tomorrow!"

"I wanted to say with Theo." He turns away from me, moving toward the front door.

"But they didn't know that," I say. "Your parents."

He shrugs.

"Oliver!" I follow after him, and he stops and looks up at me, as weary as an adult. "Your parents expected you to be by yourself for the whole weekend," I whisper. I don't know much about kids, but I know that you shouldn't do that. Not with a ten-year-old.

"They always do that," he says. "When they get tired of me."

My heart cracks. I don't know what to do. If I should call someone. If I should leave him alone.

No, I can't do that. And I can't send him to stay with Theo. Not for two days.

"Stay with me," I say. "Okay? I know that's not as good as staying with Theo, but Theo—" I search around for the right words. "Theo's not really equipped to handle a, uh, a living boy, you know? Because he's a ghost."

It feels absurd, saying the word *ghost* out here in the bright summer sunlight. Especially when I know the truth of what Theo is.

But it seems to work. Oliver squints at me.

"I wish I were a ghost," he says.

I bite down on my lip. Kids shouldn't say things like. And it especially hurts hearing it from Oliver, who had been so happy the night before, as we toasted marshmallows together.

"Come on," I tell him. "Let's get you settled."

23

THEO

After twenty-four hours without hearing a single whisper from the killing moon, I know the camping trip was a success. I feel more or less like myself again: no undercurrent of blood lust, no dark pull across the lake. I don't even look at my knives, which I tucked away back in their storage place after Chloe and Oliver went home.

Oliver comes to visit on Saturday afternoon, after I settle down in my cabin to get out of the heat. "Chloe said it was okay," he tells me, before dropping down on the swing and pulling out his sketch pad. This is somewhat unusual; usually, he brings the drawings to me. But after about twenty minutes of sketching, he shows me the drawing, and I realize the difference:

It's a picture of me. Just my face, floating on the blank white of the page in exceptional detail.

I feel a momentary surge of panic—*Don't let 'em take your picture* was one of my father's common pieces of advice—but then Theo signs, "It's for Chloe."

I breathe out, not sure what to say. So I just nod.

Oliver leaves well before sunset, thanking me again for letting him go camping. I follow him down to the beach for reasons not entirely clear to me. From the woods, I watch him row across the lake. Not to his house. To Chloe's. I hope he's handing that picture right to her and not anyone else.

After that, I settle back into my usual routine. I draw water from the well each morning and complete my daily patrols. When I finish, I take my telescope down to the beach and watch Chloe through the glass, all her movements upside down. I see Oliver, too; he's at her house throughout the weekend, although I do watch him leave during the heat of the day on Sunday, traipsing back to his house. There's a shift in him when it happens. His happiness kind of dries up, although he's not scared, really. He's not in danger. If I were better with humans, maybe I could understand.

Maybe I'll ask him about it, the next day he comes to visit, even if the idea makes me feel vaguely queasy.

Chloe is easier to watch. She works on her computer out on her patio, her legs kicked up on the balcony ledge. I watch her rattle around inside the house as the sun sets, staining Hanging Lake orange and crimson. It also doesn't escape my notice that she's been leaving the curtains open on her big living room windows since the camping trip, and I tell myself it's for me, like she wants me to watch her eat dinner in front of her TV and pace around the living room while she talks to someone on her phone. Her friend, the other Hunter? I don't know.

The nights are the worst, though. Being out in the woods reminds me of chasing her and claiming her on the lakeshore. Being in my cabin makes me feel agitated and distracted and, truthfully, nervous. With every day that passes, I worry I'll start to feel the killing moon again.

I know I should go to her, like I did that first night. The night I kissed her. But the idea of going across the lake—I don't know. It feels risky. Like it will trigger something, being so close to all the humans who live on the other side. It was fine once, but to keep doing it?

I feel like I'm teetering on a knife's edge, like one missed step will send me into the path of the killing moon, and I don't want that. Not now. Not with Chloe here, standing in the way.

I don't see Oliver again, either. He doesn't visit, but I also don't see him through the telescope. His boat is tied to his pier, bobbing in the water, untouched. He never comes out of the house, never plays down by the shoreline or goes to visit Chloe. I can feel him inside, though—quiet, reserved, drawn into myself. That makes me feel strange, too. Worried, maybe.

After a few days, I can't stand it anymore. I suppose I had been hoping Chloe would come to visit me, maybe tagging along with Oliver again. But perhaps she expects me to go to her.

The idea of crossing the water gives me a hard knot in the chest, and there's no denying that the moon is swelling overhead, although it's not full yet. Still, the killing moon itself seems to have quieted down, so one night, when I feel like I'm going to burst out of my skin, I decide to take the risk, and I drag my boat down to the shoreline.

I wait until full dark to cross. Wait until most of the houses are dark, as well, although not so long that the light in Chloe's bedroom window goes out. In fact, I keep my gaze fixed on it as I row across the lake, glowing like a beacon. It leaves a triangle of light across her patio that I focus on as I draw closer and closer to all the human life on this side of the lake. It still gets me agitated, all this humanity, but Chloe's presence is like a melody that I can latch on to until I feel calm again.

I dart through the shadows as I make my way to her back

door, my heart hammering. If I get inside, away from the lopsided moon, I'll be fine.

I pull out my switchblade, preparing to pry open the lock on her back door. But when I slide the blade into place, it notches in easily. Chloe left the door unlocked.

I suck in my breath and push it open, the door swinging in to release Chloe's sweet scent. Did she do that on purpose? Did she do that for me?

The floors creak softly as I step inside and shut the door and turn the deadbolt. Just to be on the safe side. I draw the curtains, too, although I cringe at the scraping sound the rings make against the metal curtain rod. I'm not here to kill her, but sixty years of hunting humans has ingrained in me to always be quiet.

Behind me, the floorboards sigh, and my skin prickles.

"Theo."

I jolt at the sound of my name, and I turn to find Chloe standing at the foot of the stairs, dressed in the same flimsy cotton shorts and thin top she wore the first night I broke in. Her hair is down, loose around her shoulders.

"Hello," I sign. Then, "You forgot to lock the door."

Chloe's eyes gleam. "No, I didn't," she signs back.

That's all it takes. Days' worth of desire surge up in me, and I lunge at her, moving with my unnatural speed. Chloe barely has time to shriek in surprise before I have her over my shoulder, her feet kicking out in front of me.

"Oh my god!" she cries, grabbing big handfuls of my shirt. "Holy shit, you're strong."

I carry her up the stairs and into the bedroom, relishing the heat of her body as she squirms against me, as her breath comes out soft and a little panicky. I wish I could tell her she doesn't have to worry about me dropping her. To me, she weighs almost nothing.

The bedroom is just how I remembered it. Tidy and

unadorned. One corner of the bedsheet has been pulled back, the pillow shoved up against the headboard, a beat-up old paperback on the bedside table. Little pieces of her that I can't see from my telescope.

I toss her on the mattress, and she squeals again, more excited than afraid. I can taste her exhilaration as she spreads her legs for me and peers up through the loose tangle of her hair.

"I've been waiting for you," I sign.

Her cheeks darken. "I wasn't sure," she whispers. "If you wanted me to—" She gestures in the direction of the lake. "Or if you would come here."

I growl softly in the back of my throat and kneel on the bed. The last thing I want to do is explain about the killing moon.

"You can always come to me," I sign. "You are a guest."

Then I crawl toward her, trapping her between my body and the mattress. She slumps back, staring up at my face, her lips parted. I brush them with mine, sighing at the way she shudders against me.

"What are you going to do to me?" she whispers.

I kiss down the side of her throat and think about Hanging Lake washing over her while I was buried in her cunt. Then I pull back so I can ask, "What do you want me to do to you?"

I can feel the effect the question has, that sudden flare of shame.

"I don't—" She stops, her breath shuddery. "I can't lie to you, can I? You'll know."

"This is about the lake, isn't it?" My fingers cast flittering shadows across her chest from the rosy lamp burning on her desk. "When the water washed over you?"

Her shame deepens, the scent of it so strong it drowns out everything else, including her sweet arousal.

"You liked it." My heartbeat quickens. "That feeling like you were drowning."

"Dying." She whispers the word instead of signing. "I like the idea of dying."

My cock throbs. Heat bursts up in my belly. It's yet another reason to explain why I felt so drawn to her that first moment I saw her standing there on the pier, bathed in falling sunlight. Another explanation for why I can't stop thinking about her, why she pulls on me like the killing moon. It's like we're meant to hook together. A monster made for nothing but killing, and a woman who comes at the thought of death.

I can't say all that to her. I don't have the words, not even with my hands.

"You were never going to die," I sign instead. "I won't let you."

Chloe breathes out. "I know," she whispers, her hand coming up my arm, trailing along my bicep. "You can tell that, too, can't you? When I got too close?"

She was nowhere close the other night. There's a slowing that happens when a human approaches death. A quieting, like the wind dying down. I would tear this world to shreds if I ever heard it coming from her.

I nod, though. I can sense what she wants, what she's too afraid to ask. And maybe I'm afraid to ask, too. Afraid to do it, afraid that it might stir up the killing moon.

But Chloe is staring at me with a hunger in her eyes that makes my cock ache. A gift only I can give her.

"Do you want to do that now?" I sign slowly. "Come close to death?

The room in the air buzzes.

And all Chloe does is nod.

THEO

"How?" I ask. One word, but my hands still shake. I don't know if it's trepidation or excitement.

Chloe settles back into the mattress and spreads her legs a little wider, like she's excited by the thought. I wedge up against her, pressing my erection to the seam of her shorts. Too much cloth between us, but I need to know this one thing before we can start.

More heat in Chloe's face. "How do you want to do it?"

"No. You tell me."

Her chest rises, full breasts straining against her shirt, her nipples indenting the fabric.

"Something simple," she signs, her hands shaking. "Just—cut off my air."

My cock shudders again, but I like the answer. I don't work in strangulation. Never have, just like I never work in drowning. Cutting off breath like that—well, it's too close to my first death. I like blood. Viscera. Heat.

This is safer. I don't think it'll trip any wires inside me.

I slide my hand around Chloe's long, graceful throat, gently pressing my palm against her trachea. The effect is immediate: her eyes go wide, her lips part, and her body riots. I raise an eyebrow, asking, *Like that?*

She understands. She nods.

I kiss her, then, a full and hungry kiss that makes her moan into my mouth. Then I undress her the way I did the last two times, quick and perfunctory, wanting the clothes out of the way so I can get to the beauty beneath. The lamplight makes her skin glow like starlight, and I can't stop myself from licking between her breasts and over her belly. Tasting her. Even over her skin, I taste the blood that will stay inside her.

Then I wrench myself away from her and tug off my own clothes: shirt first, then boots, then my jeans. I want to really feel her skin against mine, heat on heat. I don't want clothes getting in the way.

Chloe gives a little gasp as she looks up at me, her fingers curling up the bedsheets. Her eyes trace over my chest, thick and muscular from the work I do on my peninsula. Then she drops down over my soft belly to my cock, which juts between us, swollen and rock-hard.

"Do it," she whispers.

I fall onto her, catching her mouth in a kiss and her breasts with one of my hands. She moans and bucks against me, hooking her legs around my thighs and working her hips like she's trying to get my cock inside her. I don't let her, though. I kiss her and tease her, nipping at her throat and then down to her hardened nipples, where she arches her spine and grabs at my hair.

"Do it," she pants, brimming with force.

I pull back to look at her sprawled out on her bed, her eyes glassy and her body flushed. She lifts her chin to bare her throat. An invitation.

I accept it.

Well, not how she wants. I bite her neck, right at the place where her pulse flutters up against her skin, and my teeth come dangerously close to cutting her open. But fuck, it feels good, the promise of that blood. I can only imagine it flooding up into my mouth. But *that*, she wouldn't come back from.

"Do it!" she screams, pulling on my hair, bucking her hips. I shove her down at the shoulders and meet her gaze, all that wild, lustful fury

"Please," she whimpers.

Enough teasing. I line my cock up with her slit and am not remotely surprised to find that she's soaked, that it takes nothing for me to slide into her warm, sweet cunt. Chloe moans and shudders and brings her legs up around me, locking me in place.

I slide my hand up over her belly, stopping at her breasts —just for a few seconds, mostly because I can't help myself— and then end with my fingers around her neck, my palm pressing into the place where I bit her.

I don't move. Don't thrust. Just sit inside her while she stares up at me, desperation brimming in her eyes. I think I'm giving her a chance to stop me. To say no.

Instead, she rolls her hips, grinding herself along my cock.

It's all the answer I need

I tighten my grip, squeezing hard on the sides of her throat until her pulse is flapping around wildly like a frightened bird. A soft choking noise spills out of her lips, and she thrusts harder against me. I respond by settling more of my weight onto her shoulders, pinning her down into the mattress. Stilling her.

She sputters, lips already turning red. I slide in and out of her, slow and steady. I'm afraid that if I go any faster, any harder, I'll lose control. Her cunt is already fluttering around my cock, her muscles pulsing furiously as her body fights for air.

"Faster," she manages to rasp out, her hands wrapping around my wrists, almost like she's going to push me away. But maybe I'm only expecting that because of what I am. She actually clings to me, eyes rolling back, body jerking. "Fuck—me—fas—"

The last word dies on her lips as I squeeze just a little harder, the sound turning to a gurgle in her throat. Her face is turning red now, too, and her eyes are glassy and wet. Inside, her systems are in a panic: blood pounding, breath tight and strained. I wish I could keep her like this forever, right on the verge of death. It's the most beautiful fucking thing I've ever experienced.

I can't, though. Unlike me, her death will be permanent.

I give her another sip of air at the same time I deliver a hard, firm stroke, burying myself to the hilt inside her. Chloe cries out, still clinging to my forearm. "More!" she gasps.

I know she doesn't mean air. I squeeze again, making her convulse. Her cunt convulses, too, slicking my cock with her arousal as I pump slowly in and out of her. Chloe drops one hand to her side, her knuckles thumping against the mattress. She's still very much alive—I can hear it, her body screaming for release—but her eyes are starting to dim, and so I let her breathe again, just a little. She gulps down the air greedily and grinds against me. There's a heat building in her core. I can taste it on the air.

With my free hand, I manage a single clumsy phrase: "Come for me."

She sees it; I watch her glossy eyes follow the movements. Whether she parses it, I don't know. I tighten my grip on her throat, and her lips move, so red and swollen that I can't stop myself from bowing over her and catching her bottom lip in my teeth and biting down until I taste the hot, salty tang of blood.

It's stupid. I know it's stupid, making her bleed like that. As soon as I taste it, my cock surges, and I lose what little control I had, and I give her what she's been asking for:

I fuck her harder. I fuck her as hard as I can, hard enough that her body jostles and slams beneath me, hard enough that I have to brace my other hand around her throat, pinning her down at the neck.

And she *smiles*.

Through the glossy tears and red-veined eyes and panicked lungs, she smiles for me. Her blood looks like lipstick, garish and bright. The brightest thing in the room.

"Thank," she rasps, the rest of it strangling in her throat again. Then her eyes roll back, and she flops against the mattress in time with my angry, violent thrusts, and the strangling noises become steady and rhythmic.

She's about to die.

She's also about to come. So am I.

My muscles cord up in my arms as I bear down on her, the bed frame slamming loudly against the wall in a creaking, staggering rhythm that almost matches the panic of Chloe's heartbeat. I press my fingers into her throat, relishing the give of her skin, the staccato rhythm of her pulse, and the taste of her impending orgasm, building like a storm cloud.

Her lips move, like she's trying to say something. I'm squeezing too tightly, though, and just for a moment, fear flashes through her, bright and sharp as a knife. It's a fear I've felt dozens of times, that spark when a victim realizes I really am going to kill them.

Usually, it delights me. Not tonight, though. Tonight, I feel my own panic at the thought of losing her, and so I loosen my grip—

Just as Chloe's orgasm spills over.

She screams her first full breath, her body a riot beneath mine. I slam my fists into the pillow and fuck her as hard as I can, hard enough that I can hear the drywall splitting as the doorframe slams into it, burying myself deeper and deeper into her spasming cunt until heat tears through me, too. My cock pulses, my cum erupting inside her.

She's still coming, though. Her body pulses, and she squirms beneath me, making soft, desperate little noises. I slump down to kiss her, licking the dried blood off her lips and tangling my fingers up in her hair while she ruts against my softening cock, riding out the last waves of her pleasure. That place where we're connected is drenched with a hot, warm liquid that reminds me of blood, even though it's not.

Eventually, Chloe's movement slows, and then she stills completely, sinking into the mattress. And I feel the shift in her emotions, like I did before.

Shame.

I roll off her and settle on my side so I can smooth her sweat-damp hair away from her face. She turns her pretty brown eyes toward me, her lashes still limned with tears, her lips still swollen.

"You feel ashamed," I say, twisting my body to make room for my hands.

Chloe tenses a little. "You can sense that, too?" she murmurs.

I nod. Then, even though it makes my heart feel tight: "Is it because of me?"

Just for a moment, her shame is replaced with confusion. Then she shakes her head and reaches her hand up to her throat, already striped red and white from my fingers. It'll be mottled with bruises tomorrow, a thought that gives me a warm feeling, a little like pride.

"It's not you," she says softly. "It's—this. Wanting this when we're…" Her voice trails off, and she looks away from me, up at the ceiling. "The things I would have to think about," she says flatly, "with other guys, just to have any hope of coming—"

The shame flares hotter, and I cup her face to force her to look at me.

"Tell me," I say.

Chloe trembles a little. The tears dance on her eyelashes, and I reach up and swipe them away with my thumb, then press them to my tongue.

"You know what I am." I have to sit up to talk to her. "The things I've thought about doing to you would probably make you scream."

She smiles shyly at that.

"Tell me what you think about," I say. 'And I'll tell you what *I* think about."

My heart's pounding furiously against my ribs as I form the words, knowing I could be making a terrible mistake. But I've never wanted to share a piece of myself with a human before. Or with anyone. My father kept me at arm's distance, the way a leopard mother does her cub. I did the same with others of my kind, the few that I've met over the years. We're all solitary predators, hunting in our respective territories. The blood was what mattered.

Until Chloe showed up across the lake.

She takes a deep breath, fingers trailing along my arm, a reminder that she's real. "I would just—think about dying," she says, and there's a faint rasp in her voice that I know I put there. "Imagine being strangled, like you just did." She blushes. "Or being cut. Bleeding."

My cock pulses.

"What do you think about?" The shyness in the question makes it seem to curl in on itself.

"Blood," I say. "I think about blood, too."

"My blood?" She signs it, and she says it, making the words echo.

I nod. "Splitting you open." I wonder if she sees how my hands shake. "So I can worship the inside of you."

Chloe stares up at me, her eyes wide with fear. With something else, too.

"Are you ever going to do that to me?" she whispers. "For real?"

"No." I shake both my head and my fist forcefully. "I told you that."

We stare at each other, and she looks so luminous in the lamplight. It doesn't matter how much I would like to see her split open like that, to feel her blood on my skin. I can't destroy her.

"I just don't want you to be ashamed," I finally say. "Because I think those desires are what brought us together."

Chloe breathes out, eyes shining. And then, like I think it might prove it to her, I drag her into my chest and lie down with her on the mussed blankets. She doesn't pull away. Actually, she does the opposite, tucking herself into my chest, her warm fingers spreading against my waist. I nuzzle into her hair and trace along the outline of her skin. Along her arms, and the curve of her hips, and the side of her neck, where I know bruises are already starting to bloom. The evidence of the violence I did to her, that violence that marks her as mine.

We stay like that, wrapped up together on her bed. Chloe doesn't speak. She doesn't have to, because I can feel her contentment and her hesitation and the last lingering threads of her fear, all warring together. Eventually, though, contentment wins out, and her breaths slow until she's asleep in my arms. Vulnerable. Safe.

I'm aware of how fragile she is, holding her like this. Humans are unbelievably fragile to a monster like me. It's so easy to rip them into pieces, to creep into the places where they think they're safest and paint them red with blood. Whether I use a knife, or an ax, or my bare hands, it doesn't matter. It's always easy.

I squeeze Chloe a little tighter. She mumbles in her sleep and tilts her face into my chest, warming my skin with her breath. And I know I won't hurt her.

But there's a silvery line of moonlight spilling in through the gap in the curtains, and I feel it again. That sense of something snapping inside me.

The killing moon, calling me home.

I close my eyes against as dread coils in my belly, and I press my nose into Chloe's hair. I really thought I had chased it away. But there's no denying the way it's pulsing through the air. I only have a few more days until it rises.

I wish there were a god for me to pray to, but I know there's not. What god would listen but the devil?

So instead, I pray to Chloe. I pray to her blood and her fear and desire.

I pray that the killing moon will pass me by.

CHLOE

He's gone when I wake up.

I roll onto my back and blink at the rectangle of sunlight spreading across the ceiling toward the fan. My throat burns furiously, like when I got sick a few years ago with a cough that stripped it raw. I swallow against the pain, testing it. Nothing *seems* broken.

It's disappointing that Theo has left me alone, although I'm also not surprised. He's a night creature, that's for damn sure.

It's a weekday. And going by the brightness of the sun in the window, I should be getting ready for work right now. The idea is absolutely too much.

So I grab my phone to fire off a message to my boss, telling him that I came down with a cold and will need the day off. There are a few messages from Penelope in the group chat, too, asking about our next Zoom movie night. No word yet from Abi, but I respond with an *I'm in* and a string of emojis. I should probably tell Penelope what happened. Or both of them. Abi really ought to know about Callie, too, although I can understand why Penelope doesn't want to tell her. Abi's the county coroner down in a little beach town in Texas. She has a professional obligation to report crimes.

I leave the phone on the desk and shuffle into the bathroom, the space between my legs aching. Memories of last night flash through my head, but most of all, I think of that moment right before I came.

I really thought, just for a second, that Theo was going to kill me. And that's what tipped me over the edge. The orgasm that followed almost destroyed me, especially with how it kept going, longer than I'd ever had an orgasm last. I'd read about what a lack of oxygen can do, how it heightens pleasure, but I'd never tried it. I always wanted to, of course. Like I told him, I would think about it incessantly, trying to make sex with my college hook-ups more tolerable.

But the real thing was like nothing I ever imagined. I'm swoony just thinking about it.

At least until I stumble into the bathroom. When I flip on the light, I cry out in shock.

My neck is almost black with bruises.

"Fuck me," I whisper, staring at my reflection. My eyes are pink at the edges, too, and there's the cut on my lip from where Theo bit me. But my neck is a nightmare. The imprints of his fingerprints are undeniable, long black bars caging my throat.

I tug my hair forward. It doesn't do much to hide it.

A scarf? It'll look stupid in the summer, but I don't think makeup's going to do much, either.

I wobble back into my bedroom and over to my closet, sliding through my clothes until I find a blousy bow collar shirt I haven't worn in years. Better than nothing.

The doorbell rings.

The sound startles me, and I nearly jump out of my skin. *Just leave it*, I think, pulling on the shirt. It sits high enough up on my neck that it covers most of the bruising, especially with my hair down.

The doorbell rings again, three more times in quick succession. I frown. Penelope? Did she decide to come down here after all, completely unannounced? Her texts didn't sound like she had left her sister's place, but she would ring the doorbell like that, if for no other reason than to annoy me.

Could be Oliver, too, even though he's never bothered to ring the doorbell before. Usually just taps on my back door, although I haven't seen him since the weekend he spent at my house while his parents were away. Our last conversation was him thanking me for letting him spend the night, right before he made me swear not to come and talk to his parents. I agreed. Maybe I shouldn't have.

I bustle downstairs and into the foyer. There's no sign of anyone through the little stained glass window set in the door, and so maybe it's not much of a surprise when I pull the door open, and it is, in fact, Oliver standing on the stoop.

"Hey, bud—" The words lodge in my throat.

He has a black eye.

"Can I come in?" he signs. "Please?"

"What happened?"

He's zeroed in on the living room, though, brushing past me so quickly that the hairs on my arm stand on end. "Oliver? Are you okay?"

He sits on the edge of the couch, his knees pulled up to his chest. My heart thunders. "Oliver, you know you can talk to me, right?" I kneel on the floor to look up at him, and he flicks his gaze over to me. The bruising is around his left eye, making it look sunken. The sight of that, a black eye on a child, makes my stomach twist around in angry knots. "Who-ever did that to you, you can tell me. Even if it was—" I swallow, knowing what I have to say it even though I don't want to. "Even if it was Theo."

Oliver gives me a disgusted look. "Theo wouldn't hurt me."

I breathe out. "Then who?" I feel like I know the answer already, though.

Oliver looks away from me, down at the floor. His brow is knitted up tight, and he hugs his legs in so close that it's like he's trying to make himself disappear. I honestly don't know what to do. I have no experience with children. Certainly not with a child who is clearly being abused.

How the *fuck* did I not see it before?

"Oliver," I say softly, brushing his hair back. "You came here for a reason."

"They don't care," he signs around his legs.

"Who doesn't?"

"My parents."

A weight drops in my stomach. I suck in air, sharp and tight. "What do you mean? What don't they care about?"

"Anything," he signs. Then, with a single flick of his wrist, "Me."

A cold, sick feeling works through my belly. I hate myself for not making the connections earlier. Because I've seen all the fucking clues, haven't I, even if I didn't want to face what they were? His mother's cold, angry voice when I came by to ask about his imaginary friend. The shouting I heard when he would disappear inside his house. The fact that he was left alone to fend for himself for an entire weekend.

"Oliver," I say again, and when he turns his gaze over to me, I sign the rest of it. "Please. Tell me what happened."

His face is hard and stony, and I don't know what to do. I need a professional. Child Protective Services? Better safe than sorry, even though the last thing I want is for Oliver to tell them about Theo.

That doesn't matter, I admonish myself. Theo can take care of himself.

"Please," I sign. "I can't help you if I don't know what happened."

Oliver swallows and slowly lowers his knees down until he's sitting normally. "I want to see Theo," he signs. "But Mom took my boat away."

I take a deep breath. "We'll find a way to get you over there," I tell him. "Why did she take your boat away?" That seems a safe question, since he clearly doesn't want to tell me about his eye.

"Because she hates me."

I swallow, my throat dry. "Was it because of the camping trip? Because you spent the weekend with me?"

Oliver stares sullenly up at me. "They didn't know about that." His eyes gleam. "Can you take me to see Theo now?"

"Why do you want to see Theo?" I ask, feeling dizzy. I'm not prepared for this. In fact, I'm certain I'm going to fuck it up.

"Because Theo is my friend," Oliver says. "And he told me that if anyone ever hurt me, I should tell him."

I take a jagged breath. A million thoughts flood my head. Would Theo kill someone for Oliver? Surely *Oliver* doesn't realize that, and I don't think for a second that's what he actually wants, to be the reason someone—his parents, it seems—should die.

"He'll protect me," Oliver says, his signs becoming fast and jagged. It takes me a second to parse what he's saying. "But I can't go across the lake without a boat. Can you drive there?"

With that last question, Oliver gives me a look of such pure desperation that I feel my heart crack in two. I know telling him no isn't remotely a possibility.

"Let me check," I say weakly.

Oliver draws his knees up to his chest again, squeezing himself up tight. With shaking hands, I pull up a map of Hanging Lake on my phone. The main road does seem to wind around the lake, dead-ending near the start of the peninsula. It's going to take a lot longer than rowing across. Or even swimming across, for that matter. But Oliver's not in a swimsuit. To be honest, I'm not sure he even knows how to swim.

"It looks like it," I say, and he jerks his gaze up to me. God, it makes my heart hurt to see the bruise around his eye. "But we're probably going to have to hike over to his cabin."

"We won't," Oliver says. "He'll know we're there."

My heart flutters, although I don't say anything.

"We need to hurry," Oliver says, his eyes big and desperate. "Please. Before they realize I'm gone."

The bruising around his eyes seems to swim out at me. All I can do is nod.

TEN MINUTES LATER, I'm winding down the lakeside road, my phone's GPS glowing in the passenger seat. Oliver is curled up in the backseat, watching the trees flicker past us. It's all trees out here, standing guard against the smooth blue waters of Hanging Lake.

This is a mistake. I'm sure it's a mistake. I should have told Oliver that I was calling CPS, that someone would come help him. But I think about his big, pleading eyes and how excited he was for our little campout. I think about kind Theo is with him, and how unafraid Oliver is whenever he's around.

Callie saved me and Penelope, I think, squeezing hard on the steering wheel. *She's just like Theo, and she saved us.*

By killing our attacker, though.

The road narrows as we come to the bend of the lake, heading toward the peninsula. Gravel crunches under the tire.

"Almost there," I say, although I'm not sure if that's actually true. The forced cheeriness in my voice makes me cringe. When I glance up in my rearview mirror, Oliver's still staring out the window.

A yellow sign flashes ahead: ROAD ENDS .5 MILES. I breathe out, trying to work out what I'm going to say to Theo. *Don't kill Oliver's parents.* That's all there is to say, isn't there?

Another sign. END OF ROAD. Trees crowd in tight, and I press down on the brakes, because the road literally does end, cutting off abruptly in front of a big red and white barrier fence. A row of pine trees rises behind it. On one of them, rather conspicuously, is a large, battered sign reading DANGER. KEEP OUT.

Not that it stops Oliver. He's already scrambling out of the car.

"Hold up!" I cut the engine and jump out after him, leaving my car parked in the middle of the road. Oliver looks over at me dolefully.

"Hurry," he says.

"Don't go in the woods by yourself," I say. "Theo, um, might be able to know we're here, but it's gonna take him a while to get over to us, okay?"

Theo kicks at the gravel on the road, sending a few stones skittering into the underbrush. I look over at my car, sigh, and decide it's fine where it is. No one should be coming down this dead-end of a road.

Oliver stamps his foot.

"I'm coming, I'm coming." I look down at the map on my phone. All I can see are splotches of green and splotches of blue. There aren't any trails, because, as I damn well know, it's dangerous. But I can see, more or less, that we're standing on the edge of the peninsula, and I think I have a good sense of how I can get us over to the lake shore. Oliver *is* right; Theo will sense us, and I'm sure he'll come looking. But it'll be easier to walk along the shore than cut across the woods.

I take a deep breath and look over at Oliver. God, I hope I'm not making a huge mistake.

But I still plaster on a smile and say, "Are you ready to go find him?"

THEO

I'm drawing water when I smell Chloe in my territory.

I let the bucket clatter back down into the well and sniff, certain it's my imagination, that it's just the lingering impression of her from last night. I've been smelling her all morning—on my fingers, on my clothes, in my hair.

But no. The wind gusts, and it's not just her. Oliver's here, too. But the direction's all wrong. They're on the other side of the peninsula, opposite the lake houses.

I hoist the bucket back up and set it beside the well, frowning. Something's wrong. I don't sense that, exactly—I suspect they're too far away—but I can think of no other reason why they'd be on that side of the peninsula.

So I take off, following their scent through my woods. Tracking them. Something tugs in my chest, almost like the killing moon. But I focus on Chloe's scent, on the memory of last night, and it settles, vanishing back in the darkness where it lives.

The wind sweeping across my territory makes it easy to track them, especially since I'm used to weaving through the dense overgrowth of my woods. They're walking along the lakeshore, taking the long way around, but I'm able to intercept them not far from the edge of my territory. I stop just inside the treeline and peer out through the shadows—my father taught me caution, and I cling to it, even now. But all I see are the two of them in the distance, the wind blowing Chloe's hair back away from her face. Oliver's a small dark figure beside her.

Something *is* wrong.

I sense it immediately, the scent as sharp as blood. Chloe's worried, a tight, knotting feeling that makes my heart constrict. But Oliver's sorrow is nearly overwhelming. I haven't tasted something like that in a long, long time. Not since I was a child myself.

Not since I died the first time.

I burst out of the trees, making myself known. Chloe sees me first, and she bends down to say something to Oliver, her voice muffled by the wind blowing the trees around. Oliver jerks his head up, though, and his sorrow changes, just for a moment, into something like hope.

That's an odd feeling, someone feeling hope when they see me.

He takes off running down the beach, little arms pumping. I don't know what to make of it, especially not when he reaches me and flings his arms around my legs, burying his face in my hip. Chloe jogs up after him, her worry thicker than before.

"Something happened," she signs.

Oliver peels himself away from my leg and looks up at me, and that's when I see it. The bruises around his left eye.

Rage swells through me, fiery and terrifying. I stumble back, my blood pumping furiously, because I'm also terrified that it will overtake me and I will do something that I don't want to.

"Who did that?" I sign, my hands shaking uncontrollably.

Oliver blinks, and his eyes gleam with tears.

"Who did it?" I ask again, but this time I look up at Chloe, who stands a few paces away, the wind blowing her hair across her furrowed brow. She has on a loose, fluttery shirt with a high collar that hides most of the bruises I gave her last night. Normally, I'd want to admire them. But not now.

"He won't tell me," she says with her hands.

I look back down at Oliver, whose lower lip trembles. Then I crouch down so we can be at eye level.

"Tell me," I say.

Oliver blinks, and tears streak over his cheeks, and I hate it. He's not supposed to cry.

"My brother," he signs.

My rage flares again. When I look back up at Chloe, she shakes her head in confusion. "What did he say?" she asks.

"Brother," I sign.

Her eyes go wide, and I think I see, just for a moment, a flicker of understanding, although it vanishes before I can be sure. I don't know much about Oliver's brother. He's never brought me a picture of him, just like he's never brought me a picture of his parents, either.

"Your brother did that?" Chloe says, speaking this time. Oliver nods but doesn't look at her. He looks at me, and then his hands start flying.

"Owen hates me," he says. "Like my parents hate me. He said I was a weird freak, and that I need to talk like a normal person."

The rage ignites, sending bolts of fire shooting through my veins. Ancient memories flash through my head, from the time I was Oliver's age. From the time I thought I was human. All the children in Veritas taunting me whenever I went into town. My mother kept me out of school, taught me sign language herself. But everyone in Veritas knew how I was and hated me for it.

"Your brother said that?" Chloe asks. She's come around to stand beside me, and her presence is the only thing that comes anywhere close to helping me calm the anger surging inside me.

"He always says that," Oliver signs. "And Mom and Dad agree with him."

Chloe makes a soft, sad sound in the back of her throat. But Oliver keeps going, his eyes fixed on mine as he signs.

"His friends came over," he says, "and they held me down while he beat me up."

My muscles quiver, and I curl my hands into fists, and all I can think about is blood.

"He beat you up?" Chloe's voice is shaky. "That's why your mom took your boat away?"

Through the haze of my anger, something connects. They must have taken the road here. That's why they're on this side of the peninsula.

"She said I made him do it." Oliver's signs are fast and jagged, like he can barely contain himself. "She said he's right and that I do need to learn to talk and they've coddled me too much and that's when she took my boat away. My dad told him he did a good job, that if that's what it takes for me to be normal, that I should stop crying."

I suck down deep breaths, my hands still clenched into fists, tight enough that I can feel my nails digging into my skin. Chloe's worry has intensified. I'd actually say it's turned to fear.

Oliver's not afraid, though.

"Oliver," Chloe breathes, dropping down to her knees. "Oliver, why didn't you tell me? We can—there are things we can do and—"

"Theo can help," Oliver signs.

Oh, Chloe's fear erupts when she hears that. But Oliver doesn't know what I am, and I'm not terribly surprised when he goes on to say, "I can stay here. Away from all of them."

Chloe rocks back on her heels, staring at him. I force myself to focus on the sounds of my territory: the soft lapping waves, the birdsong, the wind blowing through the trees. The symphony of life coming from these two humans that I inexplicably care about.

"They'll come looking for you," Chloe says gently, brushing her hand over Oliver's hair. "This is the first place they'll check."

"Theo will hide me," Oliver says. "And protect me."

Chloe twists around to look at me, her expression dark and suspicious, her fear so strong it masks the scent of pine and lake water. It hurts, seeing that suspicion on her face, but I understand why it's there.

"I would," I sign, mostly to her.

That does nothing to soften the tension in her body. But I can't say I particularly blame her. We both know what my protection involves, even if Oliver doesn't. And I can feel the bloodlust surging in me, and the killing moon is echoing in the rattle of tree branches. I don't care, though. Oliver is hurting, and I can take away the things that caused that hurt. It's all I can do, really.

"Why don't we go back to Theo's cabin?" Chloe signs. "And we can talk about it there?"

Oliver looks over at me, and I nod. Then he does, too.

Chloe stands up, but it's my hand that Oliver takes. It's startling how small it is. And how easy it is for me to be delicate with it, to not crush his tiny, bird-like bones in my palm.

I tug him toward the woods, the two of us leading Chloe home.

But I can feel her worry the whole way back.

"I NEED to call Child Protective Services," Chloe signs. "He can't just run away and live with you. That's not how things work."

We're in the kitchen. Oliver is in the living room, drawing on some of my mother's old stationery with a ballpoint pen. He held my hand the entire way back to the cabin, and I feel a jolt of irritation at Chloe's words. Because why couldn't he live here? Does she think I would hurt him?

No. That's not what she's worried about, and I damn well know it.

"If you call the authorities," I say slowly, making sure my words are clear, "they will find out about me."

Chloe frowns. "I'm not calling the police."

Frustration bubbles through me. "If Oliver mentions me, don't you think they'll want to ask questions? Even if they aren't the police?"

Chloe's frown deepens. I glance past her to look at Oliver. He's still curled up on the couch, his pen scratching furiously over the paper. I do understand where Chloe's coming from. It would be better to go through legal channels, I suppose, and she'll be there, out in the real world, to make sure Oliver is safe.

But the rage is hot and steady in my chest. And all I can think about is when I was a child, all the taunts and mockery and bullying I endured any time I crossed the lake to Veritas. It didn't end until I died.

No. It didn't end until I came back and killed my tormentors.

"Please," Chloe signs. "Can we at least try it this way? You can't just—" Her hands shake, and she doesn't finish what she's signing. It doesn't matter. I know what she was going to say.

I resist the urge to ask her *why not?* Why can't I kill them, the monsters calling themselves Oliver's parents?

"I'll tell Oliver not to say anything about you," Chloe signs. "He'll understand. Or maybe you should tell him. He thinks you're a ghost, doesn't he?"

I sigh. "Yes."

"Exactly. We'll tell him he can't talk about you because you're a ghost and—they won't believe him. Right?" Chloe drops her arms to her sides, her eyes big and luminous. My own gaze drops down from her face to the marks on her neck, just barely visible above the high collar. I brush my fingers across them, the touch feather-soft. Chloe stiffens.

"And if the authorities notice that?" I ask. "I know Oliver didn't, but he's just a child. A social worker almost certainly would."

Chloe's cheeks turn pink. "Are you sure Oliver didn't notice?"

"He didn't ask about them, did he?" I rake my fingers through her hair, and any earlier irritation I felt evaporates away. I know she's trying to protect Oliver, same as me. And I know her methods are better. I *know* that.

I still feel it, though. The killing moon's icy pull across the water. My fingers flex against her scalp.

"I'll wear a scarf," Chloe signs. "So they won't see. That's if they even talk to me. Which they might not. They'll just send someone to check on Oliver's house. If there's anything suspicious, they'll take care of it."

I keep petting Chloe's hair, relishing the silk of it against my fingers. She's too naive if she thinks it's going to work that way. But I know my way has its flaws, too.

Part of me wishes I could just gather up both of them and take them far, far away from here. It surprises me how vividly I can picture it. I don't leave my territory unless I absolutely have to. And I would never abandon it like that.

Except maybe I would. For them.

Chloe and I stare at each other while Oliver's pen scratches across the paper.

"Oliver!" Chloe calls out. "Oliver, could you come in here for a sec?"

I sense his hesitation. I sense his sorrow, too, how he wants to curl into himself, and it makes my heart feel weak and fragile, like it felt when I was a boy.

But the scratching stops, and his footsteps echo softly against my old creaky floorboards. He stops in the doorway of the kitchen and stares up at us.

"Hey." Chloe kneels in front of him and signs the rest. "Theo and I were talking, and we think it's best if I call someone to come talk to your parents. Someone from the government."

Oliver flicks his eyes over to me. "I want to stay here," he signs. "With Theo. My parents won't come looking."

Chloe looks back at me, her eyes big and imploring.

"Chloe's right," I say, even though I don't want to. "If you're missing, this is the first place they'll check."

Oliver ducks his head down, looking at the floor. Then he signs, "Who are you going to call?"

"People who can help," Chloe says, speaking the words so that he looks up at her. "It's their job to help kids like you," she signs. "And I'll be right next door the whole time. I'll give you my number so you can call or text me if you need to, okay?"

Oliver nods.

"There's just one thing. You have to keep Theo a secret."

Oliver looks up at me again. He doesn't seem upset by these instructions. "Because they won't understand," he says to me. "Right?"

"Yes." I give him a smile, trying to be like Chloe—sweet and understanding and not burning alive with the need to slaughter everyone who has ever hurt him. "Remember when you first visited me? And I said no one could come into my territory because it—" I glance at Chloe, who's watching my hands intently. "Because I'm a ghost and it would be dangerous for them?"

Oliver nods.

"Well, if you tell these people Chloe calls about me, they'll want to come over here." My heart hammers in my chest. Each beat sounds like the word *blood*. Oliver blinks at me, and I hope that's good enough. I don't know if I can say much more.

"And since they're trying to help you," Chloe says, "Theo wants to make sure they don't get hurt. Right, Theo?"

She and Oliver both look at me. I nod, trying to fight against the buzzing in my veins.

"Okay," Oliver says. "Even though it won't help. They won't believe them."

"Won't believe who?" Chloe says gently.

"My parents," Theo signs. "People always believe my parents, and not me."

The rage flares like a fire doused with gasoline. But Chloe reaches over and pulls Oliver into a hug.

"I believe you," she whispers. "So does Theo. And so will the people we call. I promise."

27

CHLOE

By the time Oliver and I get back to my house, it's nearly lunchtime. I half-expect to find his parents waiting on my front porch, but there's no sign of them

"They think I'm still in my room," he tells me when I ask, once we're inside. "They won't check on me 'til dinner time."

"No lunch?" I say quietly.

He shrugs, and I make a split-second decision. "How about you stay here for lunch? I can make you a grilled cheese. How's that sound?"

Oliver nods, and I try to ignore the tight knot in my stomach as I head into the kitchen. He trails behind me and sets himself up at my kitchen table, pulling out the drawing he was working on at Theo's house. He keeps his arm looped around it, like he wants to hide it from me.

I whip up the sandwich, although my mind's distracted. I don't want to call CPS in front of Oliver, but I'm still nervous about sending him back home. Honestly, it'd be easier if he could just stay on the peninsula with Theo, wouldn't it? I said that was the first place his parents would look, but it really isn't. My house is.

My stomach twists into knots. God, I hope I'm doing the right thing. I don't know. I really don't.

I set Oliver's sandwich down in front of him, and he finally moves his hand away from the drawing and pushes it across the table at me.

It's me and Theo, sitting beside each other like we were during our campout. It's all done in a cheap ballpoint pen, but the lines are fine and delicate and capture our likenesses shockingly well, with dark crosshatching to represent the night sky and some artistic trickery to make it look like the fire is illuminating our faces.

In the drawing, Theo looks at me with a tenderness I don't remember from that night. Or maybe I just didn't see it.

"Wow," I breathe, looking up at Oliver. "This is really, really good."

"Thank you," he signs. "It's for you. Although you should show Theo when you can."

Sadness pangs at my heart. "I will. I promise, okay?"

Theo just chews his sandwich and doesn't say anything.

I let him eat, although I do put the drawing on my refrigerator with a magnet, beside the portrait of Theo that Oliver gave me the weekend of the campout. I bet there are some old frames in this house somewhere, something I can use to keep the drawings safe.

Even if I feel like I can't keep Oliver safe. Not really.

He finishes quickly and brings his plate over to the dishwasher without me having to ask. As I watch him dutifully load it into place, that low-level sadness suddenly flares into something hot, like anger. His parents don't deserve him.

"I'm going to go home now," Oliver says. "Are you going to call the people you think will help?"

My throat feels too dry and scratchy to speak, so I nod instead.

Oliver scrunches up his brow. "It won't help," he says. "I know you think it will, but it won't."

"Why do you say that?"

He looks up at me. "You'll see."

And then he turns and marches out of my kitchen, back out the front door. I follow him and watch him pick his way across the yard from my front porch. It feels too hot out here, the sun too bright, like it can lay bare to all the secrets hidden in the darkness. Not just those of Oliver's family. But mine. Theo's.

Still, I go inside and make the call.

THE CPS social worker arrives faster than I expect, pulling up a little around 5:30. I hear the car door slam while I'm out on my back patio, reading the same sentence in my book over and over again. It's easier to stare across the water at the peninsula. I wonder if Theo is watching us. Probably.

As soon as I hear the car, my heart leaps up in my chest, and I slip around the side of my house in time to see a woman walk up the sidewalk to Oliver's house. She has the look of an elementary school principal: older, her hair allowed to go grey, her A-line skirt crisp and professional. If she sees me, she doesn't acknowledge it.

I watch her ring the doorbell. A few minutes go by. The door opens. Her voice doesn't carry enough for me to hear what she says, but she's allowed inside.

For a moment, I just stare at the Jenkins' house. There's no sign of movement inside, although the trees rustle around me, having been disturbed by a hot, damp wind that nonetheless makes my skin crinkle with goosebumps.

I glance across the water, one last time. Then I go back inside and pace around my living room, my nails digging into my arms.

I'm not sure how long it is before I hear the slam of a car door again. Fifteen minutes, maybe. I rush over to my window and crack the blinds and watch the social worker's sleek car slide back down the driveway.

A heavy sense of deflation crashes over me.

That's it? Fifteen minutes? Was Oliver with her? I don't know how any of this works. If she thought he was in serious danger, she would take him, wouldn't she?

And then what? What happens to kids like Oliver when their parents don't care enough for them? Surely he has other family: grandparents. An aunt or uncle. Someone who can take care of him.

It won't help. I know you think it will, but it won't.

Oliver's been through this before.

Sickness fills my stomach. I step back from the window, my breath tight. If there's no one for him, he'll go into foster care. He'll be taken away from here, possibly whisked off to someplace worse.

But his brother gave him a black eye, and his parents didn't even fucking care. I had to do *something*. Didn't I?

When my doorbell rings, I practically shriek with fear. It's the last sound I'm expecting, and I whip my head around and stare for a few long minutes at the front door.

Whoever's there is tall enough to be seen through the stained glass window.

I swallow. I wish, suddenly, that Theo was here with me. Maybe Oliver was right to want to go to him after all.

The doorbell rings again, followed by a heavy, urgent pounding.

"I know you're in there!" A woman's voice. Oliver's mom,

I'm sure of it. What was her name again? Britney? No, Blaire. "I think we need to talk!"

I consider slipping out the back, diving into the lake, and swimming to the peninsula. But that would be cowardly, and Oliver deserves better.

So I answer the door.

Blaire Jenkins is waiting for me on the patio, that fake-looking smile plastered across her face. Her eyes, though, are cold and hard as steel.

"May I come in?" she asks.

"I'd rather you not." I step out, easing the door shut behind me. I don't know why I say that. Maybe I think if she tries something, my screams will carry enough for Theo to hear.

And then what? Anything he would do about it would only make the situation significantly worse.

Blaire scoffs a little and tugs down on her shirt. "Fine, we can sweat it out on your porch." A long pause. "I assume you're the one who called that social worker on me?"

Blood pounds in my ears. Blaire doesn't break eye contact with me, her gaze cold and unbothered. I swallow.

"She didn't find anything," Blaire says with a sickening little smile.

"Oliver had a *black eye*," I spit out.

Blaire tilts her head, her shimmery blonde hair puddling in the corner of her shoulder. "He fell," she says coolly. "On the edge of the dock."

Heat swells beneath my skin. And panic, too. I think of Oliver's weary insistence that only Theo can help.

"Liar," I whisper.

"Prove it," she says.

"You've done this before," I hiss. "Haven't you?"

"Done what?" Blaire leans in close, and a real cruelty

marches across her features. "Shut out some meddling bitch who thinks she knows what's best for my son?"

I gape at her, and she smiles victoriously. "You don't know what it's like," she says. "Attempting to raise a child who can't even be *normal*. So keep your fucking nose out of my family's business."

I suck in a deep breath. "Oliver doesn't deserve this." It's not even close to what I want to say, but it's all that comes out.

Blaire rolls her eyes. "Oliver deserves far worse than what I've done, believe me. And if you call CPS on me again, you'll learn *exactly* what my husband and I do to people who try to interfere in our business." Her eyes narrow and then, to my horror, drop down to my neck. I'm still wearing the bow collar shirt, but I can't stop myself from jerking my hand to my throat. Blaire laughs.

"What were you getting up to over here?" she says mockingly. "Who do you think they're gonna believe? I'm a devoted housewife. Everyone in Pinella knows that. I've served on the PTA since we moved here. And you—" She scoffs, flips her hand in my direction. "You live alone and never leave your house. How are you affording lakeside property again?"

"I inherited this house," I snap, but Blaire just laughs.

"A good cover story for a whore," she says. "Is that what you're doing? Whoring yourself out? What will the next social worker think about that, huh? A whore wanting to spend time with a ten-year-old boy with *special needs*."

She says "special needs" in a tone dripping with mockery, and for a second, all I feel is a hot, blinding anger.

"Better a whore than an abuser," I snarl. "If you let anything happen to Oliver, I'll—"

"You won't do shit," she says, stepping backward off the porch. "He's my son. I'll raise him how I see fit. That's not abuse. It's showing him what the world is actually like. And you can stay the hell out of it."

And then, in an instant, she transforms. The coldness goes out of her expression. She gives me a dazzling smile—the kind of smile you see on the head of the PTA, on the mother of the high school valedictorian. "It was *so* lovely talking to you," she chimes out. "We'll do it again soon, won't we?"

I'm too stunned to react, which gives her just enough time to slip away, sashaying across the grass. As she does, she raises one hand in greeting and calls out, "Evening, Janet! I hope Robert is doing well!"

I jerk my gaze over to where Blaire is looking, and I see my other neighbor, an elderly woman I almost never speak to. She waves back at Blaire. "He's doing just fine, honey! Thanks for asking."

"That's *wonderful*." Blaire looks back over at me again, still holding that picture-perfect smile. "No one will believe you," she says in a voice dripping with honey.

And then she cuts back across the grass, and all I can do is watch her go, my heart hammering in my ribs.

28

THEO

I watch it all happen through my telescope, sitting there on the lakeshore surrounded by the deep green shadows of the woods. I watch the woman arrive in her dark car. I watch her leave. I watch Oliver's blonde mother stroll across the yard and disappear into the front of Chloe's house, and then reappear as she walks back home.

And through it all, I feel Chloe. Her anger. Her despair. Her fear. It's faint, at this distance, but undeniable. And when I catch on to it, I breathe it into myself, and I feel it inside me, fueling my own hot rage.

Fueling the killing moon.

There's no denying it now. The sun has dropped below the horizon, and the killing moon is rising, making its slow and unmistakable arc over the trees of my peninsula. And I keep staring through the telescope, watching the houses on the other side of the lake.

Watching my prey.

My heartbeat is slow and steady. I don't usually watch them beforehand. I certainly didn't do it that first time, after I woke up from five years in the ground. I was driven by rage then. Rage at the death of my mother; rage at my own death. The killing moon was the thing that told me what I needed to do to cool my rage:

Just follow the moonlight until all it illuminates is spilled blood.

The other times weren't that different. I'd hear the whispers as the moon swelled, but when it hit, it hit fast. Twenty years ago, I even thought it was a normal moon at first. But its light kept burning my skin, and all I could think about was the slipperiness of entrails between my fingers. I didn't stop until I crossed the water. Until that woman shot me in the chest.

Because that's what the killing moon wants. What it always wants. Not just human death, but mine, too. It wants me in the ground to start the cycle over.

I blink. Something hot and wet drips down my cheek.

I promised Chloe I would never hurt her or Oliver. And that's a promise I know I won't break. When the frenzy of a killing moon starts, I don't lose sense of myself, not in that way. And there are always people left alive. There are enough beating hearts over there to give it all the blood it wants without me having to break my word.

There are three beating hearts in particular that I want to end, all of them in Oliver's house.

But it's *my* death that makes my eyes feel wet and heavy. It doesn't matter that my deaths aren't permanent, that I'll claw my way out of the dirt again.

She'll be gone once I do. I'm sure of it. And so will Oliver.

But maybe—maybe they can run away together. He'll have someone who will take care of him, who won't hurt him. Maybe that's enough, knowing the two of them will be safe, even without me.

I squeeze the telescope and slide it sideways on its mount, pausing on each house. It's easy to tell the ones that have people inside, and my body shudders with the need to crack the houses open one by one, dragging my victims out to the shore of Hanging Lake so the killing moon can see my prizes.

The wind stirs, and I can see the moonlight on the water, and it reminds me of the first time I did this. The screams. The begging. The orgasmic rush of pleasure as I cut down the people who hurt me the most.

I wrench myself away from the telescope and scramble back into the woods, my gaze still fixed on the lake houses. Five of them are lit up, marking the humans inside.

My breaths are thick and heavy as I slide backward into the woods, where the moonlight can't quite reach me through the trees. The darkness is a comfort, and I wrap my arms around myself and try to focus on Chloe, on the memories of fucking her, like I can convince myself that's all this is, this terrible tugging in my chest. It helped before.

It doesn't help tonight.

I lash out, slamming my fist into a nearby tree so that the branches rattle. Then I stalk through the underbrush, swinging my arms out in a wide path of destruction. It's not the right kind of destruction, though, and I know it. Broken branches and shredded leaves aren't what the killing moon wants.

They aren't what you want.

The forest expels me into the little graveyard, and I hiss at the moonlight falling across the overgrown grass. This was where the first one started. This was where I was reborn as a monster, where I first felt the killing moon's silver light on my skin, the way I feel it now.

I didn't deny it then. I've never tried to deny the call of the killing moon, because why would I? As my father told me, over and over as we stalked the streets of Schenectady, that this is what my people are designed to do.

Don't deny it, my father told me one night, the two of us

still drenched in the blood of our victims. I don't remember anything about them. Just the conversation afterward, the two of us sitting in a dusty old barn, my muscles aching from the kill. *You had control tonight, but when you deny it, you lose that control. And the wrong people might die.*

Now, dozens of years and hundreds of miles away, I roar out my frustration, the sound echoing up into the silvered night. The wrong people might die.

Like Chloe. Or Oliver.

I can't deny this. It will hurt them, what I'm going to do, even if it's not physically. But after I die, they'll be free to go far away from here, and Chloe can take care of Oliver, and that's what really matters.

I stalk out of the cemetery, blood pumping furiously through my body. The night seems tinged red at the edges. Red and silver. Over the roar of the wind, I swear I can hear the human heartbeats across the water, and the same cold whispering I always hear under a killing moon.

They aren't supposed to be there this is YOUR territory.

My cabin looms up ahead, a dark silhouette against the blazing moonlight. Has it gotten brighter? It feels brighter. Almost blinding.

I stalk inside, slamming the door open so heavily that the walls shudder. My weapons are still in storage, where I placed them after the campout. That night feels distant now. Or really, not like a memory at all, but a dream. Like I dreamed of being human one night, and that's what it looked like.

I pry the bricks of the fireplace away, their edges crumbling in my heavy grip. My box of weapons greets me, and I drag it out, muscles tightening at the metal clanking inside. Flip the lid open. Everything shines in the moonlight spilling in through the window, sharp as the blades sitting in their loose pile in the box.

I knew this was coming, deep down. That's why I cleaned them in the same slow and methodical way I always clean my blades before a killing moon. I tried to lie to myself, tried to convince myself that it was Chloe who kept pulling my attention across the lake. And she certainly did.

But it was also the killing moon. It was the poison in my blood that drives me to kill.

I pull out the axe, the largest of the weapons, and hold it with both hands, staring down at the dull grey of the blade. It looks like moonlight.

I don't want to do this. I want everything to be like it was the night of the campout, Chloe and Oliver laughing beside the fire and me feeling this strange, unfamiliar warmth deep in my chest. But if I don't do this now, then it'll be worse when I finally do. I can feel that truth deep in the marrow of bones.

At least this way, if I go across the river, I know I can keep control. I know I won't let them die.

And when I'm in the ground, maybe both of them can finally be free.

29

CHLOE

I shudder awake with a sharp gasp of air and blink at the shadows flickering from the ceiling fan. Moonlight creeps in from around the bedroom curtain, making my room feel brighter than it should.

I don't know what woke me.

"Theo?" I sit up and fumble around at my bedside lamp. Warm yellow light floods the room, but there's no sign of him.

I slump back against my headboard. *Something* woke me up. I was in a dead sleep and dreaming, although the dream is already fragmenting into nothingness. Something about a beach crowded with palm trees, a warm, salty sea, the fear of a monster lurking in the water.

A scream rings out through the night.

I freeze, my skin prickling with goosebumps. My first thought is that I didn't actually hear anything, that it was the last remnants of the dream. My next is that it was an owl or a mountain lion, some night animal.

My third, the sharpest of the three, is that Theo crossed the lake.

But he's not at my house.

I leap out of bed with a renewed sense of terror, and I'm not even to the hallway when I hear another scream, this one undeniably real. It's not coming from the direction of Oliver's house, though, but from the other side. The neighbors I never speak to. Janet and Robert.

I think of every one of Penelope's warnings: that Theo isn't human, that I can't trust him. That he's a killer.

I think of the news reports I read, the YouTube videos I watched. The killing sprees that happened along Hanging Lake every fifteen years or so.

Survivors would report seeing a large figure stalking through the street.

Terror floods through me, choking up in my throat. Acting on a sudden surge of adrenaline, I race into the living room and, without really thinking, burst onto the back patio.

The night air is thick and humid and buzzing with insects. Everything, for a moment, feels still. Dark. All the lights are off at Oliver's house, save for the back porch. And the same is true for my other neighbors. God, I don't even remember their last name.

I slip on my outdoor shoes and stumble through the marshy grass to the lakeshore and duck to look under my pier. Theo's boat isn't there, just the black water lapping against the posts.

And then, from the direction of Robert and Janet's house, is the shattering sound of a shotgun blast.

For a second, my entire world tunnels toward that house. All the wind, all the hot night air, all the stars—they're dragged into a black hole at its back door.

I bend over and vomit my dinner into the lake.

More screams. The sound of something shattering. And then silence.

I drag myself up to standing even though my legs feel

weak and boneless. The world spins around in streaks of light and shadow, and all I can think of is Theo's promise that he wouldn't hurt me or Oliver. In my head, I see his big rough hands forming the shape of the words, and I hear the translated echo in my internal voice, and my stomach knots around, and I don't know if he's lying.

I should have listened to Penelope. I should have run far, far away from here.

But I don't run away. Instead, I run *toward*—toward Robert and Janet's house, my heart hammering in my chest. Because maybe it wasn't Theo. Why would he go there and not to Oliver's house?

Why would he go there and not to me?

The back door is hanging open, the glass shattered and sparkling across their lovely stained patio, reflecting the starlight. The lights are off in the living room, but I still step inside, feet crunching on the glass. "Hello?" I call out, voice shaky. "Um, Janet? Is everything okay?"

A stupid question, and I know it.

I stop in the middle of the living room, which has the same layout as mine but looks completely different, with its out-of-date furniture and the thick throw rug in front of the fireplace. The house is quiet. "Hello?" I call out again.

This time, I'm answered with a soft, pained groan coming from the hallway. I follow it, creeping toward the square of yellow light spilling out of one of the downstairs bedrooms, wishing I had thought to grab a weapon. But what good is a weapon against a Hunter?

Especially a Hunter you're fucking.

The thought snags in my chest, makes my stomach lurch around again. And then I smell a coppery, salty stink, and my stomach churns for another reason.

I step into the doorway and retch, but there's nothing in my stomach for me to throw up.

Blood. Everything is covered in blood. There's a mess on the bed that I can't parse: so much thick blood it looks black, but with flashes of white and green.

"Help," says a weak, feminine voice, and for a second I think it's the nightmare on the bed until I realize Janet is sitting on the floor with her back against the wall, head lolling, grey hair dripping blood. She has a shotgun across her knees.

"Oh my god." I dart over to her, and she looks at me with a kind of blank confusion.

"I missed," she says weakly. "I tried to shoot him, but I missed."

Him. My thoughts buzz. "Where are you cut?" I ask, flailing my hands, not sure what to do next.

"Everywhere," she says weakly. Then she shoves the gun at me, the movement clumsy. "Take it," she says. "He's going to come for you next."

I stare down at the shotgun, the barrel streaked with blood.

"Is he here?" I ask, my voice tight with panic.

Janet shakes her head, the movement small and strained. "He goes door to door," she rasps, slumping back against the wall. "He doesn't want us here."

I can't breathe. "Who doesn't?"

Even though I know the answer.

Janet laughs weakly. Her face is so pale, and the carpet is wet and dark, and I know she's bleeding too much from some place I can't see.

And I know Theo did it.

"The boy," she rasps. "The boy they killed. Everyone here… knows the story." She coughs, blood flecking her lips, and then tries to shove the gun at me. "Kill him," she slurs. "Someone always kills him. He'll come back. But not for a long… a long time."

I let out a wet, choking sob, and somehow, my hands wrap around the barrel of the shotgun, moving like they're directed by someone else. I keep seeing Theo in my head. Theo glazed in firelight. Theo brushing his lips against mine. Theo smiling down at Oliver.

How could he do this? How could he be the same fucking person?

"Kill him," Janet says. "You've got four shots. Don't forget to pump it. Aim for the chest. Bigger target."

I pull the gun against my chest, dizzy with horror and the scent of blood. Janet drops her head back and looks up at the ceiling and smiles. "I'll be there soon," she whispers, and I stumble back, knowing she's not talking to me.

"I'm going to call the police," I say, backing out of the room.

"Okay," she breathes.

I turn and run—out of that terrible dark house, away from the scent of blood. I don't stop running until I'm nearly to the lake, and I only stop when I feel the cold water splash around my ankles.

I didn't call the police. Why didn't I call the police?

I would never hurt you. Or Oliver.

Screams erupt into the night, shrill and panicked. I whip around, clutching the gun up against my chest. The Jenkins house is lit up, the windows glowing. It wasn't like that earlier. Was it?

"Oliver," I whisper, and then I run again, tearing across the grass with my heart thudding up in my throat, Janet's voice echoing in the back of my head: *Kill him. Kill him. Kill him.*

A masculine scream rings out from Oliver's house, and I surge forward until I land on the front porch. The door is hanging open, letting out a sharp angle of white light. I choke down the tight knots of my fear and lift the gun, holding it clumsily in front of me.

Inside, someone screams again. An adult man.

I step inside, my legs shaking. All the lights are on, flooding the foyer with too much brightness. Something crashes from deeper in the house. Then something thumps heavily against the floor. Another scream.

I don't run. I'll give myself that. I keep stalking forward, holding up the gun, and the hallways gets shorter and shorter until I'm in the entranceway, and I see them.

Oliver's parents.

They're dead, bodies slack against the couch and drenched in blood. Blaire's head hangs off the edge of the couch, her eyes staring blankly at me through the too-bright lights of the house. Her husband is face-down, the back of his head a ruin.

Horror slams through me, and for a second, the world spins around and then blinks, like the power is going out.

But then there's another scream, and I drop back into myself. It sounds like it's coming from upstairs.

And so I ran again, blindly and furiously and hating myself. Because I let this happen. Despite all of Penelope's warnings, I let myself trust the monster who left a trail of blood between the houses of my two neighbors. I let myself soften for him and open to him, and this—this is what he did.

I swing around onto the landing. More thumping, coming from one of the bedrooms. I lift the gun again, taking my slow, cautious steps, my breath fast and panting. More thumping, another scream, a terrible wet squelching sound.

I don't want to, but I step into the doorway.

Owen is sprawled across the floor, clawing his way across the carpet, his face a mask of blood. He lifts his eyes to me, but I don't think he sees me, not really.

Behind him is Theo.

My Theo, I think numbly as he lifts a massive, blood-soaked axe about his head. His blond hair is loose and streaked with pink and red. His face is splattered with gore, his eyes fixed on Oliver's brother.

Until they're not. Until he lifts them to take me in, standing there, shaking like a rabbit with a shotgun pointed at his chest.

His shoulders slump down, a fraction of an inch. I think something passes through his face. Sadness? Resignation?

No. That has to be my imagination.

"What are you doing?" I scream, a stupid, pointless question. Theo answers it by swinging the ax down and implanting it in Owen's head.

I scream and jerk away from the horror and there's a terrible explosion that makes my ears ring and my whole body slam backward. Sheetrock showers down across Owen's unmoving body, soaking up the blood.

"Fuck," I whisper, fumbling with the gun. I hadn't even realized I had my finger on the trigger. *Don't forget to pump it*, Janet said, but I have no idea how to do that. I pull on the stock the way I've seen people do in movies, but nothing happens.

Theo steps toward me, his axe dripping blood at his side.

"Get away from me!" I scream, scrambling backward across the hallway until I slam up against the far wall. Theo stops, and I'm too paralyzed with fear to move.

Something clanks. I realize he's dropped the axe to the floor.

"I'm sorry," he signs. "I couldn't stop it."

"Why did you do this?" I shriek, bracing my back against the wall to push myself up to standing. "I told you I would—"

Take care of it, that's what I want to say. But I didn't take care of it. Calling CPS did nothing.

Theo signs something, but between the blood and the

bright lights and the film of my tears, I don't think I understood. It almost looks like *I knew it would be you.*

"I trusted you!" I point the gun at his chest, like Janet said, and he doesn't react at all. Just gazes at it with the same calm expression he used when we were sitting in front of the fire.

He signs again, and this time, I catch Oliver's name.

"Oliver," I whisper. "What did you do with Oliver?"

Theo's hands move, slower this time. "Oliver is safe."

I stare at him, hook my finger onto the trigger of the shotgun. Maybe it will still work.

"You killed his entire family," I whisper.

"They didn't love him," Theo says.

My chest tightens. My hands shake, and the gun rattles in my grip. "And you expect me to believe that you do?"

Theo stares at me through the mask of blood on his face, his eyes the brightest thing in the room. I think, just for a second, that I see a woundedness in them.

"You won't understand," he says, each movement slow and careful. "But if I hadn't done this, I might have unintentionally hurt him."

I swear I see his hands shake.

"Or you."

"Bullshit!" In a surge of adrenaline, I squeeze the trigger. Nothing happens. I look down at the gun in horror.

Theo moves closer to me, and I immediately jerk it up, holding it like a baseball bat. He holds out one hand, palm up, curls his fingers in. *Give it to me.*

"Get away," I snarl, swinging the gun. He catches, and the strength of his grip reverberates down my arm.

Then he drags me up to him.

The stench of blood is overwhelming, a thick wet stink that's like the inside of a human body. But I also think, just for a second, that I smell him. That scent like pine trees.

Disgust swells in my stomach. I try to jerk away. Theo

grabs my arm, his hand sticky. "No." He grabs my chin and makes me look at him. "Listen to me," he signs with his free hand.

"Where's Oliver?" I snarl.

"Hiding. Unharmed." Theo pauses. "I told him not to come out until you said it was safe."

I can't breathe. "You can't expect me to think," I gasp out. "That it's safe now?"

Theo shakes his head, his eyes never leaving mine. Then he tilts his head toward the gun.

"I always die," he says. "It's the only way to make the kill-moon happy."

"The *what?*" I shriek, terror lancing through me. How the hell did I ever let this monster touch me? How did I ever think I could trust him?

The bruises around my throat seem to burn.

"I can't stop it," Theo says. "Not until I'm dead." He looks at me through the mask of blood on his face, eyes gleaming. "Please, Chloe. Kill me so this can be over."

I tremble. "You can just stop," I whisper, arms shaking. "Just stop killing—"

Theo shakes his head. "You don't understand. It wants me to keep going. But someone always kills me. The old farmer in sixty-five. The cops in eighty-seven." His eyes gleam. "The woman in oh-one."

I let out a soft, choking sob, tears streaking down my face. Theo watches me for a moment. Then he says, "And you. Now."

He steps forward, and I shriek and try to move away from him, but the walls block me. Theo grabs the barrel of the gun and presses it against his chest. He stares at me, waiting.

"And you," he signs again. "Now."

My heart feels ragged. Ripped in two. I keep thinking about his rough hands on my skin, his hungry and devouring kisses. It feels like they came from another person, not this blood-drenched madman, the bodies of his victims littered around me.

"It doesn't work," I whisper. "The gun."

Theo pulls the gun out of my arms, slow and cautious. I try to stop him, squeezing down on it, but it doesn't matter. He's too strong.

I expect him to point at me. Or to snap it in two and wrap his hand around my throat and kill me for real.

He doesn't, though. Instead, he racks the shell into place, the sound loud and terrible in the silence of the house.

He offers the gun back to me, his eyes on mine. They're like dry ice, so cold they burn right through me.

"Please," he signs one-handed, and I think I can feel his desperation. It has to be my imagination. "Please, I want it to be you. Just promise you'll keep him safe."

Oliver. I know he's talking about Oliver even though it feels absurd. Tears drip down my cheeks.

Theo presses the butt of the gun into my chest, and I reach up with shaking arms and take it, my breath ragged.

"The police will be here soon," he says. "Please, Chloe. I don't want it to be them. I want it to be you."

The movements of his hand leave an impression on the back of my eyes. *I want it to be you.*

"Why did you have to do this?" I whisper, my voice ragged from my tears.

"Because it's what I am." Theo directs the shotgun barrel to his chest so that it points right into his heart. "I know I've lost you. Just let it start over again. Please."

I sob again. The gun shifts sideways. Theo doesn't move.

"I never hurt you," he says. "I never hurt Oliver. And now it will stay that way."

I curl my finger around the trigger, my whole body shaking. The stink of blood is so heavy around us. I can't believe all the blood I've seen tonight. All the death. It's not like it is in my imagination.

Penelope warned me. I thought I knew what Theo is, but she actually understands. And she tried to tell me.

I suck in a breath, brace my back against the wall. Somewhere, off in the distance, police sirens wail.

Theo meets my gaze. His hands move. "I'm begging you, Chloe."

Behind him, Owen stares at us from the floor with dead and empty eyes. And I think, *That's my fault.*

I let this happen. All this death. All this blood. It's my fucking fault.

I scream through my rage, and as I scream, my finger compresses down, and an explosion erupts between me and the monster I almost let myself love.

CHLOE

Blood goes everywhere. Red, hot, stinking blood. It covers my face, my hands. It splatters across the walls. Theo flings backward and lands in a pile of limbs and flesh, a faint curl of grey smoke rising from the mangle of his chest.

I let out a loud, wordless wail. The gun drops out of my hands and lands with a clatter. The room tilts, and I stumble away from the wall, pressing my hands against the pale green walls.

Part of me wants to go to Theo. To pull his head into my lap, to check his pulse. I don't want him to be dead.

They come back.

I suck down deep, heaving breaths. I can't imagine him coming back from what I just did. He looks like meat.

I force myself down the hallway, my head spinning. Oliver. Theo said Oliver was safe. Was he lying? I need to know for sure.

The sirens are getting louder.

"Oliver," I rasp. I can barely hear myself. "Oliver!" I rasp again, louder. "Oliver! It's me!" There's a current of hysteria in my voice, and I hate that Oliver will probably hear it. "Please tell me you're still here!" I scream.

I stumble down the hallway, kicking open the doors until I come to a room that seems to be Oliver's: dinosaurs on the twin-sized bed, drawings taped all over the walls, a shelf of rocks in the corner. I sob again, because it's so normal, and we destroyed that normalcy. Me and Theo.

"Oliver," I call out weakly, and then I hear it. A sniffling from the closet.

I stumble toward it, hating that I'm leaving blood trails on the carpet, hating that any of this has happened. The closet door swings open before I get to it, though, and Oliver bursts out, his face pale and his eyes wide. There's not a drop of blood on him. Not a single mark.

He screams when he sees me.

"I'm fine," I say, trying to sign the words, too. My hands don't feel like they're working properly. "I'm not hurt."

"Theo?" He uses the special sign he made for him, and my chest squeezes tight. Theo's the one he asks about? Not his parents? His brother?

The sirens scream outside the windows. Red and blue light floods through the room, staining Oliver's face with color.

"Theo's gone," I say carefully.

Oliver looks at me.

And then he bursts into tears.

I don't know what to do. I'm dripping blood on the lush carpet. I don't know where it came from; I think it might be Theo's. Police are shouting at each other outside. And Oliver's weeping because I couldn't protect him from a monster.

Because you killed the monster he thought would protect him.

"It'll be okay," I lie, kneeling down to pull Oliver into an embrace. He squeezes tight around me, his little arms like a noose around my neck, and I cling to him because the only thing I know I can do right now is keep him here, away from the bodies of his family.

Away from the body of Theo Shorn.

Something thumps downstairs, followed by a shout of, "Police! Keep your hands in the air!"

"Come here," I whisper to Oliver, rising so I can step in front of him. He's still sobbing, the sound a worse knife in my chest than anything else that's happened. I lift my hands over my head. "In here!" I scream as loud as I can. "Upstairs!"

Voice spills from downstairs. So do shouts of horror and outrage. Footsteps echo on the stairs. "We're unarmed!" I shout. "I have a child with me!"

The footsteps slow. A shadow passes over the door. The police lights flash red and blue across the wall, over and over, as one of the officers steps inside, his gun raised. I tense, but he lowers it when he sees us.

"Jesus Christ," he mutters. "What happened?"

"A madman," I say, my voice shaky. I wish I could cover Oliver's ears. Wish I could protect him from all of this in a way Theo didn't see fit to do. "He's down the hall. He's—"

I can't say it. Oliver wails, and the cop drops his gaze to him, his expression dark. I squeeze Oliver tight around the shoulders.

"He's a ghost now."

CHLOE

SIX MONTHS LATER

"I really wish you'd just come stay with me."

I slump down in the Adirondack chair on my back patio, my feet pressed against the railing. It's warm and breezy for January, although it's supposed to turn cold later this week. I think I'm looking forward to it. The warmth reminds me too much of summer. Of that night.

"You can stop asking," I say numbly, watching the lake. "I'm staying."

Abi sighs, the sound tinny on my computer speaker. I've got her and Penelope both up on a Zoom call, my computer balanced on the little table beside my chair. These weekly Zoom calls were the only way I could get Penelope to leave my house about a month ago. She showed up two weeks after that night, her backpack slung over her shoulder and her eyes hard and glinting. *I'm not letting you stay in this house alone*, she said.

Now, though, I'm used to it, being alone.

"I have plenty of room," Abi continues. "Even with Rowan staying here. You know that."

Rowan. Rowan's her new boyfriend, and I know there's a story there, although Abi's keeping quiet about it. Honestly, she's been kind of strange ever since this summer, too, like she's keeping secrets. Penelope and I talked about it while she was here—probably in some attempt to distract me. But Penelope didn't seem to think she needed to drive down to Texas to stay with Abi like she did with me.

Granted, I haven't exactly been at my best since that awful fucking night in August.

"Dude, have you even looked at the weather forecast?" Penelope says now. I tear my eyes away from the lake to look at her face on the screen. "They're saying you're going to get snow."

"You think I can't handle snow?" I laugh mirthlessly.

Penelope rolls her eyes. "*You* can. But North Carolina can't. What if you lose power? You're completely isolated out there."

I don't say anything, mostly because I can't argue with her. Penelope saw it firsthand for the few months she stayed with me: the way, one by one, every single person who had a lake house the night of the Verity Hollow Murders has moved out. We went for walks down the road, and I could see her counting the new FOR SALE signs as they went up.

There are even more now, swinging disconsolately in the January wind. No one's buying. And why the fuck would they? The subdivision now shares its name with a fucking murder spree.

The Verity Hollow Murders. Another notch in Theo's axe handle, I guess, along with the Veritas Murders, the only other one of his sprees to get a name. I know because I keep looking them up, reading the names of all his victims, the way some people drag razor blades over their skin. Because I want to feel the hurt.

"Chloe?" Abi prompts. "What do you say? Just for a few days, to avoid the whole snowstorm situation."

"There's not going to be a snowstorm." I glance over at the computer screen, my two friends frowning into their respective cameras. "Maybe a dusting, at most."

Silence. I am almost certain that the two of them are messaging each other privately, trying to work out their next plan of attack. It's been like that since that night.

That's how I think of it. Not the Verity Hollow Murders, which sounds like something from a bad horror movie. That Night works so much better.

That Night Theo Shorn murdered five people and orphaned a child.

That Night I blew a hole through Theo Shorn's heart. Fair play, though, because he certainly blew a hole through mine.

As for Oliver—well, he didn't have anyone else, just like I guessed. Another social worker, a younger one, swept him up in the aftermath and sent him to live with a foster family that won't even let me text him.

"I'm tired of hearing about the weather," I say blandly.

"Chloe, we're just worried about you," Abi says. "We've *been* worried about you."

"I'm fine." I push out of the chair and lean up against the banister, staring across the water at the peninsula. Theo's territory. My skin gets a hot, itchy feeling, an agitation that's terrorized me since that night.

"At least promise you'll keep an eye on the weather reports," Abi says. "And keep me posted if you change your mind."

"Or I can come stay with you again," Penelope offers.

I look over at them again. Penelope studies me in the camera. Abi sighs.

"I don't need anyone to come to stay with me," I tell them. "But I'll watch the weather forecasts, okay?"

And then I snap the laptop shut.

I don't go back inside, though, just keep staring across the water at Theo's territory. Whenever I get like this, there's only one thing that makes the agitation go away, and that's dragging out Oliver's old boat from where I keep it stored in my garage and rowing across the water.

It's sick. I know it is. But I can't stop myself. I don't even know what I'm looking for whenever I do it.

I snatch up my laptop and stalk back inside, tossing it onto the couch as I make my way into the garage. My thoughts grind around, the way they always do after my weekly Zoom check-in. Jumping back to that hot, August night. To the days that followed. The hours I spent at the police station, telling my story over and over, like they were trying to catch me in a lie. The time I spent on the phone with Oliver's social worker, an overworked woman named Sofia who would assure me, with the patience of a schoolteacher, that he was fine.

We just want things to be normal for him, she kept saying. *For him to settle in with his foster family.*

I drag the rowboat down to the lakeshore, my heart thumping furiously in my chest. The sun beats down on me, winter-pale but uncomfortably warm. The overgrown azaleas over at one of the empty houses nearby are starting to bloom early, blotches of bright pink that stand out against the yellow grass of the yard.

I drop the boat into the water and push out onto the lake. Despite the warmth, it's quiet out here. Of course it is. I'm the only person living on the lakefront anymore. The other families that managed to escape Theo's axe—

He goes door to door. He doesn't want us here.

—All packed their shit and fled the second they could. I

assume they're rich enough to keep paying for a lake house and afford rent or another mortgage.

I'm not.

At least, that's my excuse. It's a shitty one; Abi and my mom have both begged me to come stay with them, rent-free, until I can offload the property. Penelope, when she was staying here, even tentatively suggested we go live with her sister.

I told them no.

That's all I tell anyone these days. No, I don't want company. No, I don't want to leave for a weekend visit. No, I'm not having a nervous breakdown because I discovered five dead bodies and shot their killer, the man I had been fucking, with a shotgun.

Oliver's rowboat slices cleanly through the water and then runs aground on the peninsula's dirt-packed beach. For a second, I sit there, the warm breeze tousling my hair. I can't imagine snow falling in this place, even though the weather forecasts are all in a panic about it.

I've never been afraid of snow, though. I'm certainly not afraid of snow in North Carolina.

I walk along the narrow, overgrown path leading to the cemetery, breathing in the scent of the poplar trees. Already, my agitation is starting to slip away, although I still get a prickle on the back of my neck, like Theo really is the ghost that Oliver thought he was, and that he's watching me through the shadows.

That prickle intensifies when I step into the graveyard. Theo's old gravestone juts up, the winter having killed off the overgrown grass.

You're waiting for him, aren't you?

Penelope said that to me when the two of us came to the peninsula while she was staying with me. She said it in this graveyard, in fact, while I was staring down at his gravestone, my thoughts numb.

I denied it, vehemently. *No, of course not. Are you fucking crazy?*

A lie. And Penelope knew it, too, because she put her hand on my shoulder, and explained how it works in a soft, even voice. How when a Hunter dies, they're supposed to bury themselves in the ground because that helps them come back faster, and that's why Theo's body disappeared the way it did.

Because they did lose the body, the cops. Somehow in the chaos after the murders, as Oliver and I were wrapped in silver blankets and swept off to the Pinella hospital, Theo vanished. The cops told me about it when I had to speak to them the day after, their voices stern and hard. I was in a witness room, surrounded by stuffed animals, but there was still a sharpness in their tone that suggested I might have done something wrong.

Are you sure you killed him? This Theo Shorn?

The blood had pumped in my ears as I stared at the detective, a craggy-faced man with five o'clock stubble across his chin. His gaze kept flicking suspiciously to my neck, the bruises there already turning yellow.

I felt like I was on the verge of tears, but my eyes were dry. Too dry, almost.

He's going to come back, Penelope said to me that afternoon, the sunlight already starting to feel like autumn. *But you shouldn't be here when he does.*

I rub my arms like I can rub the memories away. They always hit me all at once like that, braided together, and the onslaught makes my heart feel heavy in my chest.

Still, I wonder where Theo is. If he really did bury himself, like Penelope said. Sometimes at night, I imagine Theo, still with the ruin I made of his heart, dragging himself out of the Jenkins house, so slowly that the cops never notice until he's gone. I imagine him sinking into the wet mud and then getting pulled into the lake, deep in the sediment and river weeds, a corpse that's not a corpse rolling across the sludge until he finally washes ashore.

I've never seen his body, though, so I don't think it happened that way.

I leave the graveyard, following my usual hiking trail up to his cabin. It looks as it always does, when everything gets to be too much and picking my way through the overgrown woods to stand in this spot is the only thing that makes me feel calm. It looks abandoned.

It *is* abandoned, the porch still wrapped with yellow caution tape from when the cops searched the house. That was the second time I got called out to the sheriff's department, after they found some of Oliver's drawings taped to Theo's wall. Drawings of me. They told me about them with solemn, concerned faces, how they found them along with a cache of bladed weapons, similar to the axe Theo used to destroy Oliver's family.

That second interview, that was when I knew the cops didn't suspect me of anything anymore. They told me I was lucky to be alive, that he was almost certainly planning to kill me, or worse. I did not ask them to explain what their idea of "worse" was.

Those drawings are in police custody now, of course, along with his weapons. I haven't bothered going inside the house. I just come here and look at it, my arms wrapped around my chest, watching it slowly rot away into the woods, its sagging porch covered with dead leaves.

CHLOE

The weather turns fast. I wake up on a Thursday to an unexpected chill in the house, and I turn the heater back on and settle into work again. By mid-afternoon, the wind starts howling, a long, sweeping moan that rattles the northern side of my house.

"Well, shit," I say out loud.

I'm supposed to be working, although I haven't been concentrating on it, just have the work chat pulled up on my laptop as I stare at the database, text and numbers blurring together. Honestly, I hope the power does go out. They can't make me work if I don't have Internet.

The wind batters against the picture window, although I can't see much of anything with the curtains drawn. I pick up my phone and discover that my weather app's icon has turned into a big snowflake.

There's a text from Abi, too.

> Just checking in! Did you get the wood I had sent over? The snowstorm's supposed to hit today!

I set both my phone and my laptop aside and pull back the curtains on the picture window. To my genuine surprise, it is, in fact, snowing. And not a dusting, either: the air is full of the kind of thick, fluffy white flakes that I've always loved. In Boston, I would go for walks in snow like this, bundling up so the flakes stuck to my jacket like white confetti and melted into water when I came back into the heat.

But I don't feel anything, looking at the snow now. It looks like static above the lake, and Theo's peninsula is fuzzy in the distance, wreathed in a soft white glow. I breathe out, fogging the glass.

I wonder if it's snowing where Oliver is.

The thought hits harder than I expect, and I yank away from the window, letting the curtain fall back into place. Sofia the social worker wouldn't even tell me what city he's in, although she did say he's still in the state. *We just want what's best for him. I think we can all agree on that, Ms. Monroe?*

Agitation works under my skin, but even I'm not feeling self-destructive enough to cross the lake in this weather. I was self-destructive enough not to do anything to really prepare, though, although Abi did in fact order a bunch of fire logs on my behalf, which were delivered yesterday. I had been annoyed at the time, although I'm feeling grateful for it now.

I should be okay on food. Cooking hasn't exactly been a priority the last six months, so my pantry is already full of canned soup and boxed mac-and-cheese, and my oven runs on gas in case the power goes out. I suppose I could go fill up the bathtubs in the spare bathrooms, just in case. It's not like I use them for anything anyway.

Blankets. I should pull the various blankets and quilts my grandmother left behind.

My laptop dings with a work notification, which I ignore. The snow howls and swirls outside. And I start to work through the things you're supposed to do when there's a snowstorm. Methodically. Numbly, which is how I've done everything since that night in August.

After all, numbness is the only thing I really feel these days.

I JAR AWAKE, my muscles rigid.

My first thought is Theo, the way it always is when I wake up suddenly in the middle of the night, even all these months later. Theo coming to fuck me, Theo slaughtering my neighbors—it could go either way.

This time, however, I realize quickly enough that Theo has nothing to do with it. The house is dead silent, my ceiling fan unmoving.

The power went out.

I slump down and snuggle deeper into my blanket. Fuck. Abi and Penelope are never going to let me hear the end of this.

I find it hard to fall back asleep. Even when I curl up under the blankets and close my eyes, a simmering anxiety puts my whole body on a high alert. My bed might feel warm now, but it's not going to stay that way. My thoughts wind around in long, complicated patterns, repeating the same things they always do. Replaying what happened that night. Theo's shaking hands begging me to kill him. Oliver's sobs. The red and blue lights.

It's worse tonight. Worse than it's been since before Penelope came to stay with me. Everything feels bright and vivid, like it just happened.

Eventually, I manage to doze off, my winding thoughts bleeding into something like a dream: Theo's corpse dragging across the floorboards like a worm. Me swimming across Hanging Lake to the peninsula, the water frigid. A hand wrapping around my ankle, warmer than anything else.

When I open my eyes, my room is flooded with grey-white light, and my nose is stiff with cold. My phone says it's nearly nine in the morning. I guess I really did fall asleep.

I drag myself out of bed and start working through the things you're supposed to do when this happens: pulling on layers of clothes, starting a fire in the fireplace, closing off all the rooms to trap the heat in my living room, which suddenly feels much too big. I push back the curtains just enough to look outside, and my breath catches in my chest. I've spent so much time staring out at this view in particular: the patio, the pier, the trees across the lake. And now they look alien and unfamiliar, buried beneath a thick layer of snow and ice. For a moment, all I can do is stare at it, my breath warming the glass.

I wonder about Theo, if he'll freeze beneath the ground.

Then I wonder about Oliver, if he's seeing all this snow. Wherever he is in North Carolina, I hope his house didn't lose power, that he's being allowed to sled and build a snowman and throw snowballs, and that, just for a few hours, he can forget what Theo did to him, and what I allowed to happen.

I make a bowl of instant oatmeal, grateful again that I have a gas stove, and then wrap myself in blankets in front of the fireplace, watching the logs crackle and collapse and turn to embers.

It's not so bad at first, being without power. I text Penelope and Abi, tell them I'm okay. Their responses are predictable.

ABI

Keep us posted, okay? And don't forget to move around! It'll help warm you up.

PENELOPE

Told you so.

Then, five minutes later:

Bet I could make my way out there if you
really needed me, though.

I sigh at that, tap out a response.

I'll be fine.

My hands are already cold just from getting that much out. I tell myself I'll text my mom later.

Since I can't work without power, I flip through the stack of old paperbacks I found shoved into the spare room when I first moved in—a bunch of Westerns and bodice rippers from the '70s, the pages yellowed and thin as cellophane. When it's time to eat, I heat up a can of soup.

Honestly, things aren't that different from how they normally are. Just colder.

A lot colder.

It pains me to put the fire out that night, but I know better than to go to sleep with it still crackling in the fireplace, even behind the mesh screen. Once it's out, the cold suddenly seems to flood in, seeping through my clothes and layers of blankets and distilling straight down into the marrow of my bones. I curl up on my couch, facing the dark, scorched fireplace. I manage to sleep a little. When I dream, it's about death. Not the hot, crimson death that Theo brought, but what comes after. The absence of heat. The cold and the dark. The emptiness.

The next day is the same. I wake up to my breath frosting in the air, great white clouds of steam puffing up toward my ceiling. It's incongruous, seeing it inside. My hands shake as I build the fire, but it seems to take longer for its heat to permeate the room. I feel like I can't stop shivering, my whole body vibrating even though I'm wrapped in layers of blankets.

I think of Abi's advice: *Don't forget to move around!* So I do, first exploring the house, testing each room to see how cold they've gotten. The answer, to my dismay, is a lot.

Then I venture outside, my old snow boots from Boston sinking into the snow piled up on my patio. There's not so much. Maybe three or four inches.

Somehow, the cold isn't as bitter outside, I suppose because I expect it out here. The wind is harsh, though, sharp and slicing, and it picks up flurries of loose snow and blows them around in little glittery tornadoes. I pick my way down to the lake, which still isn't anywhere close to iced over; there's too much movement, too much depth. The water looks black against the grey and white of the snow, though, surging like frost-tipped ichor.

Since I can't cross the lake, I walk over to the Jenkins' house. I don't know why. Punishing myself, probably. Whoever owns it now didn't even bother trying to make it look nice. They just boarded over the windows with big pieces of plywood and let the yard grow wild and straggly. The snow covers all that up, though. Even the plywood looks pretty, decorated with frost.

My breath puffs in the air, the only sound for miles. Like I'm the only living thing for miles.

I probably am.

When I go back inside, my phone is littered with alerts: another round of snow is on its way. *Up to a foot expected,* reads the headlines. *Prepare for blizzard conditions beginning around four PM.*

A dark, sick despair tugs at the pit of my stomach. Blizzard conditions? How is this happening here, in fucking

North Carolina? It's worse than what the meteorologists were predicting, at least earlier this week.

Maybe I should have gone to stay with Abi, even if the idea of leaving my house for an extended period of time makes me feel strange.

So I build the fire up higher than is strictly safe. I try to read the old pulp paperbacks, my eyes skimming over the words. I pull the blankets tighter around my shoulders.

And I wait for the storm to hit.

33

THEO

Reviving always feels like an electric shock. Death contracts like sleep does; I drift in and out of a kind of half-consciousness, only vaguely aware of the thick rot of the soil around me. But the moment of revival is bright and zapping, all my atoms firing up at once.

I plunge my arms up through the soil, clawing and digging my way to the surface. There's a hot, panicked instinct to it, a sense that I'm being buried alive. My wits aren't all about me yet. All I can focus on is air and—

And *her.*

I see her face, smiling up at me in the shadows and the firelight. Then I see her screaming at me, tears streaming over her cheeks, blood on her clothes. *Why did you do this?*

Dirt spills into my mouth, cold and steely. I spit and dig, pushing myself upward. I know she's not going to be waiting for me on the surface. No one is. I did what the killing moon calls me to do, which is drive all the humans away until I'm alone in my territory.

My fist plunges into something bright and unexpected. For a second, I think it's fire, because it burns at my skin. But

I keep squirming my way upward, and I realize that no, it's the opposite. Not burning, but freezing.

I escape the dirt only to suck down a mouthful of cold, white crystals that turn to water on my tongue. By the time I heave myself out of the ground, my hands are screaming from the cold, and all I can see is a sweeping expanse of white that glitters like diamonds.

I blink at it, my thoughts still blurry from the revival. *Heaven*, I think stupidly, squinting against the light. Like the cold, it's so bright that it burns. But it can't be Heaven, because there's no place in Heaven for a monster like me.

The closest I came was her. Chloe. The way she would cling to me as I sank into her warm, squeezing cunt. The sound of her blood rushing in her veins and her moans escaping her plump, swollen lips. But I'm not good enough for that Heaven, either.

I roll onto my back, breathing hard. Overhead, the sky is a pale, feathery grey, suffused with a soft, pale glow. It appears to be falling as well, dropping in soft, ashy flakes that look like stars. A freezing dampness burns through my ragged, blood-stained clothes.

Snow, I realize with a jolt. It's snowing.

I sit up, my heart thudding, and twist around, trying to get my bearings. More memories come to me, sudden and painful: the unblinking eye of a shotgun barrel, the resistance as I racked back the pump to load in a fresh shell. The shell that killed me.

I want it to be you.

I squeeze my eyes shut, a sudden wave of sadness welling up in my chest. At the moment, I did want it to be her. I had done my work. I split open the humans who hurt me.

No, they hadn't hurt me this time. Not her, either. The boy. The boy who reminded me of myself.

His face flashes in my thoughts, his big eyes staring up at

me, at the blood on my shirt. His parents' blood. I had killed them already, although he didn't know.

Hide in your closet, I told him, my hands quick and darting, *and wait for Chloe. Don't come out until she says it's safe.*

That had been so important to me, him hiding. Him not seeing what I had done, what I was about to do.

I drag myself up until I'm standing on uncertain, newly revived legs and turn slowly in place. I'm on the wrong side of Hanging Lake. Houses rise on either side of me, but they feel empty. I don't know if the snow is muffling things or not. It's falling more thickly now, adding a pale haze to everything. I'm not used to it, all this silence around the lake. It's like the whole world is trapped in a half-death.

I trudge toward the house, my boots sinking into the snow. I'm leaving tracks, which can't be good. Not for a predator.

No. It doesn't matter. No one's here. I don't sense any human heartbeats.

The house's windows are boarded up. I stare up at it for a few seconds, trying to remember why it's familiar. Is this her house? Chloe's?

No. It's the house where I died. It's Oliver's house.

I keep shuffling around to the back porch. No one's been here for a long time. The scent of humans isn't muffled by the snow; it's just faded.

More memories, this time after I died. The sense of being moved, jostled into a body bag. Male voices. Even in that half-state, I was still worried about them, the woman and the little boy—

Chloe and Oliver.

Something sweet and lush blooms in the air. I stop and sniff, trying to track it through the odd, icy scent of the snow. It's her scent, and just for a second, when the wind shifted, it seemed fresh.

An excitement stirs in my chest. Maybe she didn't leave.

The wind gusts again, but her scent—if that's what it really was—is gone. The snow is falling so heavily now that it feels like a curtain closing in around me. I swipe through it, trying to clear my way through. But the snow is blinding me. Not just visually, although it's certainly doing that as well: I can only really make out the dark shapes of the houses standing sentinel along the lake. The water and my territory beyond it are completely lost behind a veil of snow.

But the cold seems to impair my other senses, too. All I can hear is the howling, mournful wind. And all I can smell is water. The lake, the snow, some freezing condensation in the air. It clings to my face and makes my skin burn.

I stumble forward, moving on some half-remembered bodily instinct.

If this is where Oliver lives, then *she* lives just a few yards away.

I don't know if she'll still be there. I didn't expect her to stay when I went into the ground. Right before I died, I memorized her tearful, blood-streaked face because I knew that moment would be the last time I'd ever get to see her. And when she squeezed the trigger and the pain tore through my chest, I held onto that image of her face. I didn't let it go as I drifted in the void, dead but not dead, slowly recovering in the dirt.

So why do I swear I can smell her?

I push through the whipping, furious snow, my head tucked down, bare arms wrapped around my chest. The cold is astonishing. Even when I was up in New York, I don't remember feeling cold like this.

Maybe I only smell her because I'm about to die again. Wouldn't that be something, to revive after a shotgun blast to the heart only to freeze to death moments later?

We're stronger than humans. We can survive a lot more.

But this cold is slicing me to ribbons, each snowflake burning an imprint of itself on my skin. Ice coats my hair and the tattered remains of my shirt. The wind sounds like humans whenever they encounter death, a long and constant wail.

I keep walking through the storm, though, my teeth chattering in my skull. Because sometimes I catch it, her scent on the wind. It's probably my imagination.

But it's the only compass I have in all this white.

34

CHLOE

I gasp awake, my dreams condensing in the air in front of me. I was dreaming about Theo again. I had been in the dark, shivery lake, and he was swimming toward me, as sleek and dangerous as a shark.

I pull the blankets tighter around my shoulders, blinking my surroundings back into focus. There's the crackle and pop of the fire off to my left—I dozed off on the couch. At least the fire is still contained in the fireplace, the flames low and licking at its brick walls.

Outside, the wind howls wildly, louder even than it did when the storm first blew in. Snow plinks against the glass of the windows with an arrhythmic chiming.

"Fuck," I whisper, shivering inside my blanket. I force myself to stand up, to move around. The fire's heat beats back some of the cold, although not much; I move closer to it and breathe in the scent of smoke.

Something thumps outside.

My heart jolts, and I whip my head over to the windows, still covered by the heavy curtains. I listen. The wind screams around the house. The snow batters the glass. I don't hear anything else.

"Probably just a tree branch," I murmur, finding some comfort in the sound of my own voice. But the thought invokes a new fear: this wind is fierce, and what if it's strong enough that a tree branch falls through my window? It's a possibility I hadn't even considered.

Anxiety tightens in a knot in my stomach. I stumble toward the window, my steps shaky from my constant shivering. "Just a tree branch," I whisper, and the wind answers with a long, mournful howl.

I push the curtain back.

The sight outside is astonishing. The forecast wasn't lying about the blizzard conditions—this is a true white-out, the sort of thing I experienced a couple of times up in Boston, although always from the comfort of a cozy apartment with a working radiator. There are no radiators in North Carolina, not that it even matters without power.

I drag the curtain further aside and stare out at the whipping frenzy of snow. My porch is only barely visible through the static, and every now and then, I see a flash of the lake. But nothing else, and already snow is piling up in a drift against the window.

I pull the blanket tighter around my shoulders. It's colder here, the wind seeping through the glass. I need to get back to the fire. I need to—

Something moves in the white-out.

I freeze, staring out at the blizzard. Nothing.

It must have been my imagination. Or maybe the lake, surging through the snow.

But then I see it again: another faint flicker of movement. A dark shadow, like a bird flapping its way through the storm.

There can't possibly be any birds out here.

I squeeze my blanket tight. Fear prickles in my belly.

The shadow shambles closer. And I realize, no, it's not a bird at all.

It's a man.

It's *him*.

I jerk back from the window, my heart pounding furiously. But I don't close the curtain, and I can still see him, standing there on the edge of my yard, the wind whipping his frost-coated hair into his eyes. He's wearing the same shirt he wore the night I killed him, although it's turned to rags now, revealing the smooth, unbroken skin of his chest. There's no sign of the terrible, gaping hole where his heart should be.

He lifts his face, and I think he sees me.

I shriek again and stumble back toward the fire, never taking my eyes off the window. Outside, he moves closer, each step slow and heavy. My breath comes out in short, frantic breaths. My phone. Where's my phone?

And what am I going to do with it? What does it matter if I call someone in the middle of a blizzard? Theo Shorn is here now.

He steps up onto my porch, his footsteps heavy and loud even over the wailing wind. He moves like a zombie, slow and shambling, and it occurs to me that's what he is. Because I killed him.

I knew he would come back eventually. Maybe I've even been waiting for him, a truth Penelope saw that I didn't want to admit. But now, seeing him—

Confusion wars in my thoughts. Anger, fear.

Relief.

He steps up to the door and peers through the glass. I don't know if he sees me. All he does is stare inside, his snow-covered hair hanging in his eyes.

I watch him, my whole body shaking. From fear or cold, I don't know.

He put his hand on the window, his body heat melting the ice crawling across the glass. And something inside me snaps. The last string of my willpower. All I can think about is how warm he was when he had his big arms wrapped around me.

The cold has made me stupid. Or desperate. Or both.

I let the blanket fall to the floor. The adrenaline has warmed me up enough that it almost feels uncomfortable, and there's a thin layer of clammy sweat on my skin that I know, distantly, is dangerous.

Just like he is.

I cross the room again, aware of Theo's eyes following my movement. When I get to the door, I stop, staring at him through the glass. He doesn't do anything. Doesn't say anything. His eyes just bore into me, as bright as stars.

I turn the deadbolt with shaking hands. He pushes the door open.

The gust of wind that slams inside is shocking. It blows my hair back and brings a swirl of glittering white snow that scatters across the floor like spilled sugar. When Theo steps inside, it melts beneath his boots.

He slams the door shut and stares at me. I don't know what to say to him. All the speeches I planned over the past six months—excoriating him for what he did to Oliver, for what he did to me—fly out of my thoughts. There's only cold and dark and silence.

Theo lifts his hand, the skin red and chapped from the cold. "Are you real?" he signs.

"Of course I'm real." The words fly out of my mouth, harsher than I intend. "Are you?"

He blinks. Pushes his hair out of his eyes. There's dirt all over his shredded, rotting clothes, dirt and old blood, and as the snow melts around him, it turns to sludge on the floor.

"I thought you'd be gone."

I suck in a breath, my body shaking.

"Everyone else is gone," he continues, his hands moving slowly. "That's what always happens after a kill-moon."

I blink, uncertain if I saw that correctly. He said the same thing that night: the sign for *kill*, the sign for *moon*, melded together in a way that suggests they're meant to connect. It makes my head vibrate, and I think of the moonlight that night, bright and silver as I ran across the yards. The moon had been full. I'll never forget it.

Theo stares at me, waiting for an answer.

"I didn't have a choice." The words come out hard and flinty. "I can't afford to leave."

Theo's shoulders slump a little, and I don't know how to read his face. He almost looks disappointed. Anger surges up in me.

"You thought I was waiting for you?" I snap. Never mind that part of me was. "After what you did?" My voice trembles. "To me? To *Oliver?*"

"I didn't do anything to Oliver."

"You killed his fucking family!" This erupts out of me in a scream, and I wrap my arms around myself, even though my anger is keeping me warm. "He's in foster care! They won't even let me speak to him, so I don't even know how he's—" Tears brim on my eyelashes. "How badly you fucked him up," I snarl.

Theo blanches like I slapped him. "He didn't see anything," he signs. "I made sure of that."

"It doesn't matter! He was there!" My voice bounces off the cold, shivering air of the living room. "How could you do that?" I scream, and then I launch myself at him, rage burning like a fire through my body. I want to slam my fist into his big chest, to pummel the place where I shot him, but Theo grabs me by the waist and whips me around and throws me onto the couch.

"His family hurt him," Theo signs, anger darkening his own features. "They didn't care about him." His eyes blaze in the darkness, and the crackling firelight wraps him in an eerie orange glow. "He wanted me to protect him! Why do you think he came looking for me?"

"Not like that!" I jump to my feet, and Theo pushes me down again. Only this time, he straddles me, wedging me against the couch with his thick body.

I was right. He is warm.

Theo leans in close, his face inches from mine. I can smell him, the earthy scent of juniper and pine and cold soil, and I hate my body for flushing with a sudden warmth.

I take a shuddering breath. "He didn't want you to kill—"

"What if he did?" Theo signs the question simply. "What if he wanted to come live with—" His fingers twist *us* to *me*, so quickly I'm not sure if I really saw it.

I breathe heavily, staring up at him. He's dripping cold snowmelt all over me, all over my couch, and I want to scream at him for that, too.

"You're lying," I whisper. "Oliver didn't want that."

"Oliver wanted a protector," Theo says, "And that's what I was."

I slap him, my arm springing up on its own accord. The sound it makes is like the blast of the shotgun I used to kill him, and my hand burns from the impact.

Theo doesn't move.

"Is that what you want?" he asks. "Hurt me, if it makes you feel better."

I screech out my anger and slap him again, harder. He growls softly, and the sound bores into my chest. A traitorous heat floods through my core.

Then I start hitting him in earnest, slamming my fists into his strong, unscarred chest, raining down six months' worth of sorrow and despair upon his hot, bracing body. And he lets me. He even drags me up by the waist until we're standing in front of the couch, like he wants me to hit him harder.

And I do. I slap and punch at him, screeching through my hot, desperate tears. He doesn't try to stop me. He certainly doesn't try to fight back.

I know I'm not hurting him. I *can't* hurt him, not like this. He isn't human. But god, it feels good, all that pent-up anger pouring out of me.

"Why did you do it?" I scream, the word turning to steam in the frozen air. "Why couldn't things stay how they were?"

That question is what finally makes Theo act. His hand lashes out and catches my wrist before I can strike his face again, and his eyes burn as he drinks me. I breathe, staring at him, tears streaming hotly down my face.

"You think I didn't want that too?" he signs.

I let out a single, choking sob. And then I collapse into him, pressing my face into his cold, wet, filthy shirt, weeping out into his chest. He wraps his arms around me and holds me up against him, and I don't want him to let me go. I wanted so badly to hate him these past six months. And I did, sometimes. But right now, I'm cold and hungry and lonely, and he's so much warmer than the fire.

Theo's hand smooths over my hair and then wraps, tentatively, around my throat. I jerk back, meet his gaze. My pulse flutters, and I know he feels it, the way he presses his palm harder against the side of my neck.

"I didn't want to kill you," I whisper through my tears.

With his free hand, he signs, "I didn't want to die."

And then he pulls me up to him by my throat, his mouth crashing into mine in a fury of tongue and teeth. I scream into the kiss, and it feels like all my anger and sorrow have transmuted suddenly into a hot, baking lust. I tear at the filthy rags of his clothes until they disintegrate in my hands to reveal the hot planes of his flesh underneath. Then I claw at his skin, too, like I'm trying to dig out his new heart.

He growls and hurls me down onto the sofa. Then he pulls at my clothes, all those layers that were supposed to keep me warm. And I help him. I claw them away, throw them across the room, until we're both naked, the firelight staining our bodies red while the cold air frosts over our skin.

Theo gazes down at me, drinking me in with bright, burning eyes. And I can't take my gaze off him, either: his strong, muscular chest, the taper of his soft belly.

His cock, swollen and straining and already gleaming at the tip. My pussy aches, seeing it.

Theo reaches down and wrenches my legs apart, exposing my dripping pussy to the cold air. I buck against him, but he pushes his weight down on my thighs, pinning me in place. Even though his hands are currently occupied, the message is clear:

He's going to fuck me.

I lift my chin, baring my throat to him. He growls and falls on me, catching my neck between his teeth right before she slams his cock into my cunt.

I scream at the painful, violating stretch of him, and then I scream again as he jackhammers against my hips, his teeth sinking even deeper into my neck. I fuck him back like I'm trying to buck him off, like I'm trying to fight him. Maybe I am. I honestly can't tell the difference, not right now. It hurts, how rough he is, but it sends hot pulsing pleasure up my spine, too. Because here's the real truth of things:

Every time I hated him in the past six months, it wasn't because of the five people he killed. It was because he killed five people and then abandoned me to drown in the blood he left behind.

Theo releases my throat and kisses me, his thrusts melting into a slow, agonizing roll of his hips. It feels good. But it's not what I need.

Especially when I taste my blood on his lips.

So I wrench my head away from him, breaking the kiss, and snarl, "More" in a voice that I hardly recognize as my own.

Theo makes an animalistic sound in the back of his throat and then bites me again, this time in the shoulder, his teeth tearing down into my skin. I scream at the pain, but I also know it's an acknowledgement.

"Harder," I rasp, grinding my hips up against him. His slow, teasing thrusts aren't good enough. "And don't you dare fucking stop."

And to his credit, he listens, slamming his cock up against my cervix until it almost feels like I'm dying.

35

THEO

I had not realized how much I needed Chloe until I'm inside her, the heat of her cunt the first warmth I've felt since the shotgun shell tore through my heart.

And once I'm inside her, I don't want to leave.

There's always this primal hunger inside me after I revive, and I usually expend it with a quick, easy kill. If I don't come from the killing, I'll stroke myself off afterward.

This is different, though.

Today, Chloe is spread out on the couch beneath me, her skin flushed and golden in the firelight, blood blooming on her neck and my teeth marks implanted in her shoulder. I slam myself into her, barely able to control my movements, and with each thrust, her whole body shakes in a way that sends fire surging up my cock. I grab her by both wrists and pin them above her head one-handed as I plow into her hot, drenched pussy.

She hasn't come yet. I know that. I can feel it, the pulsing heat building in her clit. But fuck, I'm not going to last much longer. Not with her staring up at me with those angry, lust-drunk eyes. Not with the taste of her blood on my lips.

I crush her wrists together, and she makes a pained, ecstatic sound and clenches her pussy around my cock. Milking it. Milking me.

I clench my jaw and try to focus on the cold, on the howling wind, on anything else.

It's no use, though. My orgasm tears up from my belly, and I roar as my cum pulses into her, ropes and ropes of it after being dead for six months.

"Did you just come?" Chloe shrieks, jerking her hands away from me. I let her go. "What the fuck?"

I barely hear her, the way my pleasure reverberates up my spine. She hits me again, and I catch her wrist and glower down at her through my wet hair as she keeps squirming against me, fucking my softening cock.

It won't be soft for long, though. I just revived, and I know exactly what will get me hard again.

I latch my teeth into her neck, probing my tongue at the cuts I made earlier until her blood flows out. Chloe shrieks and pants and ruts against me, and I moan around the salty tang of her blood.

"Fuck," she whispers, her breath shuddery. "Fuck, I'm so close. I'm—"

I rear back, dragging my cock out of her pussy in the process. Chloe screeches and slaps her hand down on her clit, but I grab her by the wrist and shake my head. She glares at me, and I can feel it, her anger and her lust and her confusion and her fear, all twining together.

Then I guide her hand to my dick, wrapping her fingers around my still-sensitive skin. She gives a little gasp; I'm already hardening up for her again.

"Jerk me off," I sign, moving forward until I'm straddling her at the waist.

She does, squeezing my shaft hard in her fist like she wants to make me hurt. I buck into her hand, staring down at her the whole time. *Don't you dare fucking stop*, she screamed at me right before I came. I don't intend to.

Especially with that first orgasm out of the way. This next one, it'll take much longer for me to build up to it.

"How are you hard again already?" she whispers, her palm making a wet thwapping sound around my dick.

I grin. "I'm a Hunter."

Then I pull away from her so I can flip her over onto her hands and knees. I shove her head down, pressing into the cushion so her ass lifts up for me, revealing the wet, pink slit of her cunt and the pretty bud of her ass. I slide my fingers along her clit, making her shudder and quake. I bring my other hand down hard on her ass cheek, the sound cracking through the room.

"Fuck!" she shouts, lifting her head. I shove it back down into the sofa and slap her again, harder. Hard enough to leave the red imprint of my hand against her skin.

She moans into the pillows, tries to snake her hand down to her clit. I stop her. Spank her again, this time right on her pussy.

She howls. Her arousal and my cum drips down her thighs, gleaming in the firelight. It might be cold in her house, but her skin is damp with sweat. Flushed with heat.

I slide into her again, moaning as her desperate pussy clenches down on me. Then I thread my fingers through her hair and jerk her head back, bracing myself against her as I start to fuck her with slow, teasing strokes.

"Harder!" she screams.

I respond by yanking her back by the hair. She shrieks, and I taste the surge of her adrenaline. I pull her closer to me, closer enough that I can wrap my other hand around her throat. When she swallows, I can feel the movement against my palm.

Then I fuck her again, the way she wants. Hard, fast,

brutal. I hold her in place by the neck, although I don't squeeze the air out of her. Not today. I don't want to tempt death.

Chloe moans, shoving herself back and forth on my cock until we lock into a frantic rhythm. I focus my attention on her quickly building orgasm, angling my cock so I know I'm striking the right place inside her.

"Fuck," she pants, and I can feel the word against my hand, too. "Fuck. Fuck. Fuck."

I squeeze her a little tighter. Pull her hair a little harder.

"Fuuuuuck," she whines. Her body quivers. Clenches.

And then she comes, all her muscles contracting down around my cock. Chloe screams, and I let her go so she can slump forward while I keep fucking her through her orgasm, my fingers digging hard into her hips. She pushes back on me, her muscles flexing in my hands.

Then she flips up her hair, twisting around to look at me through the tangle of her hair. Her eyes blaze, and I love it: her anger, her fury, her desire.

"You left me," she snarls.

With one hand, I manage to sign, "I had to."

"No, you didn't!" She jerks away from me, dragging me out of her hot, perfect cunt. I growl in protest, try to pull her back. Not with all my Hunter's strength, though. Part of me wants to see what she does next. I can, after all, still feel her pounding lust.

Chloe twists around on the couch and slaps me hard on the chest, like she's trying to shove me back. I grin at her.

"You think that's enough to hurt me?" I say, and she screeches in vexation—

Right before she slashes at me with her nails.

That, I do feel: a pleasant, burning sting on my skin. I grin at her, feeling all my wickedness come to the surface, and try to grab at her again.

She shoves me with all her strength and knocks me onto her floor in front of the fire, on top of the mound of blankets that are piled up there. I don't move, just lie on my back staring at her as she rises from the sofa like some vengeful goddess, all the lushness of her body glowing in the firelight. My cock throbs, gleaming against my stomach.

Chloe stalks toward me and straddles my waist, grabbing my cock with a forcefulness that makes me grunt.

"You left me," she whispers, batting my cock against her clit. "You fucking left me alone."

She slaps herself harder, and my cockhead screams at the impact.

"You made me kill you," she pants, and the blend of emotions I feel from her is exquisite. She's turned on, talking about this. Angry and turned on. I buck my hips up, trying to catch her cunt. She squeezes my cock in warning.

"Why me?" she whispers, leaning in close to my face, her breasts brushing against my chest. Her eyes blaze angrily. "Why did it have to be me?"

She's still holding my cock in her fist, like she might tear it out if I give the wrong answer. But she's drenched in desire, too.

I slide my hands up between us, wait until I know she's looking at them.

"Because there's nothing more intimate than killing," I tell her.

Chloe stares at me, her chest heaving, her hair falling around her shoulders to hide the marks I made on her skin. At first, I'm not sure if she understands. Explaining what it's like, the intimacy of death, of wearing another person's blood on your skin, would take so many more words than what I have. But she's experienced it now. She gave me that gift.

And then I feel it, her realization. Her blood starts rushing. Her eyes widen. Her cunt gets even hotter.

"That feeling?" I say, my hands shaking. "I don't want to share it with anyone else."

Chloe's lips part and her eyes gleam. Beside us, one of the logs in the fire collapses, and the sparks and the ash drift into the air.

And then she sinks her drenched pussy back down on my cock.

She sighs as she pulls me into her, throwing her head back and grinding against my cock like she's dragging me up inside her cunt to trap me there. I'd let her, honestly. After six months in the ground, this is all I want—to lie down on the floor while Chloe pleasures herself on my dick, the firelight flickering along her skin. She fucks me hard, almost as hard as I fucked her, bouncing up and down on my cock with enough force that my hips ache. I don't care. I'm too mesmerized by the sight of her tits shaking as she rides me, at the dark spot of blood on her throat from where I bit her. I lick my lips and swear I can taste the salt of it again.

"You left me," she pants, squeezing her pussy down tight around my cock. "You fucking left me."

I run my hands up her thighs, the muscles taut with exertion. Chloe groans and then drops her head down, her eyes meeting mine, her body quivering. There's an accusatory gleam in her gaze, and she grinds down harder, squeezing my dick like she wants to tear it off.

Somehow, I manage to sign, "Punish me for it."

Chloe grunts and falls forward, bracing her hands on either side of my head, and pumps back and forth on my dick. Then she slaps me hard on the face. The sting is as beautiful as any kiss.

I grin. She does it again, and her fucking is wild and frantic. She's getting close, though; I can feel it in the riot of her body. Her walls flutter around me, and her face twists in the firelight.

When she lifts her hands to hit me a third time, I wrap my fingers lightly around her throat.

That's all it takes. Chloe's hand falls as she screams out her pleasure and wrenches out of my grip to sit up and sinks all the way down on my cock again, her pussy spasming hotly around me. As her orgasm fades, she slumps down, her hair falling into her eyes, her tits heaving from her still-quickened breath.

Don't you dare fucking stop.

And I don't intend to. I muster up all my strength and grab her by the waist and flip our positions, pressing her down on the floor. Chloe gasps and keens and squirms around my dick, but I pull out of her completely. I've already come in her once. I want to do it somewhere else, this time.

So I kneel, one leg on either side of her writhing body. I grip my cock and point it at her pretty, swollen lips as I fuck my hand, her sweet arousal making the friction as smooth as honey. Chloe watches me from under heavy lids, and with my free hand, I reach over and pry her mouth so I can see the lovely pink of her tongue.

And just in time. My orgasm hits me hard, and my cum spurts out in long pearly ropes across her chin, her cheeks, her waiting mouth. She jolts when it hits her, and it's a jolt of pleasure. I feel it as surely as I feel the fire's heat lapping at my skin.

"Eat," I sign.

And she does, swallowing my seed down and then licking it away from her mouth with long, clean swipes of her tongue. Then she drops her head back, breathing hard.

"Thank you," she whispers, her eyes fixed on the ceiling.

But I grip her jaw and force her to look at me.

"I've been dead for six months," I say, keeping the movements slow and measured so I can feel her understanding as it happens. "And you told me not to stop."

Something that feels like fear but isn't actually flares hot and bright in her, and she makes that soft whimpering sound again.

Then I slide down to bury my face between her legs, to lap at her drenched, swollen cunt until she's screaming my name.

THEO

I lose track of time, fucking Chloe there in the heat and light of the fire.

Eventually, we wind up cocooned together in one of the blankets. Chloe is limp and sleepy in my arms, tucked up in a ball against my chest. I'm inside her, of course, her pussy warm and wet around my cock, and our position lets me kiss and bite at the slope of her shoulder. "Don't stop," she murmurs, thrusting listlessly back against me. Her words are slurred. "Don't you fucking stop."

I brush her cheek with my fingers, then reach down through the warmth of the blanket to toy with her clit. It's hot and swollen and probably aching, although I haven't been counting how many times she's come. Or how many times I've come, for that matter. Inside her. On her. I feel like I could keep going.

Chloe, though, is clearly winding down. I press my hand on her hip to still her lazy, sleepy thrusts. She gives a soft, needy little whine that just makes me pull her in closer before I go back to brushing her clit. One more orgasm, and I think she'll fall asleep. She's already halfway there; her heart-beat is slowing down, same as her breath.

I nuzzle her neck, roll her hard clit around between my thumb and forefinger. Her body pulses. I press a little harder, and—

Chloe cries out, jerks against me, and then slumps with a sigh. Her pussy contracts around my cock, fluttering like a butterfly.

Although I don't particularly want to, I slide out of her, rolling her onto her back among the thick layers of blankets. She blinks up at me, her gaze blurry and unfocused in the firelight.

"Don't stop," she breathes. "Keep fucking me until I'm dead."

Her words send heat jolting toward my cock, but I shake my head no and brush her tangled hair out of her face.

"I wanted—" she mumbles. "I was so—you left us—"

"I'm here now," I sign, although her words make my heart feel tight and strange. I wish I could make her understand the killing moon. That it's like the tide, something that washes in every few decades and drags me out to sea.

I tried, but in the end, even I couldn't fight it. But at least I came back to her.

"Sleep," I say, and her eyes roll back, her lashes fluttering against her cheek. She curls up against me.

I don't move until her breath gets quiet and even, until I can tell from the sounds of her body that she's dreaming. Only then do I extract myself from her, and it's almost painful, that separation of our skin. Outside of the blankets, the air is frigid, and I wrap her up tight and arrange her head on one of the pillows from the couch.

The fire flickers, giving off its paltry warmth. I don't want to extinguish it, not in this dark, terrible cold. At least it sounds like the storm is over. The winds are silent. Everything's still.

I think of the rows of empty lakes houses. People always leave things behind when they flee my violence. I saw it in '65, in '71, in '87—but I mostly remember the aftermath of 2001, when Veritas finally died for good. After I revived, I spent days picking through the dusty remains, gathering up clothes and shoes and canned food.

Clothes. I'm going to need clothes if I'm going to go out in the snow.

I leave Chloe to sleep in front of the fire. If it spreads out of the fireplace, I'll smell it. And I tell myself I won't go far.

Then I explore Chloe's house, moving quietly through the cold air to open each shut door. Rooms I never bothered to look at before. Why would I? Chloe wasn't in them.

One of the rooms is being used for storage, the space stacked high with cardboard boxes. That's where I find some men's clothes, the smell of their former owner so faint I know he left them here years ago. Jeans, a flannel shirt, tennis shoes. No jacket. They don't fit well, but they'll be good enough to get me to the other houses.

I check on Chloe one more time, tucking the blanket tightly around her shoulders. Sniff the air to get a sense of what a contained fire is supposed to smell like.

I leave through the front door, not the back, so I don't risk waking her. When I pull the door open, a foot of snow is piled up in the doorway, and for a moment, all I can do is stand there, letting what little warm air is in here out. The last time I saw this place was the night of the killing moon, and now it's transformed into something beautiful and completely unrecognizable. An unmoving, alien landscape carved out of ice.

I plunge into the snow, dragging the door shut behind

me. The cold damp immediately soaks through the jeans, but I have my wits about me now, and I'm prepared for the burn of the cold. I also have a mission.

I trudge through the calf-high snow, blinking at the glittering expanse. The air is very still and very cold, and although it's nighttime, everything is far brighter than I'm used to. A nearly full moon hangs overhead, and the snow reflects its shivery light, bathing everything in silver.

Not a killing moon, though. Not even close.

I make my way to Chloe's neighbors, my first victims from that night. I had been in a blood haze when I rowed across the lake, and their pier was where I landed. Chloe's house had felt dark to me. Empty. But this one, it was full of life I was meant to snuff out.

There's no life here now.

I break the door down. Inside is empty and echoing, not a single piece of furniture in sight. I do a half-hearted search but don't want to waste my time, so I move on. Not to Oliver's house, but to the house on the other side of this one, which has a stale whiff of humans about it.

This one *does* have furniture, old and mismatched and covered in a fine layer of dust. In one of the upstairs closets, I find a rain jacket and a pair of boots, both a size too small. I put them on anyway. In the garage, I find a tank of propane, and that I cart over to Chloe's back porch. Then I continue my search.

I move from house to house, as silent as the ghost I've always pretended to be. In each one, I breathe in the old scent of the humans who used to live there, and I can't stop myself from wondering about this most recent killing moon. Do they have a name for it? They name them, sometimes. I'm curious how they reported on it, how they described me. Usually, that's one of the things I look for while I do my salvage after a revival—newspapers. Clippings for my trophy box back in my cabin.

But this time, I don't feel the urge to read the story of my murders. It felt different, this killing moon. Maybe because I wasn't really doing it for me.

I was doing it for Oliver, even if Chloe can't understand that.

Perhaps that's why I skip Oliver's house as I make my way along the lakeshore, my breath puffing out in the frigid air. I keep hearing Chloe's voice in my head — *You killed his fucking family!*

I did. And for some reason, I don't want to know what the aftermath looks like, if anyone came and cleaned the blood off the walls and out of the carpet. If Oliver's things are still inside.

He's in foster care! They won't even let me speak to him!

I wrench the lock off a house a few doors down from Chloe's. Foster care. That was not what I wanted for Oliver when I did this. I thought he would be able to stay with Chloe —that she would take him someplace far away, yes, that I'd never see them again—but I thought he'd be safe. With her.

I shove the door in, letting out cold, stale air. Another house still filled with the detritus of human life. I really don't understand them, I'm starting to realize. Humans. I don't understand why more of them aren't like my mother, or like Chloe. After all, my mother loved me even when she knew there was a chance I would turn out to be a monster. There's no risk of that with Oliver, and yet his parents treated him like a monster anyway. Of course they had to die, along with his cruel older brother. But why not let him stay with Chloe?

That was what I wanted. That was the gift I wanted to give her before I went into the ground. And it was humans who fucked it up.

These thoughts trail around after me as I methodically make my way through the house, finally ending up in the garage. And that's where, finally, I'm rewarded: a portable generator sits in the corner, covered with a fine layer of cobwebs. I breathe out.

My original gift failed. Maybe she'll like this one better.

I hoist the generator up in my arms and go back out into the strange, glowing night. I'm not used to the lake being so quiet. There are always animals and insects singing their songs to each other, always the constant rustle of leaves and the soft lapping of the lake against the shore. But the snow silences everything. There's just the starry night overhead, the bright blanket of snow beneath, and the frozen air.

I set the generator on Chloe's back porch, next to the propane tank. I used to have a generator like this, many years ago, before I learned how to siphon electricity off the power lines still dangling around the remains of Veritas. A much quieter solution, to be sure, and one that didn't require me to constantly steal fuel. But as I hook up the propane tank, it comes back to me easily, and within a few moments, the generator rumbles to life.

I shut it off, then clear a path to the back door and slip inside. Chloe's still asleep, and the fire is still where it needs to be, well within the frame of the fireplace. I go into the laundry room and switch off all the breakers, then go back outside and clear another path to her electrical panel and connect the generator directly into her house.

It won't run everything, of course, but it's enough to run the heater. Enough to give her a little bit of comfort.

I crank the generator until it's rumbling again, melting the snow into the patio. Then I slip back into the laundry room, take a deep breath, and switch over the breaker that controls Chloe's heater.

A *thump* echoes through the house, followed by a faint

electrical buzzing that I'm sure only I can feel. A second later, the heater kicks on, smelling faintly like electricity.

I don't know if it's good enough. She's human, after all, and I felt her rage at me earlier, even if it was intertwined with lust. I don't know if this will be enough to calm that rage, but at least I know I tried.

CHLOE

When I stir awake, I can tell something's different. At first, I think the power has come back on, because the house feels more alive somehow. And warmer, too.

But when I sit up from where I was curled up on the floor, the electric clock on the mantel is still dark. I crawl over to the couch and fumble for the lamp switch. Nothing happens.

So why isn't it freezing in here?

A footstep thuds behind me, and I jerk my head around to find Theo standing in the entrance to the living room. He's changed his clothes, and it looks like he might have taken a shower, too. There's no trace of filth left on him.

Plenty on me, though. From what we did.

I rip the blankets away and find I'm still naked underneath, dirt and blood streaking my skin. Warm air settles over my shoulder.

"What's going on?" I ask.

Theo points to the picture window, still covered by the

curtain. But I realize I *hear* something. A low, mechanical rumbling.

"What's that?" I sweep up one of the blankets and wrap it around me, more to hide my nakedness than to keep warm. Theo gives me a shy, pleased-looking smile, and something about it makes my heart tremble.

He's a monster, I tell myself, as if I didn't just fuck him for hours. Willingly.

I cut across the living room and drag back the curtain. The first thing I notice is the snow—piles and drifts of it, like what happens up north, all bright white and untouched. The sky is grey with early dawn, but the snow itself seems to glow.

Then I see the generator.

When I turn around to look at Theo again, he's standing right behind me. I jump, startled, and he smiles again.

"Found it in one of the empty houses," he says. "No one was using it there."

Yeah, no one was using it because everyone fled because he murdered five fucking people. I don't say that, though.

"It's running the heater," I say instead. "Isn't it?" I realize I can hear that too: a soft, constant hum in the background. I think that's what woke me up. What made the house feel alive.

Theo nods. "It's not strong enough to power everything, but I thought the heater was the most important."

He signs more quickly than he did earlier, and I'm six months out of practice. But I still manage to get all of it.

We stare at each other. I tug the blanket around my shoulders, trying to decide what to say. My entire body is aching, and I know it's not from the cold. My heart is aching, too, and I don't know if it's from his kindness or from the fact that I let myself give in to him the second he walked through my door. That I begged him to fuck me even though I'm supposed to hate him.

"Thank you," I finally say, the words stiff. Then, half-heartedly, I sign it, too.

"I don't mind if you talk," Theo says. He holds his hands still for a second, then adds, "I like the sound of your voice. I missed it."

I jerk my gaze to meet his eyes, as bright and piercing as the snow. "Missed it?" I echo.

"While I was underground." He tilts his head. "Do you know about that?"

My chest tightens, and I pull away from the curtain, back toward the center of the living room, where the fire is still casting a dim pool of orange light. "Yeah," I say. "My friend Penelope, she told me that's how you—how you come back."

Theo's footsteps thud against the floor. So he can make noise when he wants to. He puts his hand on my shoulders until I look over at him.

"Yes," he says. "I'm aware, when I'm dead. Sort of." His eyes gleam. "Usually, all I think about is the void. But this time, I thought about you."

My breath lodges in my throat and wobbles there. My eyes feel heavy.

"Why?" I whisper.

In response, Theo reaches over and brushes his hand over my hair, lank and greasy from three days without power or a proper bath. God, none of that occurred to me when he was fucking me into unconsciousness. Mostly because I wasn't thinking about anything. Just—him.

Now, with the heat on, the storm over, and some semblance of a civilization seeping back into my home, it's all I can think about.

"The hot water is working," he says. "Would you like a bath?"

Heat flushes into my cheeks. Can Hunters read minds? No, not like that. I didn't think.

"Did you take one?" I ask.

He nods.

"It would be nice." I don't move to do it, though. There's something lodged between us right now, and I don't know what to make of it. I saw this man drenched in blood. I saw the bodies he left behind, smelled the viscera staining the inside of those houses. I smelled the inside of his body, layered with cordite from the shotgun.

I know he's a monster. I *know* it.

And yet all I can feel is a warm, strange gratefulness. That he went out into the cold and brought me a generator. That he thought of me while he was dead. Or half-dead. Or whatever the fuck he was.

He still orphaned Oliver, though.

"You're upset." His hands speak, but his face is unreadable.

"Yes," I breathe out. "Can you even understand why?"

Something darkens across his features, and he jerks back a little, and I think I might have hurt him. Is such a thing even possible?

He makes the sign he did earlier, *kill* and *moon*.

"Do you mean the murders?" I snap.

Theo's expression turns steely. "Not murders," he says. "I'm not human."

My confusion hardens, then, into fear. "Excuse me?"

"A murder would be if I killed another of my kind." His eyes are cold as his hands flash out his words. "But I didn't. I killed humans. Three of them hurt another human, that I—" He stops, and I bite down on my tongue to keep tears from spilling out along my lash line. "That I care about."

I feel dizzy. "Oliver, you mean."

"They didn't hurt you, did they?"

I blink. For a moment, I don't understand what he means. And then I do.

"You care about me," I breathe.

Theo gestures toward the window. Toward the generator, as if that answers the question.

Except maybe it does. He dug himself out of the ground exactly how Penelope said he would, and the first place he came to was me.

And although I've tried so hard to stop them, the tears finally spill over, streaming down my face in long, hot rivers. I suck in a shuddery breath and squeeze my eyes shut, and all I want to do is cry—it's all too much, how I was trapped in the cold and the dark and then it's *Theo,* a fucking killer, who brings me warmth.

He wraps his arms around me, pulling me up to his chest. I sob into his flannel shirt, and he strokes his hand over my hair, soft and gentle, with not a single trace of violence. And I let him, because it feels good to be held like this. To be held by *him* like this. To know he didn't really abandon me after all.

Theo lifts my chin, forcing me to look at him. "I'm sorry I made you cry," he says. "I'm not going to kill you."

His brow is furrowed, his expression serious and concerned and a little confused, as if he thinks the only reason I might be crying is because I think he's going to murder me.

"I don't—" The words come out all jagged, and so I try to sign them instead. "I don't think you're going to kill me."

"Then why?" He finishes the question by wiping some of my tears away with his big, rough fingers.

I take a deep breath, considering all the ways I could answer that. "It's too much," I finally sign, and Theo tilts his head, his confusion clear.

"I missed you." My hands shake. "And I was furious with

you, with what you did." I look up at him, and I tell him the truth. "I hated you," I say. Out loud.

He doesn't react, not really. I expect hurt in his eyes, but there's nothing.

"But now that you're here, I—I know I didn't. Not really." My tears spill again, and I press my face into his chest again, and he squeezes me tight. "I don't know how this can work," I say into his shirt, each word releasing his scent. "You're a— you're not human."

Theo tilts my chin up with his finger. I stare at him through the veil of my tears, and somehow, I feel lighter. Because I found the truth of things, I realize. I want him, but how can I have him when we aren't the same? At all?

Theo tightens his jaw. Brushes his fingers over my cheek again, drawing away more of my tears.

"It can't work," I whisper. "You'll have to keep doing —*that*."

"Killing," he says.

"Yes!" I step away from him and draw the blankets tighter around my shoulders. "You're a murderer! You kill people, and when you die, you come back to life! When I die, I'll be dead forever!"

The words explode out of me, and with a kind of soft, squeezing horror, I realize—

That's the real truth of things. It isn't that he kills. It's that he'll never die.

Theo stares at me for a long time. Then he lifts one hand and folds his fingers slowly into a very familiar shape—one of the first signs I learned, even before I started my major in college. Everyone knows it. Kids learn it in elementary school.

"I love you."

I suck in my breath and take another step backward. He doesn't drop his hand, just keeps it there, letting me see it, like he wants me to know it's not a mistake. His eyes are wide and pleading. Almost desperate.

"You can love?" I whisper.

Maybe it's the wrong thing to say. Or maybe not. Theo drops his hand and slumps his shoulders a little, his eyes never leaving mine. "Yes," he says. "It's different, but I know what it means to love someone."

I pull on the blankets, my body shaking.

"I wanted Oliver to go with you," he says, his signs crisp and his eyes blazing. "I wanted Oliver to have a mom like I had. A mom who loves him."

I feel dizzy.

"His dad would be a killer," Theo says, "but so was mine."

My tears brim up again. "It doesn't work that way."

"Why not?"

I open my mouth, try to find the answers. There aren't any.

"Oliver came to me for help," Theo signs, the movements growing faster. "He was hurt. *I* didn't hurt him." He shoves his thumb against his chest. "*They* did." He doesn't use the general sign for *they* but instead points off to the left, toward Oliver's house. "I wanted to save him." His movements are sharp. "I wanted to save you. Why can't I do that? Why can't I save someone I love?"

I sway in my spot until the blankets slide away from my shoulders. I think of Penelope's sister, how grateful I was when she stopped that man in Miami from hurting us. How she swept in so cleanly and calmly and slid the knife between his ribs as if she were plucking up a spider that had set me and her sister to screaming. It had been nothing to her to take that man's life.

It terrified me. But I was still grateful.

And when I look up at Theo, at his steely eyes, his firm mouth, I realize he *had* done the same for Oliver.

He would do the same for me.

"You can," I whisper. "But it's still not how things work." I swallow, my throat dry. "For humans."

"It's how things work," he says, "for Hunters."

I nod. Then I fall into him again, letting the blanket drop to the floor. He pulls me into him, buries his nose in my filthy hair, and breathes it in like it smells sweet. I don't know what to makc of any of this. What any of it means. All I know is I don't want him to leave my side.

"I'm going to take a shower now," I whisper. "Come with me."

He responds by scooping me up in a bridal carry, and I cling to him, shivering. It can't be from the cold. It's not cold in here. Not anymore, thanks to him.

Theo carries me into the closest bathroom. It's one I never use, but right now, it's still damp from his own shower, and I wonder if that should bother me, him using it and creeping around my house while I was asleep.

No. It doesn't.

He turns on the water and lets it run until it's steaming. I peel his flannel shirt back, and I don't have to say anything, because he strips off the rest of his clothes. It's dim in the bathroom, the little window above the toilet letting in grey, snowy light, but I take him in, this towering, strong body I had not allowed myself to think about except in the darkest parts of the night, when my hand would creep between my legs.

"Thank you," I whisper, and I don't know what I'm thanking him for, not really. Maybe it's just being here.

He smiles at me in that small way he does, and then he takes my hand and helps me into the spray of water. It's shockingly hot, almost scalding, and after two days without electricity, I've forgotten what real heat feels like.

I tug him in after me, and he drags the curtain shut and

then pulls me up to him for a kiss. It's not like yesterday, when we didn't kiss so much as devour each other. It's slow, measured, careful. He runs his hand down the side of my throat, skims it along my arms, and rests it on my hips. I shift until I feel his cock press into my thigh. Then I wind my arm around his neck and squeeze his wet hair up in my fingers.

He said he loved me.

Right now? In this moment?

I think I might love him, too.

And that scares the fuck out of me.

THEO

The power comes on the next day, all the appliances in Chloe's house suddenly erupting back to life. It reminds me of how it feels to revive, all that energy surging through you at once.

We're in the living room when it happens. Chloe's curled up next to me on the couch, reading from a stack of paperbacks she piled up on the floor. She let me stay with her, and I am grateful for it, even if every time I look at her, I feel a dull ache in my chest. Because I know she sees me differently than she did before the night of the killing moon. I can feel it sparking on the air between us, how everything had been perfect like the night we went camping, sitting close together in the warm summer air, and I ruined it.

It's quiet, under the surface, but it's there.

When the lights flick on, Chloe lets out a gasp of delight, drops her book in her lap, and looks up at the ceiling fan with something like surprise. "Holy shit," she says. "That's faster than I thought."

I smile, like I'm pleased. But it means the generator, the thing that made her soften to me, isn't necessary anymore.

It stays cold, although the sun comes out the same day the electricity turns back on, and the snow starts to turn slushy and wet. While Chloe cooks a big dinner for the two of us, using up the food she kept out in the garage so it wouldn't spoil, I go out and clear a path from her back door down to the pier. She doesn't ask me to; I just do it. I want to be helpful to her, to make up for all the hurt I caused.

The *hatred* I caused.

It's another thought that makes me feel tight in my chest. *I hated you.* It shouldn't bother me; I have lived my entire life being hated, even before I began killing. I wrapped humans' hatred around me like a shield and used it to keep them away from my territory.

But I never wanted her to hate me. At least she put it in the past tense.

The dinner is good; some kind of chicken stew with barley and carrots, plus bread that she smears with big chunks of butter. We eat at the dining room table, and I can feel something like contentment coming off her. It's curdled, though. It's not like it was in front of the campfire.

I help her clean the dishes when we're done, loading them into the dishwasher instead of washing them by hand. Afterward, Chloe trails her fingers along my waist and looks up at me with her big doe eyes.

"Fuck me," she signs, the electricity blazing around us.

I do, there in the kitchen. I shove her up against the counter, hard enough that she grunts, and then I yank her pants down and slide my fingers up into her cunt, hot and dripping for me. Her lust is sharp and undeniable. But so is the sadness lurking beneath it.

She moans, squirming down on my fingers, and I bring her as close to orgasm as I can before replacing my fingers with my cock. That makes her cry out and spread her legs and shove back on me, fucking me like she wants to kill me. Or kill herself.

When she grabs my hands and puts them on her throat, I give her what she wants, squeezing until she's gasping and choking and her cunt spasms around me. Her desire drives me crazy; I pound furiously into her so that the edge of the counter slams into her belly.

I hurt her. She comes twice.

The second time, the ripple of her orgasm feels so fucking good around my cock that I spill my seed into her, breathing hard against her spine. When she pulls away, my hand marks on her neck are as beautiful as dark lace. When I press my lips to them, feeling the heat of the abrasions, she tilts her head back and sighs, her hand trailing along my hip.

"I have to go to bed," she murmurs. "Do you want to come with me?"

She looks up at me, and I don't know how to answer. The truth is, I don't need to sleep. And if I pretend, what good will that do? It won't convince her I'm normal.

"For a little while," I finally say, and it doesn't seem to upset her.

She falls asleep easily, nestled up against me. I stroke her hair and listen to her breath and her blood and wish I could fix all the things I broke when I succumbed to the killing moon. Because I know something's broken. It seems the same, on the surface. Eating with her. Fucking her. Staying with her while she sleeps. But my senses can feel her turmoil underneath.

I have the thought then that I wish I weren't what I am.

By midnight, I leave her. I brush my lips against her forehead, and she stirs a little toward me but doesn't wake. She could be one of my victims, vulnerable there in her bed.

For a single, terrifying second, I wonder if *she's* the one the killing moon really wanted.

No. I don't think so. The thought of killing her—really killing her—gives me a hot, sick feeling in the pit of my stomach.

I leave her instead, going downstairs to pull on the boots and the coat I stole before stepping out into the cold, windy night.

When I was doing my scavenging yesterday, there was a boat still tied to the dock of one of the houses, a few doors down. That's where I go now, following the slushy trail of my own footsteps. I need to assess my territory for the damage the cops no doubt did to it. They always sweep in and steal my things away, especially my weapons. I ought to do a better job of hiding them, like I do the newspaper clippings. But weapons are easy to get.

The boat is covered in snow and ice that I scoop out with my bare hands, not caring that it burns my palms. The water is choppy when I push off, the wind buffeting me around, but I manage to make it ashore without capsizing. Thank god for that: the last thing I want is to go into the cold depths of the lakes. With all this unsettling tightness in my chest, I might just stay down there. Hook my ankle on some rope and die again.

Maybe then Chloe would leave.

The tightness clamps down as I drag the boat ashore. Her still being here was a surprise I hadn't hoped for in the void. But I don't think it's fair to her. I can sense her sadness and confusion every time she looks at me, and I keep replaying her tearful voice: *How can this work?*

She was supposed to save Oliver, that's how. She was supposed to gather him up and run far, far away from here. That was how I wanted to save him. How I wanted to save both of them, really. From me.

I don't like it, all these churning, stormy thoughts. I don't like trudging through the foot-high snow drifts in the woods, the icy water soaking through my stolen jeans. The grave-yard is covered in glittering snow, my gravestone completely buried. I look at it for a moment, the way the snow hides everything and reflects the moonlight. Then I keep going to my cabin.

From the front yard, it actually looks nice. The snow hides all the peeling paint and rotting roof shingles. But I can tell the cops were here, and not just because the bastards left yellow caution tape across the porch steps and a CONDEMNED notice on my front door. I can smell them, faint and stale, even before I break the shiny new padlock on my doorknob and burst inside.

Evidence of their meddling is everywhere: the couch is shoved up against the far wall, my kitchen is cleared of the meager provisions I left behind. My fireplace has been smashed open, and my weapons box is gone, the brick dust still piled on the floor.

I don't feel much, seeing that, though. It's what I expected.

What sparks the fire in my blood is when I go into my bedroom and discover that they took Oliver's two drawings of Chloe off my wall.

The idea of some grubby cop's hands smearing all over the paper makes my muscles tremble in rage. The anger burns in the back of my thoughts, and I stumble backward, curling and uncurling my fists. I want to kill again, the desire coursing hotly through my body. I want to steal a car and drive to the Pinella County sheriff's office and cut my way through every single person in that building until I get my drawings back.

And what would Chloe say about that?

So instead, I tear into the closet, where I find that the floorboards are undisturbed, which calms me a little. I claw them back until I can see my lockbox, completely untouched.

Only then do I feel like I can breathe. I take it over to my bed and flip open the lid, and there, at least, are the rest of Oliver's drawings, stacked neatly on top of my old newspaper clippings. The clippings I leave, but I lift the drawings out and flip through them carefully. There's the ice cream shop. There's his BJJ class. There's a scene with his favorite dinosaur toys.

When I'm done, I put them back in the lockbox, covering up the newspaper clippings, which don't feel important the way they used to. Then I shuffle back into my living room and blink at the rearranged furniture. The idea of attacking the sheriff's office feels absurd now. I would just get myself killed again, and I don't want to go in the ground again. I want—

I want things to be like they were before. When Chloe didn't feel confused around me. When Oliver was still here, bringing me his drawings.

But I also know they can't be.

I slump down on the couch, hanging my head down between my knees until my breathing slows and the fire leaves my blood completely. I stare at the floor—dirty, scuffed, ancient. This is my place. This cabin. This peninsula. I protect this little patch of land because that's what I've always done. Because—

Because you couldn't protect your mother.

I squeeze my eyes shut. My chest feels tight, tighter than it does around Chloe. But it's true, isn't it? My mother did everything she could to protect me, even knowing I might turn into a monster. And I went and died, and then I lost her.

Sixty years later, I couldn't protect Oliver, either. All the advantages I have—the strength, the heightened senses, the constant, underlying urge to spill blood—and I couldn't make things better.

All I really did was make things worse.

CHLOE

I'm dreaming of the lake again, although this time, the water's as warm as some tropical sea. I float on my back, staring up at a bright, turquoise sky, and when strong hands wrap around my waist and pull me under, I don't fight it.

Theo, I whisper, his name turning into a stream of silvery bubbles.

Some kind of sonic jangling cuts through the water, and his hands slip away from me, and I'm left floating on my own. The jangling doesn't disappear, though. It gets louder and louder until I—

Until I gasp awake, blinking in the bright morning sunlight. The jangle, I realize, is my phone. It beeps over to voicemail as I try to get my bearings about me.

"Theo?" I sit up, tossing the blankets aside. My bed is empty, and I feel a kind of hollowness at the sight of it, even though last night when I asked him to come to bed with me, I didn't fully understand why. I didn't fully understand why I asked him to fuck me in the kitchen, either, or why I had him choke me, or why I came so hard from it. Twice.

"Theo? You here?" I grab my phone and squint down at the caller.

SOFIA SOCIAL WORKER

I freeze, suddenly not focused on Theo's whereabouts. I fumble to play the voicemail.

"Hi Chloe, it's Sofia Barrera. I know it's been a few months since we, uh, spoke, but I have some questions I wanted to ask you."

My heart thuds. She never calls me. I was the one calling her, desperate to set up a time to see Oliver, to make sure he's okay.

"If you could give me a call back when you get a chance, I would really appreciate it."

Is there a tight quiver of worry in her voice? My whole body goes numb except for my heart, which pumps so furiously I feel like I can't catch my breath. Every time I called Sofia, she told me the same thing: I'm not family. She understands my concerns. They want to smooth the transition as much as they can.

With shaking hands, I call back. She answers on the first ring.

"It's Chloe." I stumble into the living room, bright with sunlight. There's no sign of Theo anywhere. "Chloe Monroe. You just called—"

"Oh, yes. Chloe." Sofia sounds harried, I think. Worried. "Thanks for calling me back. I was just calling because—" She hesitates for a second, and I stop in front of the picture window and shove the curtain aside to look at the snow-covered trees of Theo's peninsula. I'm sure that's where he went. "Because I was wondering if you had heard from Oliver lately."

"Heard from—" I shake my head, my heart still pounding. "No, I've been out of power for the last three days because of the storm. I—he never texted me or anything. Is he okay?"

Sofia takes a deep breath. I hate that fucking sound. It's what she does right before she delivers bad news. "Please," I say, whipping away from the window and pacing across the living room. "I understand that I'm not family and that there's a certain way of doing things, but I really do worry—"

"He's missing," Sofia says.

Every system in my body seems to stop.

"Missing?" The word echoes around in my ear. "How the hell can he be missing?"

Sofia takes another deep breath that, on the phone, sounds like the blizzard. "His foster family woke up this morning to find his bed empty and some of his clothes missing. His backpack, too."

I think of that backpack, covered in green and blue dinosaurs.

"He had been—unhappy." Sofia hesitates. "He was having trouble adjusting, given everything that happened. It was— one of the reasons we didn't want him to have contact with you."

I squeeze my phone, my heart thumping. "If I heard from him," I say numbly. "I would tell you."

"I know you would. The police are aware and are out looking for him, but I wanted to give you a heads up in case he did try to contact you."

"Did he leave a note?" I ask. "Anything? Some sign of where he was going?"

He thinks Theo is a ghost.

"No, nothing that the family was able to find."

And ghosts don't die.

"Where was he living?" I ask, my chest tight.

Sofia hesitates again, the silence thudding on the phone. Then she says, "Rockingstead."

"That's only forty-five minutes away!" I'm genuinely shocked; I thought for sure they had taken him to Charlotte or Asheville. One of the cities.

"Yes. Like I said, we were trying to make the transition as smooth as possible."

I breathe out. That makes sense. Still, my heart is hammering even faster. If he's only forty-five minutes away, it's not outside of the realm of possibility that he's trying to make his way back to Theo.

Or to me.

No, I think numbly. No, it was always Theo he thought would protect him. Theo the ghost.

But god, it doesn't really matter, does it? Not in the snow and the cold.

"If I hear anything," I say. "I'll call you right away."

"I'm going to give you some other numbers, too," Sofia says. "The police contact. Oliver's foster parents."

"Of course."

She rattles off the numbers, and I scribble them down on a napkin in my kitchen. When I hang up, I stare down at them, terror gnawing at my heart.

Then I wrench away, leaving them on the counter so I can get dressed and make my way to Theo's peninsula.

I DRAG Oliver's boat into the water and row as hard as I can. The wind scouring across the lake is the coldest I've ever felt, even after living in Boston. It seems to sweep down from the north like it wants to flay my skin from my bones, and I can barely keep a grip on the oars, even with my thick woolen gloves. The waves are choppy, too, and I splash and heave my way across the water until I finally run aground on the snow-covered shore. At least I manage to get out of the boat without falling in the fucking lake.

The woods are another matter. Everything is blanketed with snow, thick and pristine, and it makes the already intimidating woods feel completely unnavigable.

I don't have much of a choice, though. I trudge parallel to the woods, trying to find some hint of the path that led to the graveyard. That's when I stumble across indentation in the snow: Footprints. Sled marks.

No. Boat marks.

I suck in my breath. So Theo found a boat to cross the water. I hadn't really thought about it until now. Part of me thought maybe he swam.

I follow the tracks into the snowy woods, my boots sinking deep enough that the snowmelt seeps in and freezes my feet. I keep going, though, fighting through the burn.

"Theo!" I call out, my voice ringing into the silence. "If you can hear me, please come out here! I need to talk to you."

The tracks take me to a clearing that it takes me a second to recognize as the graveyard. Everything's untouched, save for a delicate trail of bird tracks cutting across the open space. The wind shakes the trees around, throwing off old snow that clings to my hair. "Theo!" I shout again, more desperation in my voice. "Please! It's about Oliver!"

Silence.

I trudge on, weaving through the trees, my breath tight and panting and my feet burning. I have the thought that maybe he isn't here after all. That maybe I'm the one chasing ghosts.

And then I hear something crunch in the silence of the snow. My skin prickles with heat.

I whirl around and there he is, caged in by the skinny pine trees, wearing the coat he stole his first night back, his hair damp and clinging to his cheeks.

"Theo," I breathe out, and I'm struck with a sudden, overwhelming sense of relief at seeing him.

I plunge forward, gritting my teeth against the burning freeze in my feet. "Oliver's missing," I call out, swiping the tree branches away. "His social worker just called. He's—"

Theo catches me, grabbing me by the arms. I blink in surprise at how fast he moved. I thought he was just standing there, watching me suffer.

"You're in pain," he says.

I sway in the snow. "It doesn't matter," I gasp. "Oliver ran away from his foster family."

Theo's eyes narrow, and he studies me, like he doesn't understand what I'm saying.

"He ran away!" I cry. "Last night. I think he's trying to get back to you."

This time, Theo's reaction is immediate. He sweeps me up in his arms and plunges forward, kicking up fans of snow as he moves. I cling to his jacket, my whole body shaking. I hadn't realized how cold I'd gotten.

"I don't know for sure," I say, my breath puffing out. "The social worker told me the cops are looking for him—"

Theo makes a kind of scoffing sound.

"But I know you could find him more easily. Couldn't you?"

We burst out of the forest, Theo's cabin rising up in front of us. I stare at it, feeling vaguely dizzy. All I can think about is the polite cop who interviewed me at the sheriff's station. *He had drawings of you in there, Ms. Monroe. He almost certainly would have killed you if you hadn't killed him first.*

A falsehood I never bothered to correct.

Theo sets me down on the porch. "Where was he?" he asks, his eyes hard and glinting, his hands shaking a little.

"Rockingstead," I say. "Not far at all. I didn't realize—"

Theo shoves past me and slams into the house, the door

banging on its frame. I blink, vaguely stunned. I wasn't sure what reaction I expected from him. It certainly wasn't this.

"Theo?" I hear the quiver of fear in my voice, but I go into the house anyway. It feels stale and closed off, even more than it did six months ago. Theo's thumping around in the kitchen. "Hey, I didn't mean to upset you—"

I stop in the doorway. Theo slams open kitchen drawers, one after another, clearly looking for something, and the fear tightens in my chest. Because what else do you keep in a kitchen but knives?

We found a stash of weapons. More axes, hunting knives, a machete...

But what Theo finally pulls out of one of those drawers isn't a knife at all. It's a map, ancient and faded, that he spreads out over the kitchen table and then hunches over, tracing along it with his finger.

"What are you doing?" I breathe out, even though I already know the answer. I can feel it, pulsing in the air between.

Theo looks up at me from the damp fringe of his hair, his expression hard and determined.

"I'm going to find Oliver," Theo says, "before the police do."

40

THEO

The old highway map of North Carolina is over fifty years old, but it doesn't matter. Rockingstead is still here. I didn't wipe it out of existence like I did Veritas.

Before Chloe said the name of that town, I was consumed by something that I can only describe as terror. I am very used to the scent of human terror, of course, but sensing it in myself was alarming. What do I have to be afraid of, aside from others of my kind? But apparently, there's an answer to that question:

Oliver. Getting lost. Getting hurt. *Dying.*

But Rockingstead, I know that name. I know that Highway 74 runs through it, an artery that connects it to Hanging Lake. On this map, that highway is surrounded by woods, and I'm not sure if that's still true. The last time I was on that road was the same year this map was published.

"What are you doing?"

Chloe's voice startles me. I jerk my gaze up to her, and my fear tightens again. She was furious at me for what I did six months ago. If Oliver dies because he tried to find me on his own, she might try to kill me again. I wouldn't blame her.

"I'm going to find Oliver before the cops do," I tell her. Then I shove the map around and point to the highway. "Can you drive me there?"

Chloe holds her breath, just for a second. Then she nods. "Take me."

"Of course, but—" She puts her hand on my arm, and the touch of her palm is warm against my skin. "But I don't know what we'll do when we find him. His foster family is looking for him. We can't just—kidnap him."

Fear flares in my chest again. "Doesn't matter," I say. "I won't let him die."

Chloe's eyes go wide, just a little. I can still sense her confusing combination of emotions—her panic is strongest right now, but her confusion is still there. An undercurrent of warmth, which I think is directed at me. I also get the sense she's in physical pain.

"Are you hurt?" I fold up the map, shove it in my jacket. "You aren't bleeding."

"I'm fine. The snow soaked through my shoes. I'll just need to change my socks before we go."

Of course. Well, I don't want to make it worse, so I scoop her up in my arms again. She holds onto me, her heart fluttering rapidly. "This isn't necessary," she murmurs.

I can't say anything, not with my hands full. But it is necessary. I don't want her to hurt. I don't want either of them to hurt. And that's why I lope through the woods as quickly as I can, our breaths puffing out into the air. She told me she took Oliver's boat here, an idea that makes my heart twinge strangely. A sign, I think.

I row us across the lake, my muscles aching against the howling wind. When we make landfall at her pier, the reality of the situation slams through me—

I'm leaving my territory for the first time in fifty years. *Really* leaving it, not just crossing Hanging Lake. Going out into the wide world.

The thought makes my chest squeeze up in that way it does. *Fear,* I think, as I wait in Chloe's living room while she changes out her wet socks. This is not something I do. Always, my territory remains in my line of sight, where I can sense interlopers. I don't stray.

But I'm straying now. For Oliver. For Chloe, too.

She rushes into the living room, her worry announcing her presence as much as her footsteps. "Are you ready?" she asks breathlessly.

I nod.

"It's gonna be hard to drive," she says, leading me into the garage. "With the snow and all. But I've done it before, up north."

"I understand." I don't tell her it won't matter much, not when we get close enough to make our way on foot.

Chloe's car was conveniently tucked away in her garage during the storm. It's strange, settling into her passenger seat, breathing in the sudden and overwhelming scent of her that permeates the fabric of the car's interior. Just being in a car is strange; another experience I haven't had for fifty years.

She backs out slowly, tires crunch on the slush that the snow has become in the bright, lemony sunlight. I can sense her fear, as sweet and musky as ever, as we creep down the silent, snow-covered roads. I don't know if it's from driving or if it's because of Oliver. Or both.

"I hope he's okay," she whispers. "I wish he had just texted me."

I put my hand on her knee, and she glances over at me, just for a second. "Sorry," she breathes. "I've got to keep my eyes on the road."

We creep our way through the woods, and I try not to think too much about the widening gap between myself and my territory. It helps, though, that Chloe is in the car with me. She's like an anchor, like a piece of my territory that I can hold close.

When we pull out of the winding side road and onto the highway proper, I fumble with the buttons on the car door until the window rolls down, letting in a blast of cold air. Chloe yelps and shoots a fearful glance over at me.

"What are you doing?"

"Scent," I tell her, then point at the road through the front windshield. She looks back where she needs to, her fingers right on the steering wheel. The highway is just as bad as the side roads were, covered in a slushy mix of ice and snow that crunches beneath the weight of her car. But there's no one else out, and the wind blasting in through the window carries a wild blend of scents. Too many, I think with a faint surge of panic. Too many, and too unfamiliar. I'm used to my peninsula, where I know the tapestry of trees and animals and the lake itself. Out here, the wild is drenched in humanity, and it makes my blood spark in my veins.

Still, I force myself to concentrate, to sift through it all. I don't know if I'll remember Oliver's scent, not the way I remembered Chloe's. But there are other things I can look for: Fear. Hunger. Pain. Confusion. Those are the scents my kind are designed to pick out anyway, the scents that lead us to our prey.

The car passes by a green sign: ROCKINGSTEAD 5 MILES. Chloe makes a soft hum in the back of her throat.

"Do you want me to keep going into town?" she asks. "Do you think he would have gotten this far?"

I tap her knee until she looks over at me. "Pull over," I sigh, and I feel her relief at the words, even if she doesn't say anything. She slides into a stop on the edge of the highway, the thick, snow-covered woods towering around us.

"Do you—feel him?" she asks, worry tightening her voice.

I shake my head and pull out the old map, folded so that I can see this patch of highway. Fifty years ago, Rockingstead was surrounded by woods, and it seems it still is. I breathe in the air again, desperate to catch onto something useful.

And then, just for a second, I do—a glimmer of childish terror, as bright as the north star. And although I didn't think I would, I do remember the last time I sensed it.

It was the night of the killing moon.

I scramble out of the car, the wind whipping the door out of my hands. "Wait!" Chloe cries, and I'm aware of the engine dying, of her footsteps on the snow. "Do you have him?"

I stop on the edge of the trees, breathing deep. The terror is in the woods, I can tell that much, carried toward me on a draft of winter wind. "I have to go on foot," I tell Chloe.

"I'll come with you." She glares up at me like she's daring me to tell her not to.

"I'll be faster by myself."

"I want to help," she counters, the wind whipping her hair into her face. For a moment, I'm reminded of how she looked the night of the killing moon—the way her face flushed with that same determination as she pointed the shotgun at my chest. But it's different today. Her determination isn't soiled by abject terror and despair. It almost feels hopeful.

So I nod, not really wanting to leave her alone on the side of the road anyway. Then I take off into the woods, moving as quickly as I can, all my senses on alert as I track that little glimmer of fear. Sometimes, the scent shifts away from me, blown off-course by the wind. But I catch it more often than I don't, and it's not long before I have a clear trail that leads me deeper into the woods.

Chloe is a constant presence at my back, and her presence

is easier to keep up with. Her breath and heartbeats are loud, letting me know she's not falling behind. I keep moving.

It feels like stalking prey. Not like during a killing moon, where my victims are tucked away in their houses, but when I stalk interlopers that come into my territory. I always catch their scent and follow it until I find the right time to act. But there's so much more urgency here, because with every step, that terror grows brighter, calling out to me like a beacon. I don't even know for certain that it's Oliver, although I can't imagine there's another child lost in the woods, drowning in fear.

We weave through the trees, Chloe and I. And then I catch a whiff of blood.

I freeze in place, fear jolting through my system again. Chloe bumps against my back. "Theo?" she asks. "Are you—Is everything okay?"

I sniff again. Yes, blood. Not a lot. I don't know if it's Oliver's. It's coming from my left, the same direction as the fear. But there's something else, too. A kind of—quiet.

Like the quiet just before someone dies.

And with that, I run.

"Theo!" Chloe screams, and she runs after me, although I know she won't be able to keep up. At least my boots leave tracks in the snow for her to follow. Because all I can focus on right now is finding the source of that blood before the silence of death becomes permanent.

I duck through the straggly branches, clumps of wet snow falling in my hair. I'm not used to the snow, but my kind are strong, and I run without slipping or falling, darting between the trees. The scent of blood grows brighter.

Then I see it, a trio of crimson dots against the white expanse. My heart nearly erupts out of my chest, and the terror is now everywhere, as relentless as the wind.

I follow the blood trail, dots here and there, until I finally

—*finally*—catch onto a heartbeat. A child's heartbeat, as fast and as faint as a hummingbird's.

I give a wordless shout, the sound echoing through the trees. Behind me, Chloe cries out my name. Then, a second later, she calls out Oliver's.

The heartbeat quickens.

I surge forward, following the heartbeat now instead of the blood trail. It's the loudest thing in the dampened silence of the snowy forest, so thunderously loud that the sound seems to tunnel down until it's a clear and undeniable path. I follow that path with more fervor than I've ever hunted one of my victims, even though it feels the same—the blood, the fear, the frantic heartbeat. The only difference is what I'm going to do at the end of it.

Footsteps behind me, the soft, steady huffing of breath. Chloe, trampling through the woods. More blood on the snow. My heart squeezes up in that weird way again.

Then I see a flash of color: Oliver's backpack, the one he used to store his drawings. I snatch it up and look inside. Clothes. A half-eaten apple.

I move forward, the backpack tossed over my shoulder, my eyes on the snow, until I hear crying.

How many times have I heard someone cry in my life? Too many to count. This time makes my heart break in half, though.

"Oh my god!" Chloe cries. "Oh my god, I hear him!"

I hear him, smell him, sense him. I shove aside a low-hanging bough of pine needles, free of their snow, and there he is, curled up in a ball, his lips tinged blue.

I've never felt relief like this before.

Oliver tilts his head up at me and blinks, his gaze unfocused and his breath shuddery. When he sees me, he makes a small, soft keening sound. He lifts his hands, but his fingers are too clumsy to speak. I've seen enough anyway. I scoop him up in my arms, pulling him close to my chest. His whole body vibrates, and I can feel the wet patch of his tears seeping through my shirt.

Chloe rushes up behind us, and I turn to face her, Oliver still clinging to me. "You found him!" she gasps. Oliver looks up at her and makes that same soft sound, his tears streaming down his cheeks.

"We've got you," Chloe whispers, brushing his hair away from his face. "Theo's got you." She looks up at me, her eyes shining with tears, and I think this might be the strangest situation I've ever been in. It's certainly the first time I've ever saved someone's life.

But right now, in this moment, I want to be as far from death as possible.

41

CHLOE

Theo wraps Oliver up in his jacket and carries him back to my car. I trail behind them, my heart heavy with worry. At least the trek back doesn't seem to take as long as the trail to find him; in the end, Oliver was only about five minutes off from the freeway. It had felt like hours, following behind Theo as he glided through the snow like a bloodhound.

I don't let myself think of all the reasons why he was able to do that. All the lives he must have taken, learning how to track a scent. All that matters is he found Oliver before it was too late.

The car is waiting where we left it, sitting askew on the snow and ice. I blast the heat as high as I can as Theo settles into the passenger seat, Oliver still clinging to him. He looks at me over the snow-frosted mop of Oliver's hair, his brow furrowed with worry.

"How is he?" I sign, and I hope Theo knows what I mean. He can sense things—heartbeats, breath. I know that.

Theo shifts his arms around Oliver, who's still trembling in his thin jacket. "Alive," he says.

I swallow, my throat dry. "Oliver?" His name comes out in a rasp. "Are you able to sign?"

Oliver stirs, which does make me feel a little better. But when he looks over at me, terror slams through me again. His skin is pale, his lips still vaguely bluish, his eyes sunken. He blinks.

I look at Theo again, and I wish I could know what he's thinking. The urgency with which he tracked down Oliver—it was frightening, honestly, knowing how he knew to do it. But I'm grateful for it, too.

"What were you doing out here?" I ask gently.

Oliver lifts his hands, and that's when I see the blood smeared against his knuckles. "Where'd you get those?" I gasp, pulling his hands toward me. They're covered in cuts.

He pulls them back to sign, "Windows." Then he says, "Can we go home now?"

My blood pounds in my ears. "You mean back to your foster parents?"

Oliver's reaction is immediate. His whole body stiffens, and his eyes go wide, and he shakes his head furiously. Theo's expression changes, too. It turns dark and stern and intense. I might have been scared in any other circumstance.

Around Oliver's body, he signs, "He's afraid."

My heart thuds. "Did your foster parents do something to you, Oliver?" The heat blasts out of the vents, making the car feel too hot, too stuffy. At least for me. Oliver needs it, surely. He needs a hospital, truth be told.

"They hate me," Oliver signs. "Like my parents. Please take me home."

Theo meets my gaze, and for a second, I feel like I know what he's thinking, the way he always seems to know what I'm thinking. Home is the peninsula. But I suppose my house will do.

"You're hurt," I say gently.

"Home," Oliver signs, then buries his head into Theo's arm. Theo wraps Oliver up protectively and stares at me, his eyes bright as the snow. "Take him home," he signs against Oliver's shivering back.

And so I do. I turn the car around, inch by terrifying inch, so that we're driving away from Rockingstead. Away from a hospital. Away from the foster parents, whatever they did. I know I should call Sofia, but I tell myself I'll do it when we're back at my house.

The car rumbles across the half-melted ice. I squeeze the steering wheel. "Keep checking on him," I say aloud to Theo, too afraid to take my eyes off the road. "If anything seems wrong—"

Theo puts his hand on my thigh, a reassuring pat. *Yes, I will.*

By the time I pull into my driveway, my skin is sheened with clammy sweat from the heater. Oliver seems better, though. He shifts around in Theo's arms, and his face has much more color. Theo carries him carefully into the house, like he's afraid Oliver might break, and sets him down on the couch.

Oliver clings to him, his little fists grabbing onto Theo's jacket. But Theo makes a low, calming sound until Oliver lets go. "You're safe," he signs. "Chloe will help you."

With that, Oliver looks over at me. The snow's melted in his hair, turning it damp. He's not shaking anymore.

But god, he still looks haunted.

I wrap a blanket around his shoulders and kneel to look at him. Behind me, Theo stacks logs into the fireplaces.

"What happened?" I sign.

Oliver studies me for a long time. "I don't want to go back there," he finally says. "I want to be a ghost, like Theo."

My heart clenches, and I glance back to where Theo is

stoking the fire with a match. It flares bright, the flames licking through the ashes.

"You can't be like Theo," I say aloud. I want him to hear it.

Theo's back tenses, and I turn to look at Oliver again.

"Why not?" His eyes are big and sorrowful.

I breathe out. "Because you still have your whole life in front of you. Ghosts—ghosts have to die first."

Tears shimmer on Oliver's lash line. "I don't want to go back to them," he signs furiously, and I know I need to get my first aid kit to tend to the cuts on his knuckles. I also don't want to leave him alone. "Don't make me go back."

"I won't," I say quickly.

"I want to stay with you and Theo!"

I feel Theo's presence behind me, like a shadow falling across the room. He must have signed something I don't see, because Oliver says, "You promise?"

I jerk my gaze over to Theo. "What did you tell him?"

Theo's eyes fix on mine. "That I will always protect him." Something flashes in his expression. "Same as I would you."

I think about how quickly he found Oliver, tracking him through the snow and the cold. All that killer's intensity, all that focus, narrowed in on the one thing that mattered.

Six months ago, Theo shattered my heart into pieces, and I hated him for it. Now, I can't ever imagine hating him again.

"I have a first aid kit in my kitchen," I say slowly. "Can you bring it to me? So I can patch up Oliver's hands?"

He nods, his eyes searing into me. Then I turn back to face Oliver, still snuggled down in this blanket. "Tell me what happened."

Oliver's expression darkens.

"Please."

Theo walks into the kitchen, his footsteps heavy and ominous, the way they were that night six months ago. For me, at least. I'm not so sure those footsteps sounded ominous to Oliver. "I need to know what to tell your social worker, Sofia, so I can try and convince her to let you stay with me."

I have no idea if it'll work. But I have to try.

Theo steps back into the living room, holding the first aid kit. Oliver glances over at him and takes a deep breath. "They were mean," he signs slowly.

"Your foster parents?" I take the kit from Theo and pull out some wet wipes and a tube of antiseptic.

Oliver nods, although he doesn't meet my eye. "They told me I had to learn to talk."

My throat tightens. "Not with your hands, I assume?"

He nods while I whip the blood off his fingers. "What did they do?" I ask once I'm done.

Oliver looks over at Theo again, who nods a little. *Go on.*

"They would make me do these exercises," Oliver says. "And when I couldn't do them, they would yell at me. Just like my parents did." His eyes shine with tears, and I squeeze the roll of bandages in my hand. Maybe it wasn't the right thing to ask him to tell me. Maybe I'm making it worse.

But then Oliver says, "And sometimes, they would lock me out of the house at night. In the backyard. It was cold and scary, and they wouldn't let me come in, no matter how hard I knocked on the door."

Theo stiffens beside me and makes a low, growling sound, his fingers clenching up into fists. I put my hand on his leg the way he did mine in the car. *Breathe,* I want to say to him, because I can't have him stalking into Rockingstead and killing people, even if they probably deserve it. Not if this is going to work.

Theo breathes out. "How did you cut your hands?" he asks.

Oliver looks down at his knuckles like he's surprised to see the blood. "Trying to get back inside. It was snowing."

My heart cracks. It's the only word for it: my heart cracks like it's made out of glass, and I toss the bandages aside and pull Oliver into an embrace, burying my nose in his damp hair. I don't know what to say. All I can do is hold him and look over the top of his head at Theo, who watches us with a strange, uncertain expression.

Then he kneels down, and he wraps his arms around us both.

I EASE the door open to my bedroom and peer inside. Oliver's fast asleep, curled up under the blanket and clutching the little stuffed alligator toy I dug out of storage for him. My head is still buzzing from my conversation with Sofia. Somehow, I managed to convince her to let him stay with me for the time being. Putting Oliver on video chat to ask for it certainly helped. Tomorrow I'll get him in to see the doctor in Pinella. But for now, I let him sleep.

When I go back into the living room, the curtain that covers the picture window has been dragged open, revealing the snowy landscape outside. White, blazing sunlight pours into the room, making me feel momentarily blinded after the last forty-five minutes I spent in the spare bedroom, talking with Sofia.

"Theo?" I call out, and then I see that he's outside, pacing back and forth on the pier, his hair hanging in his eyes.

He's worried.

That the thought surprises me, even a little, is unfair to him. Of course he's worried. He was worried when I said I was going to call Sofia, his face scrunching up like he didn't want me to do it. Like we could all just move into his cabin across the lake and hide there, off the grid, pretending the outside world doesn't exist.

He can be a ghost. We can't.

I go to him, stepping onto the back porch without bothering to put on a coat. The wind off the lake is sharp and biting and cold, but the sun gives enough warmth that I don't care. He stops mid-pace and looks over at me, the wind making his coat flap around his legs.

A killer, watching from the pier.

"Oliver's going to stay with me," I call out, the wind catching my voice. "At least for the next few days."

Theo lopes toward me, unnaturally fast, and we meet in the middle of the pier. The wind is so much harsher on the water.

"Why only a few days?" he asks, hands slicing emphatically through the air.

I sigh. "Because that's how things work. But Oliver told the social worker he wants to stay with me. That he feels safe here."

Theo scowls. "He is safe here."

"I know. I told her that. This is the safest place for him." I look up at Theo, at his harsh, worried expression. "I couldn't tell her about you, but—" I breathe out. "I know it. And so does Oliver." The wind gusts around us, and I step closer to him, put my hand on his arm. "You're the reason it's safe here, for him."

Theo's expression immediately softens, and he brushes my cheek with the back of his hand, his knuckles rough against my skin. It's not until I feel his touch that I realize how wound up I'd been, too, and I fall against him, pressing my face into his chest.

"I'm going to fight for him," I whisper, clutching at Theo's shirt. He wraps his arms around my waist. "I'm going to try for custody. Okay? I promise. But I just—"

I look up at Theo, who's listening intently, his pale eyes boring down into mine. This is the part that I know I need to say, even though I'm afraid of it. I'm afraid of what it says about me that this is what I want.

That *he's* what I want.

"I don't want to do it alone," I whisper. "I don't want to leave. I want to stay here." I swallow, tears edging into my vision. "I want you to help. And so does Oliver."

Something like astonishment washes across Theo's face, and for a long time, he just stares down at me, the lake wind blustering around us. Then he says, "Are you sure?"

My heart squeezes. Part of me thinks I shouldn't be sure, that I'm crazy for even considering it. Maybe I am. Maybe it doesn't matter.

I cup Theo's face, and he tilts it into my hand, his eyes fluttering closed.

"You asked me why you couldn't protect someone you love." My voice trembles, and Theo's eyes open and burn right through me. "And I didn't answer then, but—of course you can." I take a deep breath. "But so can I. Which is why you've got to promise not to kill Oliver's old foster parents. I don't want them hunting you down."

Theo gives a little quizzical tilt of his head, then breaks into a smile, which is not remotely the reaction I'm expecting.

"You want to protect someone you love?" he asks. "You want to protect me?"

I nod.

"So you're saying you love me?"

Heat blooms in my chest. In my cheeks.

"Yes," I whisper.

Theo's grin widens. Then he swoops me up in his arms and swings me around until I'm clinging to him, and all I can feel is that love, impossible and terrifying and exhilarating all at once.

When Theo sets me down, he kisses me, and it's not

angry or devouring. It's sweet and gentle. The kind of kiss that Oliver could see.

"I love you," I whisper against Theo's lips. "I know it's fucking crazy, and I still don't know how it can work, but—"

"It'll work," Theo signs against my chest. "I promise."

And then he kisses me again, wrapping me in his strength and his warmth, as the cold wind swirls around us.

EPILOGUE

CHLOE

SIX MONTHS LATER

"**D**on't swim out too far!" I yell from the edge of the pier, the warm summer wind whipping my dress around my thighs. Oliver gives me a thumbs up from the soft swell of the water and then promptly dives back under.

I sigh, although I'm honestly not too worried. He's actually quite a good swimmer, as I learned when the first really hot day of the year hit, and he wouldn't stop begging me to let him go out into the lake. Eventually, Theo just rowed the boat out to the middle of the water and sat there to keep an eye on him while I finished up work. When I joined them a few hours later, Oliver was swimming in circles around him, using a pretty impressively executed breast stroke. And Theo was smiling—*really* smiling. He didn't look much like a ghost at all. Or a murderer.

I've seen that smile more and more these last six months.

Still, I don't like leaving Oliver unattended, even here at Hanging Lake, where he feels safe. Where he *is* safe, a fact I keep having to remind myself of—although less often, these days.

I walk backwards down the pier, keeping an eye on where Oliver is circling around in the water. As long as he stays nearby, I can watch from the back porch, where I've got a brisket slowly cooking away in the big propane grill-smoker that Theo liberated for me from one of the still-abandoned houses along the lakefront.

It's been nearly a year since that night. The killing moon, as Theo calls it, and my house is the only one still occupied. Me and Oliver have the whole lake to ourselves. It's still astonishing to me that I was able to convince the state to let me take on Oliver as a foster while I work toward real custody. I'm sure Sofia played a role, especially after she came to visit shortly after Oliver ran away from his ex-foster family. She told me, the two of us standing in the driveway while the snow melted around us, that she had never seen him so content.

Theo, of course, is off the books entirely.

"Our guests will be here soon!" I call out to Oliver. "You're gonna need to come in for at least a little bit to meet them!"

That earns me another thumbs up before he dives under the water.

I'm about to turn around when a big, rough hand scoops around my waist, and warm, familiar breath blows against the side of my neck. I breathe out, sinking into that firm chest.

"You caught me," I murmur.

Theo spins me around, making my skirt flare out.

"I always do." He brushes his hand over my hair, his face serious. Nervous.

"Are you sure you're okay with this?" I ask. "If you want to go back to your cabin, they'd understand. They're mostly here to see me. And that one." I tilt my head back toward Oliver's splashes.

Theo's hand tightens against my belly. But then he nods, right before he kisses me, with that slow, gentle sweetness he uses whenever Oliver is around. Well, mostly sweetness. He does nip hard at my lower before he pulls away—not enough to draw blood, but enough to hint at the darkness he saves for when we're alone.

"Just don't leave me alone with them," he signs.

I laugh. "What are you afraid they'll do?"

"The humans?" he asks. "Nothing. The Hunters…"

He drops his hands to his side. Yes, the Hunters. Penelope is bringing Callie. And Abi—

Well, it turned out Abi was keeping secrets of her own last summer. That new boyfriend of hers, Rowan?

Another Hunter. Like the two of us are cursed. Or blessed, depending on how you look at it.

"You'll be fine," I tell him. "You're the oldest one, remember?"

That actually earns me a grin back, and my heart flutters around. I really do like seeing him smile.

The wind gusts, and Theo suddenly snaps his head toward the house, his muscles tensing beneath my hands. I suck in my breath; after six months with him, I know what it means. He senses them. Whether he senses Abi and Penelope, the two humans, or Rowan and Callie, the two Hunters, I don't know.

"Showtime," I murmur against his shoulder.

It was Abi's idea, the four of them coming to visit, although I suspect Penelope played a role in it too. Abi finally confessed the truth about Rowan back in February, when she and Penelope came to help me wade through the bureaucracy of getting temporary custody for Oliver. Penelope lost her shit for about thirty minutes, pacing furiously up and down the lakeshore. It wasn't until I coaxed her back to my pier with a baggie of weed and a Thermos of homemade hot chocolate that she finally calmed down.

That's when we decided the three of us really are cursed/blessed.

They've been planning *this* trip for ages, though. Abi wants Rowan to meet Theo because, in her words, "they need mentors." And then Penelope said she could drag Callie out, too. My two best friends and their two Hunters. One big fucked-up family.

Honestly, I'm glad to see them, after all that's happened in the last year.

"Oliver!" I shout. "It's time!"

His head pops out of the water, only to slap back down on the surface in frustration. I sweep my arm for him to come in.

"Theo's doing it, and so can you!" I shout.

By now, even I can hear the car tires on my driveway, and a flare of light flashes from around the side of my house, the sunlight bouncing off the car's windows. Oliver begrudgingly starts to swim back toward the pier. I turn to Theo again, winding my arm around his. I can feel the tension in his muscles, tight and nervous. He takes a deep breath, his chest rising and falling.

"Thank you," I whisper to him. "Thanks for meeting them."

He looks down at me, his gaze soft. "You think I would let two Hunters anywhere near you and Oliver without me?"

I roll my eyes at that, even though I don't blame him, really. Then I reach up and tuck a loose lock of his hair behind his ear. He did get cleaned up for our little reunion, I'll give him that. He's wearing the new clothes I bought him a few weeks ago—clothes he didn't have to pilfer out of a murder site. He almost looks presentable.

Almost. There's still that predatory wildness in him—those big, rough hands and hard, glinting eyes. It's the same wildness that seeped into my bones and led me home: here on Hanging Lake, in the place he's haunted for sixty years.

I don't know what the future will look like. All I know is I want to stay with him for as long as I can.

Oliver climbs out of the lake, huffing and dripping water everywhere. When he shakes his head like a dog, the droplets splatter across my dress.

"Hey!" I tell him. "Watch out!"

Theo laughs. Oliver grins up at both of us, and his smile makes me happy, too. Like Theo, I never saw him smile like that—as big and bright as the sun. Not until spring came, at least. Not until he knew for certain that neither Theo nor I was going away.

Voices carry on the wind. I breathe in deep and take hold of Oliver's hand. Theo squeezes mine—just a little too tightly, crushing my fingers together, exactly the way I like.

And we stand like that, on the edge of the pier that juts over a haunted lake. All of us linked together, a little family of ghosts.

THE END

Thank you for reading *Under the Killing Moon!* I hope you enjoyed it.

The series continues with Penelope's story in All the Words for Forest.

If you'd like to read an extended (spicy) epilogue with Chloe and Theo, you can access it by signing up for my newsletter here: rosebitterly.com/newsletter.

ALL THE WORDS FOR FOREST

COMING 10.30.26

PENELOPE

I've made plenty of cross-country road trips in my life, but this is the first one where I've had the pleasure of getting kidnapped by a masked psycho at an out-of-the-way gas station.

He thinks he's got the upper hand, but I have a big secret that puts me on top. Which is how I go from being a chained-up damsel-in-distress to riding shotgun with the Rocky Mountains' most notorious serial killer, the two of us heading to a Halloween party for the ages.

Now all that remains is for me to get out of this without losing my heart—

Literally *and* metaphorically.

VINCENT

A pretty woman traveling alone who pays for everything in cash? I couldn't ask for a better victim.

But there's more to Penelope Noble than meets the eye, and it's enough for me to stay my hand, at least for the time being. Especially when it turns out that her little road trip might give me a chance for vengeance that's a long time coming.

So yeah, I let her live. I even say I'll help her. It's a mutually beneficial arrangement, and nothing more.

Even if she does get under my skin in a way no woman has for years.

And even if I don't know that I like what it's waking up inside me.

Get It Here

ABOUT THE AUTHOR

Rose Bitterly is a hopeless romantic who has been reading and writing scary stories since elementary school—imagine her excitement when she learned you could blend the two! Today, she writes dark, immersive horror romances featuring slashers and other monsters, all shot through with a hint of the occult. Visit her online at rosebitterly.com.

Never miss a new book! Sign up for Rose's mailing list and receive free bonus stories: https://www.rosebitterly.com/newsletter.